DEEDS
OF
TRUST

Previous Chase Randel mysteries by Victor Wuamett

Teardown

DEEDS

OF

TRUST

Victor

Wuamett

ST. MARTIN'S PRESS
New York

Library of Congress Cataloging-in-Publication Data

Wuamett, Victor.
      Deeds of trust : a Chase Randel mystery.
          p.   cm.
      "A Thomas Dunne book."
      ISBN 0-312-05413-0
      I. Title.
      PS3573.U38D44 1991   813'.54—dc20   90-15541

First Edition: April 1991
10 9 8 7 6 5 4 3 2 1

DEEDS
OF
TRUST

chapter **one**

··

Frank Baker didn't mention dying when I talked to him on the car phone at one o'clock. In my office earlier, he was loud, excited, almost hysterical at times, enough so that I was worried about his heart. But after lunch he was quiet, firm, and definite.

"I'm going to get the money back," he said, among other things, "one way or another."

"Where will you be?" I asked him.

"Downtown San Jose. What about the foreclosure sale?"

"I'll get the sale stopped," I said. "The lawyer's working on it right now."

"Who'd you get?"

"One of Billy Blake's people. Supposed to be a real hotshot. No sweat on the first postponement, Billy says. After this they get harder."

"This one better be the only one," Frank said. I didn't understand the last bit of the conversation very well. The cellular reception kept breaking up. Finally, we got cut off.

I was glad I didn't have to tell him his lawyer's name was Hilda. Frank was too old-fashioned to understand that women can be hot-shots, too, in today's legal world. I have a little trouble with the concept myself, but I'm working on it.

I probably never would have met Hilda, or Frank either, if I didn't have the nasty habit of showing up at my real estate office at seven-thirty in the morning. Somebody must have leaked my work pattern to Baker, because he was waiting on my steps when I drove up Friday morning. I had a hard time getting him to shut up long enough to let me take him inside. Finally I pointed to the downtown rush hour traffic, and then at my ear.

"I can't hear you," I lied, shouting at him. I pointed inside and then pushed past him to unlock the door. I didn't stop moving until the coffee was started. There's nothing that can't wait that long.

"I'm Chase Randel," I said, "I'm a real estate broker. You probably already know that, or you wouldn't be here. I just want to make it official in case you're looking for a bail bondsman or something."

"I'm looking for help," he said, and told me his name. "Otherwise, I'm gonna lose everything I have."

"How come I get the honor?" I probably shouldn't have been so cynical, but it had been a hard week, and I was looking forward to a weekend at Santa Cruz. If saving Baker's ass was going to take more than ten hours, he needed to find another broker.

"Lieutenant Marty Braynes told me to see you."

"Why are the cops sending you to me? You got legal problems, you need to see a lawyer."

Baker sat back in his chair, then, and fire seemed to leap out of his eyes. His voice, though, got real soft.

"I don't have much time, son, and if you'd shut that mouth of yours and listen, this would go a lot faster."

Now it was my time to lean back and look him over. It's been a long time since anyone's called me son. His face looked about seventy years old, and there wasn't a lot of gray hair left on his head. What he had was cut real short, like he'd started getting crew cuts in his teens, and gone to the same barber for the next fifty years. His agitated manner brought the blood to his face, and gave it a falsely healthy glow, and there was a confused look about him. His eyes still carried authority, but he wasn't sure what to aim them at.

"I'll be quiet, if you'll talk fast," I said. "I guess I owe Braynes that much."

I kept my part of the bargain, but he didn't keep his. It took him an hour to tell me his problem. After a few minutes, I started taking notes to keep it all straight. He seemed to calm down as he talked, so I tried not to interrupt the rambling story.

"I'm not exaggerating my situation," Baker began. "My wife and I worked for forty-five years so we'd have a little something put away for ourselves. I was superintendent, you know, the last fifteen years, at Southside Union district, as well as being principal of the high school. Betty taught chemistry, too, you know, after the kids were old enough. That's where I met her, in fact, in the college chemistry lab."

Frank Baker talked like a school principal, like a man accustomed to captive audiences. He told me about every piece of real estate he ever bought. He told me how many hours it took to fix each one up. I got a quick history of rent levels, taxes, garbage expenses, and the skyrocketing cost of waterbed insurance. I found out what he paid for each property, and how proud he was of avoiding the payment of real estate commissions on most of his deals.

I wrote it all down. Every boring fact, every address, every purchase price, every date. It's a habit, I guess. I'm a salesman. Most of you probably think I make my living with my tongue. Wrong. A few may even think I make it with my brain. Wrong again. I make it with my ears. I listen, I write it down, I play it back. Because you can't sell a guy something he doesn't need, and the only way to find out what he needs is to listen to him. You think I should have been a psychiatrist? Wrong again. I'd get bored making that much money for doing nothing.

"Anyway, to make a long story short," he said, "when I added it all up two years ago, I had a considerable sum in real estate equity to show for my long years of hard work."

"About nine hundred thousand dollars."

"That's real close," Baker said, looking surprised. "How did you know that?"

3

"You told me what you have. I know what it's worth. What I still don't know is what your problem is. Most people would be happy to have all that real estate bought and paid for."

That's when his newly won composure crumbled. The satisfied look drained off his face, his shoulders slumped forward, and he laced his fingers tightly together. I guessed he was watching a flashback of a part of his life, and that he didn't like what he was seeing. He closed his eyes and almost sobbed before he got control of himself.

"I was happy," he said. "I should have been satisfied. But I wasn't."

"What happened?"

"Somebody told me about the Silicon Investment Group."

"That doesn't sound too bad. They're one of the hottest companies in the valley. Bit of a fast-lane crowd for me, but lots of people swear by them."

"That's what I heard, too. They even showed me their client list. Athletes, movie stars, doctors, lots of blue bloods, too. I called at a lucky time, they said, because they had just started taking new clients again." His breath caught in his throat, and he turned pale. His right hand started rubbing his chest and throat, while his left hand stabbed for a pocket.

"Can I have some water?" he said, hoarsely.

I got him the water and he took a pill before he sat back and made a visible effort to relax. Finally he looked up again.

"I was such a fool," he said.

"This is going to sound like an old question," I said, "but what happened?"

"They told Tom I was there. He came rushing out of a meeting and greeted me like I was a long-lost uncle. I taught Tom Endman chemistry, you see, when he was in high school. I hadn't seen him since. I'd heard of him, of course, when he started building a reputation at the Silicon Investment Group, but I never ran into him until that day."

"Let me guess," I said. "Tom Endman put you into a deal that's gone sour."

"It's worse than sour," Baker said, "I think it was rotten . . . rotten right from the start."

4

"Look, everybody makes a mistake sometime. So a deal went sour. You got lots of properties left."

"Not for long," he said. After a pause, he continued. "Endman put me into a condo project that was going belly-up. I was stealing it, he said . . . I borrowed against my properties, and bought out the builder."

"And the condos still aren't worth what you paid for them?"

"They're not worth the trust deed notes I owe the bank."

"How many did you buy?"

"Thirty-six."

"How much cash did you put in?"

"Twenty thousand dollars apiece."

"Holy shit," I said. "Seven hundred and twenty thousand dollars."

"With loan fees and commissions," he said, "it's over eight hundred thousand dollars."

I waited, but for once, Frank Baker didn't have anything else to say.

"Does this condo project have a name?" I said, finally.

"Fair Valley Place."

"That's in the middle of the war zone!"

"Tom said there was over two hundred units of new housing planned on three sides of my project." He shook his head slowly. "The developer couldn't get financing to build them."

"Can't you rent them for enough to pay the mortgages until the neighborhood improves?"

"My negative cash flow is about three hundred dollars a month on each unit. Ten thousand dollars a month. Plus I have to make the payments on the loans on my old property."

"Are you in foreclosure yet?"

"The first trust deed sale is at two P.M. today."

"What'd you want me to do?"

"Help me find a way out of this mess."

Now it was my turn to sit quiet. Baker finally read my mind.

"Mr. Randel," he said, "Marty Braynes said you're the smartest real estate broker in town. . . ."

"Too bad cops don't buy much property."

Baker ignored me.

"If you'll help me dig to the bottom of this, I'll list two million dollars of property for sale with you in the next ten days. Full commission. You could make a hundred and twenty thousand dollars.

"The market's hot now. Let's do it today."

He sat there sizing me up some more.

"You get today's sale stopped," he said. "If you deliver, we'll work out the game plan tonight, and put the duplexes on the market tomorrow."

"Fair enough," I said. "I'll start with the sale. What are you going to start with?"

"Tom Endman," he said. "He got me into this. He better know how to get me out."

chapter two

....

I should've told Baker that people who get you into jams are rarely any good at getting you out of them. But it wasn't my job to tell him what to do, anymore than it was my job to tell him not to sell his duplexes. I knew he was willing to gamble what he had left to save what was threatened. What I didn't know was that he was gambling his life as well.

After Baker left, I called Marty Braynes. I wanted to check Baker out, and also to find out why a homicide cop was interested in a real estate deal.

"Baker used to be my coach in Little League," Braynes said. "I bumped into him over at the DA's office. I figured you might do him more good than the DA. Sounds like the old guy is in a real mess."

"Why's Baker talking to the DA?"

"The DA's taking a look at some real estate deals. Personally, I wish the creep would spend more time putting away the scumbags I send to court, but . . . you can't argue with the people's choice."

"So Baker's OK, then?"

"Hell, yes. Look, Chase, the guy caught me stealing the cash box from the Little League hot dog stand. Know what he did? Took me down to the county jail where a buddy of his gave me the big tour. Treated me like a very important kid, that deputy did. When it was over, he showed me how to lock the outside door of the cell block. Then he looked at me and said, 'Which side of the door you like best, kid?' That's when I decided to be a cop. So, yeah, Baker's OK. In my book, he's more than OK."

"I'll give it my best shot," I said.

"Oh, by the way," Braynes said, sort of as an afterthought. "This thing with the DA is pretty big. Keep it quiet, OK? And, Chase . . . watch your backside, too. Some of the people getting looked at are a little bad tempered."

After Braynes hung up, I drank another cup of coffee while I made an appointment to see Billy Blake. Blake's one of those rarities, a lawyer who still remembers where he came from, and who seems constantly amazed that he's making as much money as he is for doing something that comes so naturally to him.

His firm is in a post-earthquake mansion on an avenue called the Alameda that has been converted into swanky offices. It's laid out like most small law firms. A lot of little cubicles filled with energetically scrubbed young faces make the first floor look like mother rabbit's winter home, while upstairs there are three or four spacious suites for the partners, clustered around a central conference room and reception area, with roomfuls of furniture groupings that could have been lifted intact by Leland Stanford from an 1880 London townhouse.

I made it upstairs to the reception area. I was just looking through the conference room to the French doors opening out onto a fern-covered balcony, when Billy's secretary, Amy Lou Madison, intercepted me.

"Mr. Blake's been called to court," she said, with a smile that seemed to say, with a sigh, "you know how busy he is. . . ."

"One of the judges probably needed some advice," I said.

"No," said Amy Lou, "but the daughter of one of his clients does, most desperately." Amy Lou's the fifty-year-old daughter of a London insurance broker and a Macon, Georgia, lady—and her voice carries a wonderful mixture of accents that can coat the bleakest message with a glaze of Southern honey. I'm convinced her first words as a baby were, "Have a nice day."

"Since when is a millionaire's daughter more important to Billy than I am?" I asked Amy Lou.

"She's not, dear. Billy's got you all set up with a young lawyer you're just going to love. Best real estate brain we've ever had around here, and that's no lie." Amy Lou took my arm and steered me to a small conference area just off Billy's office.

"There's coffee on the burner, and I'm going to send you up one of those apple turnovers I know you love so much while you're waiting." She patted me on the hand like a good boy and slipped out. I could swear she left behind just a wisp of jasmine . . . or was it magnolia?

I know what you're thinking. Your lawyer never treated you like that. Your lawyer's secretary probably doesn't even talk to you, just looks at you over half-rim glasses and finds you woefully inadequate. Well, I've got an edge on you. A few years ago, Billy Blake, who I always thought was a decent, upstanding, family-oriented pillar-of-the-community type guy, committed a major indiscretion with a younger woman who was a law professor at Stanford. Billy was crying in his cups one evening at the Athletic Club, which is where I knew him from, and he ended up telling me his sad story. Fortunately, I was still pretty sober, even though it was after six o'clock. That was fairly rare for me in those days.

"Sounds like you better buy your wife a really nice gift fast," I said, "like the Hope Diamond or something. That's what Prince Edward would have done. He'd buy his wife Ceylon, or Tasmania, when he got caught, and that seemed to cool her out . . . at least until the next time."

8

"But she doesn't like anything," Billy almost screamed. "All Mary wants to do is take that damn easel out somewhere and paint."

"Artists are tough." We ordered another round, and Billy was sinking fast when the idea hit me.

"What's she paint, Billy? Abstracts, watercolors, landscapes?"

"The sky, mountains, the ocean, you name it. At least I can understand what she's doing, so I don't have to guess what it is."

"Landscapes, huh? Listen, I know something that might interest her."

"I'll buy her a cloud," Billy said.

"I got something mo'betta."

"Yeah? What?"

"A place where she can paint."

"Where?" Billy looked suspicious.

I looked around dramatically, then whispered in his ear.

"A beach house?" Billy roared. "You're outta your fuckin' mind."

"Santa Cruz, Billy, it's not Malibu, it's Santa Cruz. You can afford it." There was a house unofficially for sale just down the beach from a place I owned. I got mine at a foreclosure sale, of course, and this other one was seriously overpriced, but Billy wouldn't miss the money.

"How much?" he asked.

"You can probably get it for three or so."

"Three hundred thousand dollars?" I thought he was going to faint. "I only slept with the woman three times."

"What are you worth, Billy? Two or three million dollars? Mary'll get at least half that, if there's a divorce. The question isn't, can you afford to buy her a beach house where she can paint and be happy and learn to forgive you? The question is, can you afford not to buy it?"

Billy slumped forward, elbows on the bar, head in his hands. Finally he looked at me.

"What d'you say?" I said. "You going to go for it?"

"What I say, Randel, is thank the Lord you're not Mary's lawyer."

"Take my advice, Billy, and you're the only lawyer Mary's ever going to want."

Well, he did, and she loved it, and I've never heard a whisper of a rumor about Billy since then. Amy Lou knows all about it, of course, because she saw my fat commission check in the escrow papers she typed up for the deal. I think she connects me with her getting to keep the job she loves so much instead of being thrown out of work by a lawyer losing his practice over a simple midlife crisis. Anyway, to this day, Billy returns my calls, and Amy Lou gets me apple turnovers. What more can a man want from a lawyer?

A good-looking brunette brought in my turnover and a cup of coffee.

"How do you take it?" she asked.

"Just like my women," I said, "sweet and light." I used to answer that question with, "Any way I can get it," but that reply seems to have outlived its usefulness. I'm saving it now for my thirty-year high school reunion.

She didn't crack a smile, but came back with sugar and milk and a second cup of coffee. I offered her the spoon, but she shook her head and sat down.

"I like my coffee to be just like my men," she said, "black and strong." She smiled at me, for about a tenth of a second, and then sat silently, staring.

"Nice of you to join me," I said. "You on your break?"

There was a great sigh across the table.

"Mr. Randel," she said, "I'm Hilda Straton. I'm not only an attorney, I'm also a junior partner in the firm. Mr. Blake asked me to see if I could help you this morning . . . in between my other five appointments."

"You're the real estate hotshot?" I said.

"Hotter than a Saturday night special. Now, if you could tell me what the problem is, perhaps I could get warmed up a bit."

I took a sip of coffee and tried to concentrate. Hilda Straton was a nicely rounded brunette with big brown eyes set in a face worthy of them. This situation is getting more interesting by the hour, I thought, as I tried to remember what the problem was.

"A new client of mine has an urgent problem," I said. "He bought thirty-six condos late last year with a down payment of twenty thousand dollars on each one. He says he thought he was paying at least ten percent under the appraised value of each one."

"Was this a distress sale?" Hilda asked.

"That's what he was told."

"And now they're not worth what he thought they were."

"Worse than that. He says he can't sell them for the amount of the trust deed notes he assumed. Which means they're worth at least twenty thousand dollars less than what he paid for them."

"It sounds like there may have been fraud involved," Hilda said. "I'll need to see some proof."

"Proof of fraud comes next. First we have to stop the foreclosure sales."

"When is the trustee's auction scheduled?"

"The first sale's set for two o'clock today," I said.

Hilda looked at her watch.

"You don't believe in rushing things, do you?"

"I just met the guy two hours ago."

"Well, give me the details, and I'll get the trustee on the phone."

I gave her the Notice of Sale I got from Baker. Hilda read it quickly through some reading glasses that hung around her neck when she wasn't using them.

"I'll take care of this," she said, "but we better meet the auctioneer on the courthouse steps at two, just to be certain he doesn't sell it by mistake."

I got up to leave.

"Nice meeting you," I said. "Could I ask one more question?"

"Quickly," she said.

"Do you really always drink your coffee black?"

chapter **three**

···

Hilda stopped straightening her papers and gave me a look that was intended to inflict injury. When I didn't flinch, she softened it a bit.

"Sometimes," she said, "I drink it sweet, and sometimes I drink it light . . . but it always has to be strong."

"You'll like the coffee I make," I said. "Strong, dark, and Italian, with a real fine grind. It'll be interesting to see how you take it."

I smiled and opened the door when she didn't answer.

"See you at two," I said, and walked on out.

My sports fan friends are always comparing life to one game or another. They say things about getting in the first punch, and hitting them out of the park, and so on. One remark that always intrigued me was the one about the best offense being a good defense, or was it the other way around? I usually figure that the best offense is to be offensive, but I suppose your point of view depends on who's got the ball. Come to think of it, most of life seems to revolve around who's got the balls and who doesn't. Maybe I should have been a sports philosopher. I wonder what they get paid? I'll ask my bookie. He should know.

By the time I finished with Hilda it was getting on toward lunch. Normally I work out at the Athletic Club and grab a salad there, but today I stopped at Zinfadel's market and got a turkey and Swiss on a French roll to go. I never used to eat in the Mercedes, because it set a bad example for the kids. Now that I don't live with Emma and the kids anymore, I don't pay so much attention to rules and good examples . . . or to keeping the leather seats clean. Let the mustard drip, I thought, who cares anymore if Emma gets a spot on her precious ass? That would teach her not to ride around with brokers from working-class backgrounds. Which is exactly what she is not doing right now, but that's another story.

I drove down Almaden and over Stanley Street to South-Central San Jose, where Frank Baker's condos are located. It's early summer, and the hills are a sort of yellow-green, heading toward brown. The lawns that get watered are still green. Most of them are brown. The houses get smaller in this part of town, and I passed three blocks of deteriorating four-plexes before I turned down McKesson to inspect Frank's condos on the cul-de-sac at the end called Fair Valley Place. The number of cars parked along the street and in the yards has tripled since I left downtown. There were several groups of adult males sitting on front porch steps, an intriguing mix of age and color and race. It wasn't too hot yet, but I hit the switches to roll up the car windows, and pressed the automatic lock button. The door locks clicked down like the sound of closing jail doors. I felt secure now in my armored vehicle, and turned into the condo entry and parked.

I sat in the car first and looked around. Now I understood Frank Baker's despair. The driveways are done in fake cobblestone that's made by molding the top of the concrete while it's still wet. It's beautiful when it's done right; it cracks like dried mud when it's done wrong. As I looked around, I could imagine I was parked on a spider web. I got out and hit the switch on my key holder that locks the doors. I figured I'd only be out for a minute, so I skipped the switch that arms the alarm and slipped the keys in my pocket.

The crinkled drives spread out like spokes from a little landscaped central court where I parked. The condos were grouped in fours in nine separate buildings. Two leaning wooden poles in the courtyard used to hold up a For Sale banner that was now hanging tattered by one end. Ropes that held colored plastic flags between the buildings were draped along the ground. The bushes in the landscaped areas looked dead, and the sprinkler system was missing most of its pop-up heads.

There were lots of wheel toys scattered around the buildings, and not so many cars, which was a good sign. There were families living here, and some of the adults were driving their cars to work—in the daytime. As I got out and walked down the drive, a little breeze kicked up and carried the sound of laughing children from one of the back-yards. I walked over to the fence and looked in. A woman came over right away and stood between me and the kids.

"¿Que paso?"

"Do you live here?" I gave her my best smile.

"¿Habla español?"

"Me no habla español . . . para . . . uno poquito."

She brightened and started firing Spanish at me at a machine-gun pace, until I held up my hands in surrender.

"Me no comprende . . . por favor . . . me no comprende." I laughed and shook my head. She laughed, too, and I walked on toward the back of the little development. I feel like a dinosaur sometimes, stuck with only one tongue in a multilingual world. I tell myself I'm too old to change, but a hundred words of Spanish can't be that hard. I think I'll get some Spanish tapes and play them in the car instead of Brubeck. I'll write that on my to-do list for next week.

The buildings are all the same. Most places look lived in. The houses and private yards are pretty neat, just the common areas are neglected. Baker isn't helping himself by letting the outsides go to hell. He probably thinks things can't get much worse. He's wrong.

When I turned back toward my car, I wasn't alone anymore. There were two guys leaning against the passenger's side, and a third, bigger one was pacing back and forth in front of the hood. When he saw me walking back toward them, the third guy hopped up on the fender, leaned across the hood, and sighted me through the Mercedes hood ornament.

"Bam, bam, bam, bam, bam, man, the Red Baron fuckin' wins again."

I kept walking until I was about ten feet away. I wrapped my fist around the key holder, hoping it would add some zing to my punch if they made a move on me.

"Get off the car," I said, in an even voice, edging in toward him. The big guy sounded Hispanic, and his two friends definitely were. They didn't look scared of me. The big guy sat up on the fender as I eased in, and I saw the car bounce a little. My hand came out of my pocket, and I armed the alarm with my thumb as it cleared my pants.

"I said, get off the car."

Big boy grinned.

"You didn't bring no army," he said. "You could call the federales, but you don't got your telephone with you." He laughed again. "You gotta nice telephone in the car, man," he said. "Maybe you could show me how it works."

I was close, now, about three feet away from big boy. His friends were grinning at me and each other, waiting for the show to start.

"You sure you want to see the phone?" I said to them. "I'm going to stick it up his ass."

Big boy stopped grinning and was putting his hands on the fender to hop off, when I faked a wide left to his gut. He flinched and bounced off the car. His motions set the alarm off like a police siren, and froze him with surprise, and I buried a right cross in his face, followed it with a left and a right to the gut, and a left hook to his jaw that dropped him by the front tire.

His friends started to run at the sound of the alarm, but were now stopping after four or five steps and starting to come back for me. I hit the lock button on the key holder, jumped to the door and got in, locking the doors behind me. One of the men started beating on my window with the butt of a knife as I started the car and slammed it in reverse and backed out the drive with the pedal on the metal. Big boy let out a yell. I guess I drove over some part of his body, but he was still able to shout, so it couldn't be too serious. If he needs surgery, I thought, as I backed into a drive and peeled out down the street, he can go to his friend with the knife.

chapter **four**

....

The portaphone rang before I drove a block. It was Frank Baker, looking for good news. I didn't have any.

"I saw your condos," I said. "We better talk about this after I make sure the sale's stopped." It was after one o'clock already. "Meet me at the courthouse steps at two."

"I may not make it," Baker said. "I'm meeting Tom Endman downtown, I'm going to try to settle my part of it with him today. I'm going to get my money back."

"What do you mean, your part of it?"

"I'm not the only sucker, Chase. I've found several others in the same boat I'm in. Tom Endman is starting to disappoint a lot of people. If they all go after him, they'll take him down. I'm afraid they're gonna take me with him unless I settle up with Tom today."

The phone started to fuzz out. It does that sometimes when you get passed from one cell to another. The next words were the last I ever heard Frank Baker speak.

". . . like you, Chase. I told Betty to trust you, no matter what happens."

"I'd didn't get all that," I said. "Frank, can you repeat that? Frank? Frank?"

He was gone. I didn't know where he was. I got the Silicon Investment Group number from directory assistance, but they said they hadn't seen Frank. I gave them the portaphone number. I didn't know where he planned to meet Endman. It was getting close to two, so I swung on over to Market Street to meet Hilda and the auctioneer at

16

the courthouse, just to make sure nothing went wrong at the trust deed sale.

Trust deeds, in case you're wondering, are what we call mortgages in California. If someone doesn't make their payments, the lender calls the trustee and tells them to sell the property to the highest bidder on the courthouse steps. There are lots of legal notices and procedures to go through, but the upshot is, you don't have to go to court, and foreclosure only takes one hundred and twenty days—unless you hire a hotshot like Hilda. Then you can stretch it out for months.

Trust deed sales are the salvage yards of real estate. Figure it out. If the property's any good, and you can't make the payments, you should be able to sell it in four months, and pay off the loan with the money from the sale. Any property that goes to the courthouse steps has got to have something wrong with it, doesn't it? Most of the time, yes. But not always. Sometimes the owner just walks away. Maybe there's an accident, or the wife leaves and the guy spaces it out. Or sometimes the owners fall prey to the most disastrous two words in the English language: "fuck it." When that happens, some real bargains pop up.

Foreclosure is always a growth industry. In real estate, like all human enterprises, one man's failure becomes another man's fortune. Many projects never succeed until their third or fourth sale. The people involved succeed, but not the projects. The guy who sells the land succeeds, he gets his price. The builder succeeds, he makes his profit during construction: What does he care if no one buys or rents the project when it's finished? The development lender usually earns loan fees and tries to sell the loan to an unsuspecting out-of-town bank. That bank forecloses and resells the property. Maybe this time it succeeds, maybe it fails again and the cycle repeats itself. Eventually, rents go up, or prices go up to a point where an honest man can make an honest profit. Until then, watch out, because the development game is just like a bunch of kids playing with an electric fence. One kid grabs a friend's hand and then grabs the fence. The second kid tries to grab a third, and on down the line to the end. The juice flows in one hand and out the other—until it gets to the end of the line. That guy gets burned.

Every growth industry has its gurus, and the foreclosure game is

17

no exception. You see the ads every week: Learn How to Buy Foreclosures—You Can Get Rich Even If You Don't Have Any Money . . . , etc., etc.

It takes a weekend and about $295. When it's over, you're supposed to be a guru, too. The seminars work. The graduates really do get to look at bargains. What they don't teach, however, is how to recognize a bargain when you find it, and what to do about it if you do recognize one. I wonder why they don't have seminars to teach those skills, too. Are the gurus saving the real bargains for themselves? Or is recognizing opportunity really an art form, one of those elusive entrepreneurial talents that seem to hide in genetic material, rather than textbooks? If you know the answer, call me. If I'm not in the office, have them page me at the foreclosure seminar. You're never too old to learn . . . I hope.

I got to the courthouse about fifteen minutes early, just to be sure. It seemed like a lot of trouble and extra precaution, but if for some reason the auctioneer doesn't get the word, he could drop the gavel and accept a check and we'd have another lawsuit on our hands, because Frank Baker as much as said he was filing suit against Silicon Investment Group. I parked in the new city garage down the street and walked the last block.

I like to walk in the city. I used to carry a pocketful of change to give to the panhandlers. Now a lot of them look younger and healthier than me. What they get now is a you-got-to-be-kidding look, and not much else. Today there's a guy with a two-wheel cart that has sacks of cans and bottles hanging down. He's OK. As far as I'm concerned, he works for a living just like me. If a guy like that asks for some silver, hey, no problem. He's got a different line of work from me, but he's got some of the same values. But the rest of them, forget it.

I like the city sounds, though. Today there's the horn blasts of the new trolley cars behind me as they roll through the intersection. There's another high rise going up over by the old De Anza hotel. Sounds like they're using pile drivers today, down in that fifty-foot-deep hole where the cars are going to park. Underneath it all is the steady hum of traffic, while a set of sirens converging from two directions layers an obbligato across the top of my decibel range.

The courthouse really does have steps. They're wide and made of granite paving blocks colored a fine gray that's speckled with black and gold. They're flanked by broad stone planters filled with blooming perennials. There are a few lounging men leaning against the planters as always, and up at the top of the steps are a couple of short, fairly round men with clipboards and attaché cases. They're the ones I need to talk to. Coming down the street from the other direction is a quick-striding Hilda Straton, looking in her gray pin-striped suit to be every inch the officer of the court that she is.

I waited for her at the foot of the stairs. There was the blasting horn of a fire truck in the air behind her, sounding like it was rolling to meet the sirens I heard a moment ago.

"You're right on time," I said. Smooth opening lines are my trade-mark. Hilda gave me a thin smile.

"Where's Baker?" she said.

"He may not make it," I said. "He's trying to see Endman."

"If he wants me to be his lawyer," she said, "he needs to be seeing me."

"He's a panicky old guy with a bad heart," I said. "Don't be too hard on him."

Her reply was drowned out by an ambulance racing west on Julian.

"Lots of sirens," I said. "Must be an accident."

Hilda paused a moment, then pushed past me and up the steps. She looked totally focused. I don't think she noticed the sirens or anything else going on around us.

"Let's get this over with," she said.

I followed her up almost immediately, but she was already in an argument by the time I reached her side.

"I can't believe you didn't get the message," Hilda was saying. "I spoke to the trustee, Interstate Foreclosure, just before noon. Don't you check with them before you sell a property?"

The auctioneer looked pissed, probably not so much at Hilda as he was at his office for not getting the word to him.

"Lady, I checked in about thirty minutes ago and they didn't say nothing to me about a postponement on the Baker sale."

"Two things," Hilda said. "First, my name is not lady, it's Ms. Straton. Second, I've told you who I am, and why the sale's been postponed. If that's not good enough for you, I suggest you walk into the courthouse and telephone your office. Because if you hold this sale, I'm going to walk you into that courthouse myself in front of the biggest lawsuit you ever imagined."

"OK, lad . . . Ms. . . . uh . . . Straton," he said. "Don't get your knickers in a twist. I'll call, I'll call."

Hilda was about to blow a valve as the auctioneer turned to go up to the courthouse. Just then there was a ringing sound in my brief case.

"Hang on," I said. "After I take this call, you can use my phone."

I pulled the phone out of the briefcase, popped up the aerial, and clicked it on.

"Federal court," I said, with a wink at Hilda. After a few seconds, I looked away from her and gazed out across the city while I listened. There was a line of clouds coming up over the hills in the west. That meant the beach was covered with fog that would be spilling across to the inland valleys. That meant it was bad summer weather for Santa Cruz, but as I hung up the phone I didn't feel like going to the beach anymore.

I guess your body shows bad news even before you speak the words. The auctioneer was looking at me real funny, and even Hilda was paying attention.

"Frank Baker's dead," I said. "Apparently he fell from the eighth floor at Silicon Investment Group. I tried to call him there earlier, and left them this number."

Hilda looked shaken. I handed the phone to auction man and put an arm around Hilda.

"How can he be dead?" she was saying. "He was my client and I never even got to meet him."

She looked lost.

"He never even signed a retainer agreement."

I grabbed her arm and squeezed tight. Hilda spun toward me with her mouth open, but my tongue was quicker than hers.

"Baker was meeting us here with a hundred and twenty thousand dollars," I said, to the auctioneer. "You're going to have to postpone this until the court names an executor for his estate. Right, Ms. Straton?"

20

Hilda was too shaken to do anything but nod. I pointed to the phone round-man number one was holding.

"You need to call your office to confirm the postponement?" I asked.

"Not today," he said. "I don't know about all the other stuff you said, but I ain't selling Baker today. Not after all this."

I looked at Hilda.

"Good enough for you?"

She was biting her lower lip now. Again, she just nodded. I took her arm and pulled until she started walking with me. Round man handed me the phone as I moved.

"I'm sorry guys . . . you've been a big help," I said, over my shoulder. "I know we can count on you."

When we got down the steps to the sidewalk, I stopped and looked at her again.

"How old are you?" I said.

"Twenty-eight."

"Have you ever known anyone who died before?"

"No. Never."

"You never even met Frank Baker."

"He was my client. We had a relationship. I was involved in his business. You told me all about him and I felt like, like he was an older uncle I was going to take care of."

"Walk up to my car with me," I said. "I'll give you a ride back to your parking lot." I put an arm around her and started walking. We got about halfway up the block when she started laughing.

"Oh God, it's so silly," she said, "I never even saw the man."

She's getting over it, I was thinking, just as the laughter turned into sobs, and she stopped and buried her face in my shirt. I held her until she calmed down.

"There's a first time for everything," I said, "I know how you feel. I wish it was the first time I had been touched by death." I pulled her face up gently with one hand until she was looking at my eyes.

"Why don't you ride around with me for a while," I said, "until we find out what happened and what we have to do next to protect his family. Frank may need us more now that he's dead than he did when he was alive."

chapter **five**

....

I gave her a little smile and she finally returned it, reaching up to wipe the tears off her face. We turned and walked on to the car, and her pace seemed to quicken after a few steps. She's started thinking again, I thought. she's going to be her old self again now; she's got her feelings tucked away again. It made things easier, but I was a little sad, too. She'd been a little more human there for a few minutes. You could see the scared kid beneath the armor of the woman lawyer.

It's not her fault, really, at least not yet. She's grown up cut off from real things. She grew up in the suburbs, probably, where everyone's the same age, and where the future's always a receding line on the horizon. If something breaks, you fix it. If there's a problem, you solve it. When relationships founder, there's counseling, and no-fault divorce, and remarriage, and lots of stepfathers and new-style extended families where nobody remembers who really belongs to who. Grandparents don't get old, they move to Leisure World, or to Florida, where they write postcards from, or to Heaven, where they don't.

America's young, and bright, and enthusiastic, and it doesn't take death sitting down. So I understand how Hilda feels. I felt that way, too, the first time someone I knew died. But that was before Freddie didn't come home from Vietnam, and Jimmie Keene died crazy in the Indian caves, and Jeff Bogue fell off the fishing boat in Alaska stoned out of his gourd. I found Mike McCrae with the needle still in his arm, and I was there when Richie Evens didn't pull the rip cord on his 362nd jump. And I held my mother's hand while she died, eaten up with cancer and completely willing to go, and when

22

my brother was on life support and the brain-wave curve went flat, I made the doctor let me pull the plug.

So, yeah, now that Hilda's reminded me, I remember how it was the first time death touched someone I knew. But I had to sort through a lot of memories to find that one, stashed back behind a lot of years and a lot of faces. Now Frank Baker's face is in my files, and something's not quite right about how he got there.

It was only ten blocks over to the Silicon Investment Group building, but I took my time getting there. I figured Hilda could use the extra minutes, and Frank Baker wasn't in a hurry anymore.

They had moved his body by the time we arrived. The police had an area blocked off with yellow ribbon, and there were a few onlookers, but it was mostly cops doing their job. There was blood and other gore still on the concrete, and a black loafer about fifteen feet away. A coin was tucked under the flaps. It looked like a dime, but it was too tarnished for me to be sure. There was a smell of bile in the air. I guessed someone had vomited at the sight of Baker's body. I wasn't sorry we missed it. A uniformed cop was about to send us on our way, when I heard Marty Braynes's voice.

"Hold that man," he said, "I want to talk to him."

I had taken Hilda's arm when we got out of the car, and I still kept her right beside me. Braynes finished giving a photographer directions before he came over. A reporter stopped him five steps away from us.

"I know what you're going to say," Braynes said, to the reporter, "and I've got an answer for you."

The news hound had his mike and tape recorder ready.

"My answer is, how the hell do I know? I just got here too. Any more questions?"

The reporter didn't blink "Did you ID the victim?" he said.

"We'll release details after we notify next of kin." He pushed the mike away. "Now if you'll excuse me, I have to talk to my broker."

Braynes pushed on over to us, and took my other arm.

"What the hell's going on, Randel? I sent the man to you for help. The DA's trying to build a case for fraud, and you let his best witness die."

"What happened?" I said. "I talked to Baker less than an hour ago."

"Who's this?" Braynes said, looking at Hilda.

"Lieutenant Braynes, Hilda Straton. Hilda is Billy Blake's real estate brain. We were over at the courthouse stopping Baker's foreclosure."

"I hope you got your retainer, Ms. Straton," Braynes said, "Frank Baker's turned into a real deadbeat."

Hilda grew pale again, and turned away. I shot Braynes a dirty look and led her into the Silicon Investment Group building to find a bathroom.

The receptionist saw us coming, and jumped up to intercept us at the ladies room door.

"I'm afraid this is not for public . . ."

I pushed her to one side until Hilda was safely through the door.

"Very well," she said, "if you insist on disrupting a place of business, I will be forced to ask the police for assistance."

She actually started for the front door. I grabbed her arm and stepped in front of her.

"One of your customers just died falling off the top of your building," I said, quietly. "Didn't that disrupt your day? We were friends of his. We just need a few minutes to get over the shock."

She hesitated, studying me over her turquoise double-arch glasses.

"In fact," I said, "I'm feeling a little shaky, too. May I sit down for a minute?"

I was still holding her arm, and I tugged at her sleeve a little and frowned. I guess I did it pretty good, because suddenly she got afraid I was going to faint on her.

Of course," she said, "come right over here."

Just then the elevator opened on the other side of the lobby. A burly, balding man in his fifties got outflanked by two plainclothes cops I recognized as detectives I'd seen with Braynes. The balding man towered over the other two, and he had his arm thrown over one cop's shoulders, talking and gesturing with his other hand to make a point. The cop didn't look pleased about the embrace, but he couldn't seem to find a graceful way out. The trio was almost at the front door, and I was starting to follow, when a fourth figure got out of the elevator and stopped, uncertainly. We saw each other at the same instant, and I altered course to meet her in the middle of the lobby.

She had red hair that hung long onto her shoulders over an off-white linen jacket and a kelly green blouse that seemed to be held together by gold chains strung down off her neck and not very many buttons. She tossed her head to get the hair out of her face, and in the motion flashed some creamy white cleavage as she stopped in front of me. Our eyes met. Hers were big and grayish-blue, like the eyes of a Persian cat, and I couldn't see very far into them. She blinked slowly, and then raised one brow inquiringly.

"What's your business here?" she asked. "We've had a tragedy here, and unless you have an emergency, it would be better if you came back another day." She followed that with a brief formal smile, and then reached for my arm to turn me toward the front door. I held my ground.

"It was an emergency," I said. "Now it's just urgent. I need to see Tom Endman . . . right now."

"I'm afraid that won't be possible today. I'm his assistant. Perhaps you could tell me your problem and I can relay it to him."

"I'm Chase Randel, Frank Baker's broker," I said. "Who are you?"

"Yes, I talked to you on the phone earlier, didn't I? I'm Elaine Endman, Tom Endman's daughter." She thrust out her hand to me for a handshake. I took her hand in both of mine and held it after the shake.

"Can you tell me what happened?" I asked.

She let me keep her hand while her eyes searched my face. Then her face seemed to crumple a little, and she moved closer.

"We don't know what happened," she said. "He was having a drink on the balcony outside my dad's office. Dad said he just suddenly acted like he was choking, and then he stumbled back over the railing and fell." She stood there shaking her head and biting her lip. "Dad's awfully upset," she said.

"Was that your father with the cops in the elevator?"

"Yes. Dad loved Frank Baker. He was one of his high school teachers, you know."

A door opened behind me and Hilda Straton came out. I did the introductions. Hilda arranged to meet Elaine the next morning and then left to walk the three blocks to her office. She looked eager to escape, so I didn't try to stop her. A walk in the warm fresh air would be just the thing, I told her, and watched as she bolted out the front and down the steps. I bet Hilda writes a mean document, and can structure a deal that's tighter than a fish's ass, but I wouldn't want to be in jail waiting for her to bail me out.

chapter six

....

Mr. Randel . . ."
   "Please, call me Chase."
"Chase . . . Can we talk privately for a few minutes?"

I looked out the door and pretended to hesitate. Braynes and End-man seemed to be talking loudly outside, pointing and gesturing, first at the ground and then up at the top of the building. I looked back at Elaine.

"OK," I nodded, and followed her to the elevator.

The elevator doors rolled through the confusion and shut us into a more normal world, a room filled only with the sight of an attractive woman casually posed against a wood-paneled background, where the air smelled only of that scent they put on the pages of *Vogue*—I think it's Obsession, and the only sound was the quiet whir of an electric motor moving the elevator. I stared at Elaine a little too long. She noticed, smiled a little, and looked away. Her left hand unconsciously pushed her hair back off an ear. The atmosphere in the little moving space was so normal I could taste it. After spending most of the day with Hilda, normalcy tasted damn good.

Elaine took us all the way to number eight, the top floor.

"We can talk in Tom's office," she said. She noticed my eyebrow jump before I could control it.

"I often call my dad Tom," she said. "He's my stepfather, really, but we're very close."

One hallway was blocked by police when the elevator doors opened. A uniformed cop saw us get out and hurried over.

"Sorry, Ms. Endman," he said. "This will probably stay sealed off until tomorrow."

"What's the problem, officer?"

"It's just routine. We want to preserve the integrity of the scene until the coroner's had a look at the body."

"The man's death was either an accident or a suicide," Elaine said. "I don't see why you need to treat this like a crime."

"Suicide's a crime in California, Ms. Endman."

"Very well. I suppose you're doing the right thing." She turned to me, and led me down the other hallway. "Let's go this way, then, we can talk in the conference room." She tucked her arm through mine, pulling my elbow in against her wonderfully firm young breast, and off we went to confer.

It's one of the sexiest moves around, to my way of thinking. Just picture Scarlett O'Hara or Emma Bovary in a nice low-cut gown with lots of cleavage showing—décolletage, I think they call it. Now imagine her arm sliding in along yours. There's a slight tug as she pulls you down against her so she can whisper in your ear. You feel her . . . generosity. She laughs lightly in your ear and then she pulls and starts to walk. What did she whisper? I don't know. Maybe it was, "Let's have some champagne on the veranda." Or maybe she said, "I have to go to the bathroom." Whatever, am I going to follow her? My feet were moving before hers hit the ground.

The conference room was half-paneled in a dark mahogany that ended at about waist level in a nicely detailed chair rail. Chalk-white plaster upper walls, and a ceiling strung with black wrought-iron chandeliers gave the room the California Mission atmosphere. It's an appropriate decor, I guess. In most conference rooms, some of the conferees pray that they won't get fleeced, while the others prey on the prayers. Elaine flicked on the overheads. She looked comfortable in the room. I sat at the head of the table and waited. Am I to be the fleecer or the fleecee, I wondered. The more I watched Elaine, the less difference it seemed to make. Obsession is like that.

Elaine's voice broke the spell.

"May I get you a drink?" she said.

"A Coke is fine," I said.

I'm going to have some brandy," she said. "Sure you won't join me?"

"I'd love to join with you, but I'm an alcoholic—a recovered one, that is."

She came over and touched my hand with her fingertips.

"I'm sorry," she said. "Will it bother you if I drink a brandy?"

"As long as you touch my hand like that, you can drink anything you like." I don't know where she learned about touching, but somehow Elaine has got hold of one of the elemental truths of the universe.

She looked at me appraisingly, and then crossed to the sideboard and poured herself a double brandy. She got me a Coke from a little refrig built into the bottom, opened it, and handed me the bottle.

"You're not quite what I expected Frank Baker's real estate broker to be," she said. "Sit down, please."

What you see is what you get, I thought. Middle sized and middle aged. Too many gray hairs, from a color point of view, but too few if we're talking numbers. Not overly attractive; but not overweight, and definitely not over the hill.

She took a couple of big hits of the brandy before she said anything else. She lost the forced smile and the studied casualness, and stared out the window, seeming to forget I was there. She looked like a person choosing the last lottery number on a pick-six card, you know, like they're getting a message from outer space, pulling in a number from the ether and materializing it out of the ends of their fingertips. I guess I was the number she chose, because when she started talking again, she got right to the point.

"Frank Baker thought a lot of you, Chase."

"I just met the man today."

She gave me another of those straight-ahead looks supported by a sincere smile.

"You evidently make good first impressions. The point is, somebody put something over on Baker, and on us, too. I need to find out who did it, and why, and whether it goes any further into any of our other investment portfolios."

"How do I fit into that?"

"Somehow, some doctored appraisals slipped through, indicating Frank Baker's condos were worth too much money. It would help Mrs. Baker . . . and me, too . . . if you could ask around about this appraiser we were using. Do you know Mickey Peachton?"

"I know who he is."

"If I start asking questions, all the other appraisers are going to shut up. You know how everybody protects their own profession."

She looked straight at me again, and leaned a little closer, and reached over and rested her fingers on the back of my hand.

"What I would do," she said, "and this is just a suggestion, what I would do is approach some of the other number boys like you're thinking of buying Baker's condos at foreclosure. They'll give you a straighter answer if they think your money is on the line, and not just your client's. See what they think the property's really worth. If Peachton's appraisals were really off base, we can start looking for connections to the builder, you know, kickbacks and that sort of thing."

I moved my hand away and took a drink of Coke.

"You know what I think?" I said. "I think . . ." and then I reached over and touched her hand, all the while shooting her a piercing look in the right eye, "we should talk about it over dinner."

The bad news was she didn't smile, nod, sigh, or blush. The good news was, she didn't move her hand.

"I'm suggesting a business arrangement, Chase. One that would not only help Frank Baker's family, but also help us find out if other investors are at risk."

"I can get started in the morning, if I have enough information to know what I'm looking for. It's almost four o'clock already today. If we have dinner, you can give me the background I need on how your operation works. Otherwise I might as well spend the weekend in Santa Cruz and take a shot at it next week sometime."

This time I was the one who didn't move his hand. She looked at me thoughtfully, and then nodded.

"We'll have to be quick," she said. "I have to be back here at seven-thirty to help Tom with an investment seminar."

"We could skip the food, if you'd rather, and just keep on, uh, working, the way we are now." I tightened my my grip on her hand a little.

"That might be fun, but I think we need to keep the right side of your brain occupied with some smells and colors, so the left side can process some information."

Finally she retrieved her hand.

"Meet me out front at six?" she said.

I nodded.

"Watch where you step," I said.

"You watch yours," she said.

chapter **seven**

....

Downstairs Braynes was just finishing up. There was still a chalk outline of Baker's body on the sidewalk, but the mess had all been cleaned up. There was no sign of Tom Endman and the detectives. A TV news van was just pulling away from the curb. I glanced at my watch and it was just after four o'clock. Channel Five would be "First at Five" again. They liked *f* words there. But would the news be "fair," or "full," or "factual?" Their commercials don't mention those *f* words. Am I being too finicky?

Braynes saw me, and waved me over.

"Shit like this makes me appreciate white-collar crime," Braynes said. "Baker say anything to you about killing himself?"

"Not at my office," I said, "but I got a strange call from him just after one o'clock."

Like most cops, Braynes was always about a sentence behind. He held up his hand like a traffic cop to stop me while he dug out a notebook and pen.

"If I don't write this shit down," he said, "I might as well start wearing a wire," he said. "When that word got out, not even my own wife would talk to me . . . which wouldn't be all bad. . . ."

I made some small talk until he was ready.

"You guys are spending a lot of time on a man who falls off a building," I said. "Things must be slow downtown."

"Why do you think it was an accident?"

"I think he had a heart attack, and fell. Endman's daughter said he was choking just before he stumbled over the railing."

"That's what they said. What did Baker say to you?"

"I got a call on the cellular, real bad connection. He was saying something about settling up with Endman, and talked about some other investors that were in the same boat he was . . . then it started cutting out. I think he said something about telling his wife to trust me, and then he was gone. I never got the connection back."

"That's it?"

"That's all there was. This morning he was spitting fire. No doubts, no questions, full speed ahead. Then on the phone, he was different, somehow, but I don't know what it means. Any ideas?"

"I got lots of ideas, Randel. What I wanted from you was some answers, not more questions."

"At least you got a live case. I got a dead client. Now they want me to do a whole lot more work, and for what?" I stopped and took a deep breath. I glanced at the SIG lobby, behind the glass doors. Elaine was making a vigorous point with the receptionist, waving her arms and pointing. I looked back at Braynes. "But what the hell, Marty, there's more to life than money."

"There may be more to this than an accidental death, too." Braynes looked around and then took my arm and led me aside. He talked quietly, and held my eyes with his.

"A lot of people are sniffing around, Chase. State people. Corporations lawyers. People from the Attorney General's office. Maybe the auditors from the Real Estate Commissioner's office. Hell, even the DEA's in town. It's kind of like a bunch of prison guards stomping around the getaway trail before the bloodhounds arrive. If you hear anything . . . see anything, hell, if you even *think* anything, let me know, right away. Otherwise I'm going to have a lot of sound and fury here, and not a hell of a lot else."

"Relax, Marty. Chase Randel's on the case now. But if anything comes of this, you better share the glory, because I don't know if there's going to be a lot else in it for me."

I shrugged and smiled and started toward my car. "I'll call you tomorrow if I hear anything worth talking about," I said over my shoulder.

As I walked toward my car down the avenue they call the Alameda, I glanced at the stately mansions that have been converted to offices for lawyers, accountants, doctors, and even a real estate broker or two. They're old, for San Jose—fifty, sixty, even a hundred years old. You almost expect to see Gatsby getting out of a Pierce-Arrow. For the most part, the houses were built for people on the way to somewhere else on the social landscape; and when their owners left, the economic climbers replaced their society cousins, just as money replaced birth as a marker of status.

Tom Endman has pushed his way into the pecking order, and now he's fighting to hold on to his spot. His stepdaughter Elaine wants me to help. Maybe we can help Mrs. Baker's memories at the same time. And her bank account. And what about my bank account? Mother always told me if I went into a situation with dollar signs in my eyes, I wouldn't come out with money in my checkbook. I've always tried to live like mother told me, but I do wonder sometimes, why she didn't die rich?

chapter **eight**

··

I had about an hour and a half until I was due back for my "working" dinner with Elaine, so I took a run out Stevens Creek Boulevard. There's no sign of the creek anymore, or Mr. Stevens. I've often wondered what it would be like to get someplace early enough so that they named the landscape after you. Not much chance of that these days. Even half the moon's been named already, and the part that's not named nobody's ever gonna see anyway, at least not from where I'm sitting.

I think Mr. Stevens would like the street they named after him, though. It's a street of little stores, some open, some closed up. There are some bright spots, businesses fifty years old or more, with big expansive fronts, newly repaved parking lots, and nicely lighted signs. In between are the used car lots, and the liquor stores and bars, and all the little specialty shops, like you find on the lower cross streets in New York: coin shops, magic shops, comic book stores, Civil War memorabilia, Asian restaurants, discount appliances, and a hearing aid repair shop. A few will survive, most will die and be replaced. Kind of like Mr. Stevens and the pioneers. For every one who's remembered, thousands lie in forgotten graves.

One bright spot for the living, though, is LiddyPools, a postchrome revival pseudo-English pub full of Beatles posters and twenty-year-old juke box hits and aging rockers, like my appraiser friend Irving Greene, who I know will be hiding in the back room. It's still early enough to talk to Irv without an interpreter, although there are four Watneys bottles on the table already. Irv won't let them take the empties. He knows when he starts knocking them over, it's time to go home.

When he's not too sober, Irv is one of the best real estate appraisers in town. Show him a picture of a house and give him the address, and he'll guess the sale price within a thousand dollars, ninety-nine times out of a hundred. With Irv, when his blood chemistry is right, the paperwork is just a formality. He knows the value as soon as he sees the property. Sober, though, he worries, and it affects his accuracy. But in LiddyPools, you can count on Irv to be relaxed, and that's the way I need him today.

Irv's face lit up when he spotted me, and he started to lurch up to say hello, when his thumb caught on the edge of the table, pulling him off kilter so that his other hand stabbed out for balance and tipped the bottom of an empty Watneys, which rolled across the table and off the end. With the instincts of a waiter, my foot jumped out and slid under the bottle as it fell, and my toe flipped it back up into the air. I caught it about a foot off the floor, twirled it around in front of Irv, and set it down softly in front of him.

His face was white.

"Thank God you caught it, Chase; I thought I was on my way home in the middle of the afternoon. I've never broken a bottle this early before."

He sat for a moment, savoring his rescue, then suddenly looked up at me again and shouted down to the end of the bar.

"Terry, two more Watneys down here, love, before the drought starts again."

He waved me to the other side of the booth, and ever so gently moved the empty bottles against the wall at the end of the table. There was a little chrome and neon remote selection box for the big Wurlitzer across the room. Irv tossed a couple of quarters on the table.

"Go on, Chase, pick three good ones. I'm buying."

Flipping through the songs was like looking at your high school yearbook. Each song had some faces tied to it. Shirley always liked to listen to the Stones in bed, especially "You Can't Always Get What You Want." That wasn't true of Shirley, thank God. I gave that a spin. My mind flipped to Beverly, who later changed her name to Kali and started riding motorcycles. Bev and I spent most of one summer walking down Hollywood Boulevard arm in arm, harmonizing "I Want To Hold Your Hand," and saying "wow" a lot in the breaks. I guess heterosexual relationships are a bit strange in that part of LA these days, but that, too, is another story.

I found a third song, too, that froze time for an instant. Music can do that, and I don't think it's an acid flash any more; it's been too many years, but there I was, lying in my bed late on a summer night, radio turned way down so my parents wouldn't hear it, and "Randy's Records" was coming in strong at midnight from Gallatin, Tennesee, beaming out the first waves of the rock and roll revolution—a near fatal mix of black rhythms and white words being master-mixed into a fifteen-year-old's brain. Later that summer, we danced to the song self-consciously, because it was neither slow nor fast, not jitterbug, not bop, it just was what it was, and Catherine and I didn't care, we found a way to hold each other and sway and laugh, and when it was over, we kissed on the screen porch and nothing was ever the same after that.

The waitress interrupted memory lane by setting the lagers down loudly on the table.

"Bring me a Coke, would you?" I said.

Irv looked a little sheepish, like he'd been caught out in a bad joke.

"I'm sorry, Chase, I completely forgot you're not drinking these days." He looked at the waitress. "It's OK, Terry, two at a time makes your life easier, doesn't it? I won't need another one for five or ten minutes now."

Irv sang along with the Stones until I got my Coca-Cola. He especially liked the "you get what you need" part. He liked to wave at Terry while he sang that bit.

"God, I love that music, Chase," he said. "That really says it like it is." Irv sat musing at his own profundity, and then looked up at me suddenly. He had that drinker's way of suddenly tuning in and out of various realities.

"What about you, Chase? What do you need today?"

"I need some free advice."

Irv leaned across the table, and talked right into my face.

"Don't stay on the wagon too long, Chase, that's my advice. Now, what else do you need to know?"

"I'm thinking of buying some condos, Irv. Fair Valley Place. You know it?"

Irv shook his head. "That place is the shits, Chase. Stay out of there. Buy in Los Altos Hills or something. You can afford it now. You're too old to go slum picking."

"They're in foreclosure, Irv. I can get them for a hundred and twenty-five apiece."

"One twenty-five! That shit's not worth a hundred and ten."

"Hell, Irv, the bank loans are a hundred and twenty."

"What bank?"

"Shorham Commercial Savings."

He slumped forward, elbows on the table, head on his hands, his head shaking back and forth.

"Where the hell you been, Chase? If you're going to stop drinking, you got to start thinking." Irv mouthed a few bars of "I Wanna Hold Your Hand," before he went on. He was well into the second Watneys.

"Shorham Savings is an Orange County outfit that came up here first of last year and threw money at every project in town. The feds closed them up two months ago. I think three of the officers got indicted for fraud. Who the fuck appraised those things for them?"

"Mickey Peachton."

"C'est le guerre, c'est la derriére."

I'd forgotten how Irv's prep school background starts to come out after a few bottles. He waved two fingers at Terry, and emptied the second bottle. I waited him out.

"Mickey blows his nose a lot, Chase. Not many banks up here will have anything to do with him these days."

"Does he inflate appraisals?"

Irv shrugged his shoulders.

"I hear stories," he said.

I sat and finished my Coke. Somehow I didn't think I was going to get much more out of Irv. Nobody likes to knock someone in their own profession. It's bad for business. Like there're no crooked real estate brokers. Just some guys who seem to make some crucial "mistakes."

"I'm sorry, Chase," he said. "You asked me, I told you."

"What else do you hear, Irv?"

"When did all this shit go down, Chase?"

"First of last year."

Irv sat lost in thought. He didn't even look up when Terry brought his beers.

"Look," he said, "it's probably nothing . . . but Mickey got a new BMW last year. Now Chase, I'm not prejudiced about cars or anything, but Mickey was always a Plymouth man, maybe an Oldsmobile, but Mickey in a BMW? Something changed last year. That's all I'm going to say."

I smiled and nodded thanks. The Beatles went off and there was a short break, then a trio of black falsetto voices came waltzing in from thirty-five years away. Irv looked at me dumbfounded.

"What the shit is that? Did you play that? That's incredible!"

I stood up, took the latest empty and twirled it up in the air like a baton, caught it neatly, and set it down in front of his face.

"It's your song, Irv. The year . . . 1954. The group . . . the Jive Bombers. The tune . . . well, sing along, you'll figure it out."

I walked out singing.

I'm just a bad boy
lalalalalalalalalala
All dressed up in fancy clothes
I'm taking the trouble
To turn my nights into day.

The hot blazing sun
Won't hurt my head
'Cause you'll always find me
Right here in the shade

I can see all the people
They're laughing at me
'Cause I'm just naturally
    crazy.

I guess Irv will run out of time someday—or out of liver—but until then, he seems to have made his peace with whatever demons are following him around. I hope they're happy with him. I've got enough of my own.

chapter **nine**

....

The police were gone from the SIG building when I pulled in at six o'clock. There were a couple of guys in maintenance uniforms scrubbing down the concrete sidewalk with long-handled brushes. The grass looked like an army had marched through. Over at the edge of the shrubbery, the penny loafer still lay deserted, like a dog whose teenage master has grown up and gone away to college, and isn't coming back.

I saw Elaine in the lobby and tapped the horn. She was waving her arms and gesturing to a security man at the front desk. She saw me, paused for a few more wig-wags at the guard, and then came through the doors. She had one arm in her linen jacket, and was trying to put it the rest of the way on, when she noticed something to point out to the maintenance men. The arms started again, and the jacket dragged the walk, but the men snapped to attention until the windmill stopped.

I was out of the car by this time, and opening the passenger door.

"Flowers," she was saying, pointing at the broken shrubs. "And I want them in by tomorrow. And for God's sake, get rid of that shoe over there."

She finally finished her instructions, and walked on over to the car. I caught her arm as she started to get in.

"You want that jacket on or off?" I said. She looked surprised, then noticed the sleeve trailing the ground.

"I want the jacket off, and the air conditioning on," she said, sliding her arm out of its sleeve.

"Yes, ma'am, right away, ma'am," I said. I shut her door, put the jacket on a hanger in the back seat, and walked around and got under the wheel. Elaine looked concerned.

"I didn't mean to sound so bossy," she said.

"Don't apologize, I respect a woman who knows what she wants."

"I'm not sure that's a compliment."

I glanced in the mirror, and pulled out into the traffic before I looked at her.

"Japantown OK?"

"Will they have something that's cooked?"

"I'll have them double-steam the rice, just for you."

"As long I don't have to eat a raw eel."

Japantown was close, and I knew the food would be quick and edible. The owner was making sushi behind the bar, just as he did in the ten-seat hole-in-the-wall place he first had on Hedding Street. He called to the waitress in Japanese as she led us to a table, and she smiled apologetically and bowed. About thirty seconds later she was back with a pot of tea, and two cups. Tusuro knew me before I found AA, so he sends the tea over before I can start thinking about saki.

"You want some saki?" I asked Elaine.

"That's too fiddlely for the way I feel tonight. If you don't mind, I think I'll have a beer. Is that cook a friend of yours?"

"That cook owns this joint. I did him a favor once, so he takes good care of me."

"What did you do?"

"When he wanted to move up to this place, this yo-yo landlord didn't want to let him sublet his old place. So I helped Tusuro make the guy an offer he couldn't refuse."

Elaine put on a Godfather voice.

"What'd you do, threaten to make him into sushi?"

"The guy's mother-in-law lived in an apartment over the cafe. Tusuro told him he was going to start cooking authentic Korean food."

"What kind of a threat is that?" Elaine asked, looking puzzled.

"You ever smelled kimchi? It's fermented cabbage. The Koreans love it, but to me it smells like bottled dog fart."

"What an appetizing story, Chase. You really know how to make a girl feel special." Elaine picked up the menu and started studying it closely. I felt like the frog prince without a happy ending. All the snappy comebacks suddenly sounded limp. I was feeling put down, and then I felt put out.

"Tusuro felt special . . . and as far as I'm concerned, that's where the rubber hits the road in this business. Now, it occurs to me that you're the one here with a problem, not me. All I've lost is a commission that I haven't earned yet."

"Chase—"

I held up my hand. I hate it when someone interrupts me in the middle of a good speech.

"Chase nothing! You probably play a mean game of princess, but save it for the guys on the maintenance crew. Like you said, this is business. I don't know what you need, but I know what I don't need, and that's to sit at the wrong end of a long crooked nose that's stuck up in the air at too steep an angle."

Elaine looked stunned. She's probably used to scolding servants and kicking house dogs. Things are different out in the junkyard.

"You probably feel like getting up and walking out of here," I said. "I'll lose a lot of face with Tusuro if you do. But you might lose something, too. You just don't know what yet."

The waitress came back just then.

"You ready order?"

I knew Elaine hadn't read much of the menu.

"You like deep fried shrimp?"

She nodded. I gestured at the waitress as I gave her the order. Tusuro brings the girls over from Japan for six months at a time. They don't have much English when they get here, but they know how to convert dollars to yen by the time they go home.

"The lady will have tempura," I said, "and a Sapporo beer." I pointed at the menu, too. It would be embarrassing for her if she had to ask me to repeat anything. I ordered teriyaki salmon with lots of tea and water, and answered the girl's shy little bow with a head nod and a smile.

I kept the smile as I turned back to Elaine.

"Wanna start over?" I said.

She smiled back.

"I was being awfully bitchy, wasn't I? I guess I'm used to being treated like the boss's little girl."

"How long have you worked with him?"

"All my life. It's the only job I've ever had."

"How long a life have you had?"

"What? Oh, how long have I worked for him. Ummm, about fifteen years, I'd say, since I was seventeen. I worked almost full-time while I was in college, even."

"Where was that?"

She looked surprised, and a little guarded.

"Houston," she said, after the slightest hesitation.

"Why did your folks decide to come back to San Jose?"

"Just my dad came. My mother got a divorce and stayed in Texas. I liked my work, so I decided to move here, too."

Just then the miso soup broke into the interrogation. It had been a long day, with little time for food. I didn't talk again until I was spearing the chunks of tofu with my chopsticks. Elaine watched me pick up the bowl to drink the soup, and then did the same.

"I worked some real estate syndications in Houston in the late seventies. What was your dad's company called? Maybe we were competitors."

"I doubt it," she said. "We were in oil and gas leases, mostly. But what about you? What was a San Jose broker going to Texas for? Wasn't there enough money right here?"

"I worked out of Los Angeles then, and no, there wasn't enough money, not in Los Angeles, and not in Texas, either."

This time I got rescued by the food, arranged in square wooden trays with little dishes of sauce for dipping. I'm not embarrassed about my past, but I don't volunteer information, either. The ride to the top had been so fast and furious I hadn't even known I was there until I was plunging down the other side. I rarely think about those days now, the days of magic, the days when everything I touched turned to gold, the days when even the gold we touched turned to more gold.

We were the bright ones, the new leaders, the bold entrepreneurs;

we did the things they later wrote the self-help books about. We didn't just buy real estate with no money down, we got cash back out of the deals. We bought property on an option and a handshake, got sub-divisions approved, and made deals for the lots before we ever had to pay for the original land. Not only that, we sold the lots to the limited partners, the doctors and the dentists and the lawyers—the lawyers were the best, the easiest to fool—together with a contract for our builder to build the houses, our bank to finance the deals, our real estate broker to sell the suburban wonders, and our escrow company to handle the paperwork. And you know what? The people lined up to buy the product. They camped out for days to earn the right to buy our split-level ramblers, because no sacrifice was too great to get on the magic real estate merry-go-round.

And at every level there was the cut, the rake-off for the bold ones. We paid ourselves a commission on the land purchase, a developer's fee for getting the subdivision approved, a syndication fee for putting the partnership together, five percent for supervising the builder, ten percent gratuity from the lucky decorator, we furnished our own homes with leftover "samples" from the model homes, we got a point (that's one percent) for arranging the mortgages, we got a commission for selling the houses, we split up the profits of the escrow company, and when the reporters and ghostwriters came for interviews, the "wise ones" made the journalists pick up the tab for lunch.

When our investors asked us about the oil and gas deals their friends were talking about at cocktail parties, you know what we said? Stay away from those guys, we said, they're a bunch of crooks.

So I knew more about Tom Endman now than Elaine thought she had told me, and I speculated that Endman's journey from Texas may have been sparked by some of the same motivations that caused my migration northward from Los Angeles. Failure. Financial col-lapse. Questions of fraud. Suspicions for theft. Evidence of bad faith. Even loss of confidence. Hunger for a second chance, a fresh start, a new attempt for the gold ring.

Yeah, we were the wise ones; and I bet Tom Endman was one of us, too, believing in the magic, believing in our own genius, certain that we had rediscovered the long-lost secret of Midas, and only learning too late, much, much too late, that all we had found was inflation—a treacherous mirage of quickly shifting sand that swallows believers who hang on to their own myths too long.

Is Tom Endman still a believer? It's possible. After all, the doctors and the dentists are still generating all that excess cash. The lawyers are still the easiest to fool. People still talk at cocktail parties. And the oceans are deeper than we suspect, and the sharks still follow the schools of little fishes.

At the moment, however, Elaine and I were devouring the fishes, and not much else happened until we finished.

"How many appraisals did Mickey Peachton do for you?" I said, casually, while I worried a bone out of the last bite of the salmon.

"I don't know. Why, have you found something already?"

"No," I lied, "I just want to know what I'm looking for, so if I do hear something, I'll be able to make the right connections. Can you remember any other properties?"

"God, Chase, I think he did some other work for us, too."

"Any problems that you know of?"

"No, not that I've heard of."

I started on my fifth cup of tea and tried to look pensive.

"What about your investors? Anyone else squawking about problems?"

"Chase, we're probably the most respected investment company in the valley. Tom got the mayor's Golden Fleece award last year for civic and business achievement."

"High profiles make good targets. Isn't Silicon Investment Group a publicly traded corporation?"

"Yes, but—"

"So if a raider wanted to come after the company wouldn't a couple of publicized problems hurt the stock price, and make you a sitting duck for a takeover?"

Her look of surprise was so genuine I couldn't doubt it.

"How do you get your investors?" I asked, quickly.

"Mostly word of mouth," she said. "You know, doctors, dentists, they go to the same cocktail parties, they have the same financial planners, sooner or later someone they trust mentions Silicon Investment Group. We even have a lot of lawyers as clients, that's how respected we are."

"And where do you get your product?"

"That's getting harder and harder. For a while there were plenty of good apartment properties we could syndicate. Also some foreclosed properties, like the one Frank Baker bought. We've even thought of becoming developers, so we could create a quality product for our investors. You know, buy the land, get the permits, find the builder, get the financing, create the whole product in-house."

She looked away across the restaurant, considering the vision she had just shared with me.

"I guess this Mickey Peachton thing shows there're lots of potential problems," she said. Elaine reached across the table and took my hands.

"Chase," she said, "please try to get to the bottom of this quickly. Tom's so worried. It would break my heart to see him get hurt by all this."

She glanced reluctantly at her watch, and slowly pulled her hands away.

"I have to go," she said. "Can you get started tomorrow?"

"I'm already started," I said. "Would you mind if I sat in on the seminar tonight? I want to get a feel for your operation. If anyone is setting you up, it might help me recognize the situation."

"Of course," she nodded. "I'm sure Tom would love to have you sit in."

"And what about you?"

Elaine looked at me appraisingly, and sighed visibly.

"It's going to be hard to keep this business, isn't it?"

"It never has been just business for me," I said.

"Thanks for dinner," she said. "As for the rest of it, let's just play the cards and see what turns up. OK?"

"You're the dealer," I said, as I left much too big a tip. And she was the dealer, too. But that didn't mean I wouldn't be cutting the cards, calling the bluffs, counting the money in the pot, and yeah, looking up her sleeves for extra aces. That's the danger, I thought. There may be more hidden there than aces. And when it came to searching, I just didn't know if I'd be able to stop with her sleeves.

44

chapter **ten**

···

There was a special seminar room at the SIG building that was as clever as anything I've seen. I expected the usual auditorium, maybe a couple of hundred seats, a lapel microphone that you can't see, a back-screen projector, the whole high-tech works. Instead, it was a room about the size of a grade-school classroom, with two horseshoe-shaped tables, one inside the other, both facing a little low lectern table in front of a clean green chalkboard.

There were seats for about thirty people around the two horseshoes, on sturdy wooden desk chairs with arms and good gray vinyl-covered padding on the seats and backs. A rim of indirect lighting circled the walls about a foot from the ceiling. Light panels overhead focused on the seating area, so that even in the smallish room the seats seemed to be clustered together for warmth and protection. Speakers hung high in the four corners. I could hear the "Water Music," even though the volume was turned down way low.

We were early, but not by much. Elaine left me on my own and started circulating among the guests immediately, taking their invitations and seating them at the tables. Each place had a packet and name tag in front of it, together with a pencil, ballpoint pen, and a water glass. Each place had a little light by it like those lights for reading in bed. I picked up a folder and leafed through it. It was the simplest presentation I ever saw. As you opened the folder, the left-hand page contained graphs and illustrations about real estate values, interest costs, and appreciation rates. Each right-hand page was blank except for the SIG logo and the word "notes." By each folder was a card specifying that no tape recorders were allowed, and that no other papers or notebooks were permitted. Obviously, if you wanted to refer to your notes from the seminar, you were going to have to see the SIG materials each time you looked something up.

I heard a small commotion at the door.

"I'm sorry," Elaine was saying, "but no one is allowed in without an invitation."

A middle-aged balding man in a casual leather jacket wasn't taking this news quietly. A woman hanging on his arm looked outraged.

"We were referred to you by Maxie Turbot," the man was saying.

"You do know Maxie Turbot, the football player, don't you?" the woman chimed in.

"Maxie is a dear friend of Mr. Endman's," Elaine said, "but Maxie doesn't write invitations. I do, and—"

"You folks know Maxie?" A voice from the hallway made all three turn to the door. Tom Endman came in, outstretched right hand taking first the man's and then the woman's hand in turn. He wore an expensive-looking suit that didn't seem to fit just right, and held a wine bottle with a fancy-looking label in his left hand.

"Maxie's a wonderful man," Tom was saying. "More of an example now off the field than he was when he was playing, if that's possible." Endman's right arm was around the man's shoulder, now, and the smaller fingers of his left hand were softly touching the woman's arm for emphasis, while he held the wine bottle effortlessly with just his thumb and the palm of his hand.

"Any friend of Maxie's is always welcome here . . . but you know, this seminar isn't really the way to get started. Everyone here tonight has already had a personal interview and a review of their portfolio by one of our account executives. You'd miss out on a major portion of the program if you sat in tonight without the other preparation."

The couple were both nodding understandingly. While he talked, Endman had slowly rotated one hundred and eighty degrees so that the three of them were facing the door.

"The best thing we can do," he continued, "is set you up with a personal appointment as soon as possible next week. Talk to Elaine here, she's my alter ego, and tell her to put you down for a time when I can talk to you also, just so the account executive will know you're a special client. Elaine?" He beckoned to his "alter ego," who scooted right over.

"Set these good folks up for next week when I can see them," he said. He turned back to the couple, now halfway out the door.

"Please do me a favor," he said, handing the man the bottle of wine. "Let me know what you think of this when you come in next week. This is one of the first bottles of our new private-label chardonnay . . . we've got a little vineyard up in the Santa Cruz mountains off Summit Road. Tell me if we should bottle up the rest of this, or just make it into salad dressing."

By this time Elaine was on the spot. I noticed she took the man's arm snugly in her own as she steered them on out. I listened as they started down the hall.

"Did Dad even get your names?" she was asking. "No? That's just like him. He always says a stranger is just a friend he hasn't met yet. . . ."

A late arriving couple pushed between me and the receding voices. I saw Tom Endman notice me out of the corner of his eye as he seated the clients. The room was almost full, and the clock showed seven-twenty-seven. Endman came up to me and took my arm.

"I've seen you, but I don't think we've met," he said. "I'm Tom Endman."

"Chase Randel. I talked to Frank Baker this morning about his condos. Elaine asked me to help her verify some appraisals that Mickey Peachton did."

A shadow crossed Endman's face.

"I got so busy I forgot about Frank for a few minutes," he said. "A tragedy, a terrible tragedy. I wish you hadn't reminded me. I shouldn't do this seminar tonight, but some of these people have waited weeks to get started on their investment programs, and I just can't let them down." He stood quietly for a moment and then shook his head before he looked straight at me again with sharply focused eyes that were still a bright blue. I just glimpsed the edge of a contact lens on his cornea, and I briefly wondered if the color was genetic or commercial.

"Elaine's told me what you've offered to do," he said, "and I want you to know how much we appreciate it." He looked at his watch, a stylish gold Rolex. "Time to do it," he said. "Can you sit in on the

47

seminar? Maybe we can talk a little afterward." And with a pat on the arm and smile, he turned and went to the front of the seminar. I grabbed a vacant stair and waited for the show to begin. Endman fiddled with a switch that lowered the light level everywhere except where he was standing. I saw Elaine slip into the room and take a chair in a corner. There was a trumpet fanfare just concluding one of the allegro movements of the "Water Music." He punched a switch to kill the music, and then stepped around in front of the lectern and leaned on the table. After a moment he held his hands out to the people at the horseshoe tables.

"Would you join me for a brief prayer?" he said. "Lord, bless what we do here tonight so that it may lead to benefits not only for ourselves, but also that we can take these blessings forth from this room and spread them out into the world so that it may become a better place for us all to live. Amen."

Just after the prayer, a late-arriving couple slipped into their seats. I couldn't really see them in the dim light, but I got an impression they were lean and well dressed. There was now a full house. As Endman worked into the seminar my thoughts drifted to other seminars I have known. It's an interesting word, "seminar." The dictionary says it comes from seminary, and means to study in a cloistered place. Well, we're pretty shut away in here, and I can tell we're going to be "studying" the advantages of real estate investments, particularity those made through the Silicon Investment Group.

Did something happen to the language twenty years or so ago? Maybe I just lost my innocence, and didn't really notice it was missing until the last few years. But I can remember when we pursued the "truth" in gatherings like these, I recall this willingness to let the chips fall where they would. Do I have a bad memory? Or is everyone engaged in selling something these days under the guise of studying the facts? God knows I've done enough selling these last few years. But it's worked. The clients have made money, and they're happy. Maybe the mistake is mine. Perhaps I really didn't lose my innocence after all. Maybe I'll just always be the naive farm boy groping his way through a fast-lane world in low gear, immersed in a fog of cultural shock that hides the stark reality of today's urban California.

48

I expected Endman to bring the overhead lights back on so everyone could take notes, but apparently that's what the little book lights were for. A few clicked on, and a few people took notes, but most sat and listened.

"It's not what you have that counts," he said, "it's what you do with what you have. It's not where you start that counts, but the fact that you get started. The greatest fortunes in America have been made in real estate, but you know, my friends, nobody makes money in real estate until they own some."

Endman was pacing back and forth behind his little lectern, apparently talking from memory, or maybe just from a desire to communicate the information that was in his head. Every face followed his movement. Even in the half darkness, I couldn't hear anybody yawn.

"The problem for most people," he said, "is that they think they have to be rich to buy investment real estate, or that they have to do it alone . . . and that's frightening—I know it's frightening, trusting the savings of your lifetime to an investment you don't know much about. That's why the Silicon Investment Group is here. To create an investment family for you that takes the worry out of participating in the greatest money-making opportunity the world has ever seen— Silicon Valley real estate.

"At SIG, we make real estate investment just like the stock market. We find a big piece of property, we allow investors like yourselves to buy small shares of ownership through limited partnerships, we manage it for you, handle the rents, the maintenance, the insurance, all the little painful details that make individual ownership such a headache, and when the market's right, we sell it for a profit.

"If something comes up for you so that you need to sell your share, we find a buyer, or we buy it ourselves at the price you paid for it. It's one hundred percent safe. Nobody owns too big a piece of any one property, so your risk is spread out over several properties. You have our expertise to count on. You've seen our track record when you met with your account executive. If you didn't like our record, you wouldn't have come back tonight."

Endman had more than their attention now. He had their expectations and their hopes hovering over the gathering. Their hands were restless, ready to reach for pens, and to sign where they were told.

"Some of you may scoff a little when I talk about SIG being an investment family, but that's the way we treat people around here. Some people say I'm the old man of the family. I guess I think of myself as the uncle, really, the one who went off and discovered a marvelous secret that he now wants to share with the rest of the family. It's a big family " he said, "and there's still room for more. If what I've said tonight sounds interesting, I want you to join us—right now—because now is the only time you ever have to get started on protecting your future through real estate investment."

Now, almost imperceptibly, the lights overhead were starting to brighten. Endman looked down at his notes briefly, and then scanned the room with his eyes. He stretched out his arms to include us all.

"I'll be happy to answer any questions," he said, "and I'll stay as long as it takes to clear up any concerns you may have about the program."

I almost expected them to break into applause. Instead, we got some fairly good, if rather simplistic, questions.

"What about interest rates?" said the man in the mostly green plaid golf pants. "What if interest rates go back up?"

"That's a good question," Endman said. "It's a universal question. Those of you who suffered in the Great Depression have spent the rest of your lives defending yourselves against its return. It's never come back.

"Some of you suffered from inflation in the seventies. You bought gold to protect yourselves from inflation's return. It hasn't come back.

"Some of you suffered from high interest rates at the start of the eighties. You're still worried about them, but they haven't come back.

"Last year there was the stock market crash. You vowed to stay out of that market, but it's done well since the crash.

"There's a lesson here. We can't predict disasters. The best we can do is put our money in the safest, most profitable place we can find, and that's Silicon Valley real estate."

The back row was still quite dim. A familiar-sounding voice asked the next question. I couldn't quite make out her face.

"Why did one of your investors commit suicide here today?" the voice asked.

Endman turned pale. He seemed to slump forward, and had to catch himself with his hands on the lectern. There was a buzz of whispers around the room.

"That's not just a lie," Endman said, "that's a damn vicious lie. Frank Baker had a seizure of some kind and fell to his death. As far as we know, it was an accident, and you have no right to smear his name with your lies."

The lights came the rest of the way on with a jolt. I saw the face behind the questions, and I sat back in my chair in shock.

"But wasn't Frank Baker losing everything he had on a property you found for him?" The voice belonged to Molly Gish, the tall, blonde owner of a neighborhood newspaper, and someone I had "known" quite well quite recently.

"Whoever told you that told you another lie," Endman said. "Elaine, get security in here and get those two out before I lose my temper."

"Aren't other SIG properties in trouble, Mr. Endman? Don't you think the public has a right to know the facts before they put more money into your schemes?"

Endman was recovered now, and was walking quickly toward Molly and her escort, who was dressed like Johnny Yuppie. I'd heard she was keeping company with someone I wouldn't like. He looked like one of those people my grandmother said looked like butter wouldn't melt in his mouth. More like snot wouldn't stick to his nose, I'd say, but grandmother had more class than I do.

"I'm warning you, lady, leave now or be arrested for trespassing. You're not an invited guest. Elaine," he almost shouted, "get security in here right now."

Elaine was already talking on the wall phone. For a minute I thought Endman was going to take a swing at Molly, but she was holding a camera at waist level, and it suddenly flashed in Endman's face. He stepped back in surprise, and Molly and her unisex drone slipped out in the confusion. She left behind a buzz of shocked, whispering voices, and a shaken Tom Endman. Elaine was at his side instantly, her arm around him, guiding him back toward the lectern. She watched him for a minute, waiting for him to take the lead, and then she started to talk.

chapter **eleven**

L adies and gentlemen," she started, after glancing at him again, "today one of my father's oldest friends and clients, Frank Baker, suffered a seizure while he was standing in the roof garden off our eighth-floor office. Sadly, he was standing by the railing at the time, and somehow, when he collapsed, he fell over the railing to his death."

Everyone was quiet again. Elaine had taken control of the room, and I could see in her the power her stepfather must have taught her. She paused, looking at everyone in turn. Her arm went back around Tom Endman's waist.

"I asked Dad not to do this seminar tonight, but he insisted. He knew you were counting on him.

"That woman was not an invited guest. I believe she's a reporter of some kind. She's obviously trying to invent a story where none exists. Unfortunately, that seems to be how the press operates these days.

"Usually at this point in the evening Tom and I would talk to you about some of the investments available at this time. But . . . with your permission, of course . . . I really think it would be best if I had your account executive contact you to present the opportunities privately. Does anyone object to that?"

Elaine scanned the little audience. Tom stood beside her drinking a glass of water. For a moment, he seemed totally unaware that any of the rest of us were there. One hand tugged absently at his collar. He put the glass down and rolled his head around while he rubbed the back of his neck. His eyes stayed shut until he finally heard Elaine speaking his name.

"Tom? Tom? Do you want to say anything before we call it a night?"

He opened his eyes slowly, looking first at Elaine and then around the room. Amazingly, as he saw everyone staring at him, he seemed to grow in stature and presence, and his face started to glow again. When he spoke again, he talked softly, although his voice echoed around the room.

"Thank you very much for being here tonight," he said. "I know it seems like bad timing, but there really isn't a bad time for making new friends, is there? And sometimes, you know, the relationships we form under stressful conditions turn out to be the longest-lasting and the most meaningful relationships we have."

Tom paused to radiate at the audience, slowly turning his brilliant, sad smile from one side of the room to the other. I heard someone coming in behind me, but I didn't take my eyes off Tom Endman.

"My friends, I hope you've learned all you hoped to learn tonight, but if there was one thought I would want you to take away with you, it would be this:

It's not where you start that counts, but the fact that you get started;
It's not how much you start with that counts, but what you get started on.

So start here, start now, to take control of your lives back from the planners and the brokers and the bellyachers.

Start now to protect your future with some good old Silicon Valley real estate.

We hope you'll join the SIG family, there're thousands of your friends and neighbors out there who swear by us . . . you can count on us . . . and

> I know we can count on you, to get started now in
> Silicon Valley real estate investments.

Endman was about to continue, when Elaine took his arm again. He looked down at her as she interrupted him.

"Good night, everyone," she said. "Thank you for coming. Your account executive will be calling you right away."

I stood frozen in place, feeling I was at the end of a very familiar scene that I couldn't quite recognize. Then it hit me. Blue Mountain Presbyterian Church, Yadkinburg, North Carolina, July 1955. The Reverend Bob Earnest—"Earnest Bob" Earnest, they called him. The summer revival that always followed vacation Bible school. It's on toward ten o'clock on a Wednesday night and the preacher's been going at it for over two hours, and now it's time for the call to the altar.

"It doesn't matter what you've done," Earnest Bob's saying, "what matters is that you're ready to come to Jesus.

"He doesn't care who you are. He doesn't care what you've done. What he cares about is that you join him now. That you join us here tonight at the great baptismal font and start to swim in the ocean of Life. Cast your bread now upon the waters of the Lord, and he shall make you Fishers of Men. That's right . . . come on up . . . get your new life started tonight . . . Amen, brothers and sisters, get started now. . . ."

That's it. I haven't heard anyone give the call to the altar as good as Tom Endman did tonight since I last saw Ernest Bob thirty-three years ago. That's why Endman was surprised when Elaine interrupted him, he was reaching for the collection plate, he was ready to sign up all these sinners here tonight. That's always the next move after the call to the altar, you pass the collection plate. For Tom it's probably as natural a reflex as reaching for the butter plate after you pass the bread.

Tonight, though, Molly had interrupted the altar call with her positively hostile questions, kind of like Satan showing up at the front of the church with some dancing girls. Elaine had wisely postponed

54

the collection of the offering until another time. But there would be another time. Like Tom said, you can count on him.

I slowly moved to the front of the room as the investors filed out. Several paused to say comforting words to Tom and Elaine. The others I watched, though, left more quickly than I might have expected. They looked like bank depositors who had heard an uncomfortable rumor just as they were filling out the signature cards. I don't think the account executives are going to be very successful when they call back on this crowd.

I was just about to start talking to Tom Endman when I heard Elaine's voice behind me.

"Oh, hello," she said. I turned, and there was Hilda Straton. I hadn't seen her slip in. I wondered how much she had witnessed. She looked a little recovered from the afternoon, but still appeared agitated and worried. I did the introduction to Tom right away. I didn't know if Elaine would remember Hilda's name, and lawyers are so touchy about being remembered.

"Tom Endman, Hilda Straton," I said. "Hilda was Frank Baker's attorney from Billy Blake's office."

"Ms. Straton, it's a pleasure." Tom beamed his biggest smile. "Any associate of Billy Blake's is always welcome here."

"Mr. Endman, I know—"

"No, please, call me Tom. Mr. Endman makes me sound so old."

"Well, you could be my father."

I flinched. Sensitivity is obviously not Hilda's strong suit. Tom, though, didn't miss a beat.

"Do I know your mother?"

Hilda blushed.

"That's not what I mean. I mean, you're in your fifties and I'm in my twenties, so therefore—"

"Hilda, you are refreshingly honest. And it's true, I am old enough to be your father. But I would prefer you to think of me more as an uncle. Not a Dutch uncle, but perhaps a French uncle, if you see what I mean.

"Now," Tom said, "you didn't come here to talk about our relationship . . . or did you?"

"Mr. Endman—"

"Please, Tom."

"Tom, then." Hilda looked quite flustered. "I know it's late, but I need to talk to you about Frank Baker. His wife is very upset, and she's saying a lot of unpleasant things."

"Ms. Straton," Elaine tried to interrupt.

"It's all right, Elaine," Tom said. "But let me suggest something. It's been a long day. Let's go upstairs to the office, sit down, relax, have a drink, and see if we can't work together on this. What about it, Chase? Sound all right to you?"

"Lead the way," I said.

Tom held out his arm to Hilda like he was taking the Queen of Denmark in to dinner. Hilda had sort of a blank look on her face, as if it were all a bit too much for her, but she took his arm and walked out the door toward the elevator. Elaine had a fixed look on her face, too, but it wasn't blank. Still, I offered her my arm, and out we went, too.

chapter **twelve**

··

This was turning out to be one of the stranger situations of my life. I'm here to find out how Frank Baker got bamboozled. Baker's lawyer is supposed to be after the same thing, and here we are, two plump little flies riding up the elevator with the suspected spiders. Next thing you know we'll be hanging upside down in the web, getting fattened up for next week's menu, and Tom will be asking us if we enjoyed our meal.

Still, I shouldn't complain. Poor me, sandwiched in between two very attractive women, and a man who is either one of the brilliant minds of our time or one of its outstanding scoundrels. Life could be worse. I could be bored.

The cops had given Endman his office back, but there was still a yellow tape sealing the French doors that led to the balcony. We sat in deep leather armchairs, the kind that feel so smooth on the bottom of your pants that you don't lean back for fear of sliding off onto the floor. The whole room was accented in various shades of burgundy, from the red leather seat covers to the massive cherry desk that Endman sat behind to the deep red frames on the photographs covering the walls. The photographs were mostly of Endman posing outdoors with wealthy men, or women and horses who both looked overgroomed. There was a deep pile Persian carpet over the oak floors, and a fireplace with no ashes on the hearth and no soot on the bricks.

Elaine got brandy for herself and the others, and club soda for me.

"How long have you been practicing law in San Jose, Ms. Straton?" Tom asked.

"Since I left McGeorge School of Law in 1984."

"You must have known Justice Kennedy, then, before he left for the Supreme Court."

"He is the school's claim to fame."

"Well, if that's where you learned that it's all right for a lawyer to work at night, then it must be a good school." Endman beamed gently at Hilda. "Now, what can I help you with, that can't wait until tomorrow?"

"Well, Mr. Endman—"

"Tom."

"Tom, then. Well, uh, Tom, I spoke to Mrs. Baker tonight, and she's adamant about filing a lawsuit of some kind first thing Monday morning. Now, normally, this isn't something I would discuss with a possible defendant, but Mr. Blake suggested I ask to go through the Baker files so we can give some accurate advice to his widow. We would get to see the files anyway on discovery. Perhaps everybody could save a ton of legal fees if we cooperate at the beginning."

"Well, Ms. Straton—"

"Hilda. Fair's fair."

"Thank you, Hilda. It's a beautiful name, by the way. It was my grandmother's name. I don't think there's any way you can say the name Hilda that doesn't sound pretty. And you certainly do the name justice."

Hilda sat looking at Endman like she was in a trance, a faint smile on her face, and her body completely at ease in a way I had never seen it.

"Elaine," Tom said. Elaine jumped like she was waking up from a trance, too, except that she wasn't smiling.

"Do we keep the Baker records in current files?" he said to her.

"They're more than current. They're right on top of my desk."

"Could you bring them here so Hilda and I can take a look at them. You, too, Chase, if you think you'd be interested in that sort of thing."

"Are the appraisals in there?" I asked.

"The lender keeps the appraisals, I'm afraid."

Elaine had gotten up abruptly.

"Can you help me, Chase? There is a file for each individual condo. It's quite a stack."

I got up and followed her into the hall. She didn't look back or slow down until we got to her office, where Elaine spun around and pointed a glaring finger at me.

"What's she trying to pull?" Elaine said. Her eyes were narrowed like they were being seen from the wrong end of a gun sight.

"He doesn't have to go along with it," I said, holding up my hands. "Neither do you."

"What the hell can I do about it without making us look guilty to little Ms. Nicely. With her great big law degree and her short little skirt. It looks like a napkin, and it doesn't cover much more than a napkin." Elaine was picking up a stack of files, which she handed to me. She scooped up the rest and pushed me back out the door.

When we got back to Endman's office, Hilda's chair was pulled over beside his behind the desk. Tom was showing Hilda the pictures on the wall. She had her glasses off and was gazing intently with her face about six inches from the photo. Her right hand was holding lightly onto Tom's upper arm.

Elaine dumped her stack of files across her father's desk. I set my load beside hers, straightening them carefully so they wouldn't fall. Tom and Hilda didn't turn around. He was finishing some story about a horse going the wrong way around a steeplechase course, and the way Hilda was looking up at him, I was sorry I missed the beginning. Elaine went over to her brandy and tossed it down. I walked up behind Tom and Hilda and cleared my throat.

"Do you think you're going to need any help going through those files, Hilda?" I said.

She was still laughing at the story as she turned to face me. She put her glasses back on a little sheepishly. One arm of the glasses didn't quite get tucked over her ear. Hilda didn't notice.

"No, Chase," she said, sweetly. "I don't need any help. Besides, you'd just get bored. You know how escrow files are."

"It's a good thing you'll have some funny stories to lighten the work." I turned to Endman. "Tom, I think it's great the way you're helping out. I'll see that Mrs. Baker hears about it."

Endman looked at me sharply before he held out his hand. "Keep in touch," he said.

I waved to Elaine as I walked to the door. She held up a hand as she emptied the snifter. I stopped by the door.

"Why do you need to do that tonight, Dad? Let her come back in the morning." She smiled at Hilda. "Surely it can wait until then, Ms. Straton. My father's had a long and stressful day. He needs his rest."

"Of course, if that's what you think. What do you think, Tom?" Endman looked at his watch.

"It won't take that long, Elaine. Why don't you have the guard downstairs run you home. You don't need to wait."

I knew that was my cue, of course. But like an actor with a great line, I let the silence stretch out after the key words. John Wayne, of all people, was a master at that. Remember how he would look off to the side in disgust, take off his hat, and wipe his face before he made his devastating response to the villain? I let Elaine set her glass down, pick up her purse, and head for the door before I delivered my best line of the play so far.

"I can give you a ride?" I said.

"Could you?" She stopped, and I could have sworn the surprise was almost genuine. She turned back to Tom and Hilda. "Chase will give me a ride, Dad. Don't be late." She gave Hilda a tight-lipped smile, and marched out the door. This time I took my cue and ran with it. If I hadn't, I don't think Elaine would have waited.

We didn't talk much until we were on the street.

"Where do you live?" I said.

"Just up in Los Gatos. You?"

"I have a house downtown, over by the William Street Park."

"That's the opposite direction."

I took her arm as I steered her around the front of my car.

"No problem," I said. "I'm going on over to the beach house in Santa Cruz tonight. It's been a jammed up day. I need a little ocean breeze to air my head out."

"I wish you'd take that attorney of yours with you. Take her for a moonlight swim. I hear the great whites are running."

I opened the car door, tucked her in, and shut the door firmly. Chivalry's not dead. It's just been living in a granny unit out behind my garage.

I got the Merc out on the freeway before I spoke to her again.

"You don't much like Hilda."

"That's what I like about you, Chase, you're so perceptive."

"If you tell me I'm sensitive, I'll punch you in the mouth."

"Remarks like that are one of the things I don't like about you."

"What's with the Hilda vendetta?"

"Are men born blind, or have you been practicing?"

"Men are born to solve riddles, but females are beyond me."

Elaine looked out the window as we passed the airport. San Jose International Airport, they call it now. They even have planes that fly nonstop to Canada now. What's in a name? Most everything, it seems.

"You think I'm jealous?" she said, finally.

"I don't do labels."

I looked over at her. She met my eyes and didn't look away. I glanced at the road occasionally, but mostly I stared at Elaine. Her hands were folded quietly in her lap, and she smelled the same way she had in the elevator this afternoon. The scent filled the car. My hand reached over and touched her cheek. I wanted to slap it for being so fresh, but my other hand was busy with the steering wheel. She looked away for a moment, and then back at me, smiling.

60

"What's so funny?" I said.

"You are."

"Are you laughing because I'm so suave and you're so lucky to be with me?"

"No, because you missed my exit."

"Oh, shit, so I did." I pretended to be concerned. "Why don't you just come to Santa Cruz with me. It's miles to the next exit, anyway."

"No, it's not . . . and, yes I'd like to come to Santa Cruz . . . but not tonight."

"The moon's up, there's a warm breeze tonight, I'll even bet the tide's out. We can walk on the beach in the moonlight."

"I'm allergic to moonlight."

"What about warm sea breezes?"

"Them, too. There's the next exit. Don't miss it."

I shot her a hard questioning look. She looked back, and didn't blink. I slowed and took the exit, made a U-turn across the highway, and headed back down the mountain to Los Gatos.

"What about fun?" I asked, after a minute. "You allergic to that, too?"

"Maybe I am."

I took the right exit this time.

"What about love?" I said.

chapter **thirteen**

W hat about love?" She looked at me evenly as she said it, hands still folded in her lap. The car's air conditioning had shut itself off, like the smart little machine it is. I could catch a faint trace of her perfume again.

There were still a few people on the streets of Los Gatos. It's a town that likes to think of itself as a little Beverly Hills for political liberals. The lights from the shops splashed across Elaine's face. Her eyes stayed on me. Not staring, but more like they were creating a force field that wrapped itself around me so it could examine me from all directions. I didn't answer her question until the red light caught us at Highway 9.

"I've known people that were allergic to love," I said. "They take all kinds of strange medicines for it. Drugs, sex, politics, no sex . . . What's your medicine?" I turned left toward Monte Verde without her direction. It's the richer part of the rich part of town. I'd heard Endman had a little spread up there in the middle of it all.

"I'm not sick," she said. "Medicine is for sick people."

"You damn sure don't look sick."

She finally smiled again.

"Turn left just past the light," she said.

I drove up a long driveway that wound around short, fat oak trees. The curves were marked by little low-voltage lights shaped like tulip blossoms. I put my window down. The air was cooler here, and had that little tang that oak trees give it. The grounds under the trees looked unkempt in the headlights, which didn't surprise me. The Endmans don't look like the manicured-lawn type. Nothing much will grow under those oak trees, anyway.

"Thanks for the lift," she said, with another smile.

"I could walk you in, make sure your bath's hot enough, tuck you in . . . I could even get your bed warm for you."

"I'm sure you could. Who knows, you might even cure my allergies. But I'm just too tired tonight. Most of all I don't want you to get distracted from asking questions tomorrow."

She got out then, and walked slowly up to the steps. I lowered her window as she went, hoping for just one more whiff of that wonderful woman smell she had. She stopped and turned before she went up to the door, and raised an eyebrow at me.

"Call me at the office tomorrow," she said, finally, and went on in.

There's a Hollywood movie that has a scene like this. The sort-of hero watches from his car and then goes up to the French doors and smashes through them and takes the woman right there on the floor in the middle of the broken glass.

There was a newspaper story last year that had a scene like this, too. This time, after the guy breaks in, the woman runs to the kitchen, gets a butcher knife, and stabs the sort-of hero.

Hollywood versus the real world. I love the movies, but I guess, deep down, I'm a reality man. That's one reason I rolled up the window and drove off. The other reason was, the door looked like solid oak.

When I got to the highway, Santa Cruz didn't seem interesting anymore, so I turned east and headed for home. I'd been ready for bed a few minutes earlier, but not because I was sleepy. Just on a whim, I called Information on the portaphone and got Mickey Peachton's phone number. Then I called a friend at a twenty-four hour answering service and got the address that goes with his number. She said she got off at midnight. I said I'd call her back.

The address she gave was just down in Willow Glen, an older part of town that's never stopped being popular—or expensive. I swung off the highway at Meridian and headed down to drive by his house, just because I wasn't sleepy and because I wanted to see if there were any outward signs that the house was occupied by a bent appraiser. By all accounts, the only straight thing Mickey Peachton was doing these days was lining out cocaine. I just wanted to see if it showed. I'm like that. I want the world's outer appearance to reflect its inner reality. I don't expect it to, mind you, I just want it to. I want Mickey Peachton's yard to be overgrown, I want the paint to be flaking on his house, and I want his car to be parked in the driveway with a flat tire and its hood up.

Houses in Willow Glen, of course, are not like that. I think there's a law against exposing your inner reality in public. Mickey Peachton's front yard was neat, the trees had been recently trimmed, and the front porch looked pretty enough to welcome a Girl Scout cookie drive. The porch light was on, a dim yellow glow diffused through a Spanish-style black wrought-iron hanging lamp. There was a real estate sign stuck in the ground beside the little front porch. I guess Peachton has ideas about moving. It looked pleasant along the tree-lined sidewalk, so I parked and got out for a stroll up the street. A little spaniel-looking black dog was sitting in front of Peachton's front door, barking about every thirty seconds like he forgot his key.

As I crossed the street toward Mickey's house, a next-door neighbor stepped out and glared toward Peachton's. As I watched, he walked over and started banging on the front door. Finally he started yelling.

"Open the door, you idiot," he shouted. "Let your dog in."

Ordinarily I don't talk to strangers, but I remembered Tom Endman's proverb that a stranger was just a friend he hasn't met, and walked on up behind the neighbor pounding at Mickey's front door.

"What's the problem?" I said.

"This damn dog's been barking for an hour. The son of a bitch won't let his dog in." The neighbor had on a robe over pajamas and slippers. He'd already taken his teeth out, and talked without opening his lips very wide. His bifocals glittered under the amber porch light.

"Who are you anyway?" he added

"I'm a real estate broker, I'm a friend of Mickey's."

The neighbor didn't look impressed.

"This guy's got a lot of friends," he said.

"Why do you think he's home?"

"He was here earlier. There were some people here. His car hasn't left. The lights are on. He's probably passed out again. This little yapper will bark all night if he doesn't get inside."

"Has this happened before?"

"I thought he was your friend. Do you know the guy or don't you?"

The real estate sign gave me an idea. I looked down off the front porch and saw a real estate lockbox hanging off the water pipe. You know, the little steel box the realtors put your front door key in so that other realtors can show your house to buyers when you're not home. I unlocked the box and took out the front door key.

"Tell you what," I said, "I'll let the dog in if you'll come in with me to check on Mickey."

"I'll do anything to shut this little fucker up for the night."

When you've opened the front doors of as many unfamiliar places as I have, you get a sixth sense about it. Some houses welcome you as you drive up in your car. Others seem to vibrate with malevolence. This one just seemed to say, be careful.

The front doorknob opened as I turned the key in it. The little spaniel pushed it for me and raced on in. I eased it open to the wall and slid the key out without touching the knob. A rhythm and blues tune was playing quietly in another room. The air smelled stale and smoky. There had been some pot smoked there recently. A dim red neon table lamp in the living room corner was the only light, and it gave a filmy pink tint to the walls. You felt like you didn't want to touch anything.

I looked at the neighbor and he looked at me. I walked across the living room to a hallway, glanced through an open door into an empty kitchen, and walked slowly on down to the bedrooms. I flicked the hall light switch as I passed, and that helped a little. The last door was half open. The music was coming from a CD player sitting on top of a dresser, one of those that hold a stack of five disks. The last one finished as I watched it through the door, and the house was suddenly quiet—deathly quiet.

I stopped to take a breath. I visualized the fear I felt running down my arms and legs and out my fingers and toes. You probably think visualization is a load of crap. I don't care what you think. It works for me. Then I took another breath and eased through the door.

Mickey was there, all right. He was sprawled out across his bed, still in a dress shirt and half-opened tie. His pants were getting pretty wrinkled, and one shoe was still on, a Bass Weejun from the looks of it, cordovan loafer with a silver dime in it. That's the second one of those I've seen today, I thought, as I stared at Mickey.

After a minute I moved slowly over to the bed. Mickey didn't notice me come in, and as I approached him through the dim light from the hall, I guessed that his sightless staring eyes wouldn't be noticing anything ever again.

The little dog jumped up on the bed, and was sniffing at Mickey's face. I'd only seen the man once before, but he looked like he'd gained a lot of weight recently. His clothes looked expensive. He lay almost spread eagle on the bed, with one hand curled over. The fingernails were polished and manicured. The CD player was top of the line. The carpet on the floor was stained and cheap. Mickey's values were pretty obvious. His version of life in the fast lane. He should have checked his mirror before he pulled out to pass.

The neighbor was still in the living room. I walked back out.

"Mickey's got a problem," I said. "I think he's dead."

The neighbor shook his head.

"We've been praying he'd move," he said. "The Lord works in mysterious ways."

"Why don't you call the police from your house," I said. "I don't want to touch the phone."

"You know their number?"

"Just dial 911. Look, I'll stay here with the body to make sure no one disturbs anything. After you call, could you get my portable phone out of that Mercedes? It's not locked, and I don't want anyone to rip it off."

He just nodded and walked out. Not the curious type. Well, I am. As soon as he was gone, I slipped out the kitchen door into the garage, taking a paper towel with me. Mickey's BMW was sitting there, pretty as a picture, a still life, that is. I opened the passenger's door with the paper towel, and flipped open the glove compartment. It was empty. I sat on the seat carefully. Something was spilled on the soft black leather that looked sticky. I pulled down the sun visors. Over the driver's side was the registration and insurance card. I slipped them out and into my pocket, closed the car door, and was back in the house inside of sixty seconds.

There was no sign yet of the neighbor, so I took a quick look around. One bedroom was full of unpacked boxes and steel files. It looked dusty. The third bedroom was set up as an office, with a desk, computer, printer, and fax machine. It looked kind of dusty, too. There was a gold-framed picture of a squinting woman sitting on a beach towel beside two little girls and a sand castle. A checkbook was stacked against the letter trays. I fanned through the check stubs.

Just the normal stuff. There were checks for the utilities, checks for Safeway, monthly payments on the credit cards, and a big check every month to the Willow Fund II, whatever that was. Some months there was a check to Laura Peachton. Child support? It had been a few months since he wrote one of those. Maybe now the kids can get Social Security. They can't, however, go to Uncle Sam's for the weekend. Seeing how Mickey lived now, maybe it was best the kids wouldn't be coming anymore to visit. I doubt if the kids would agree with that. Which would you rather rely on? Adult wisdom, or the logic of a child's heart?

The sound of the neighbor's return interrupted my philosophical musings. I walked back out into the hallway to meet him.

"There's no one else here," I said, to explain my exploration of the house to the neighbor. I reached for the portaphone.

"They're on their way," he said. "She said not to touch anything."

"We were smart not calling from here, huh?" The neighbor looked pleased with us.

"Did you notice anything about Mickey's visitors?" I said.

"Mickey had lots of visitors, lately."

"Anything unusual about tonight?"

"Just three guys, about nine o'clock."

"Did you see what they were driving?"

The neighbor was talking with his whole mouth now. He had stopped to put in his bottom plate. I smiled at him. I think he knew why I was smiling, but he didn't say anything about it. Mickey's death seemed to have cheered him up.

"It was just a big old blue sedan."

"Two door? Four door?"

"Well, it must have been four door, cause they had to help the guy in the back get out of the car."

"Why did they have to help him?"

"If you were on crutches, you'd need help, too."

"One of the guys was on crutches?"

"What are you, anyway? I thought you said you were a real estate man."

"I am. I'm just trying to help out a friend. Here, I'll show you," I said, and started dialing the phone. We could hear a siren in the distance. I called the police again, and asked them to get Marty Braynes on the phone. They got my portaphone number so Braynes could call me back.

"He's a lieutenant in homicide," I said, knowingly.

"You think it's a murder?"

"Maybe."

"Shit," the neighbor said. "That'll be worse for property values than Mickey was."

We heard a car stop in the driveway. Two uniformed cops came in the front door.

"What's the problem here?" the first cop said.

"We think the guy who lives here is dead back there," I said.

"Want to show me?"

I led her and her partner down the hall to Mickey's bedroom. My portaphone beeped just as they saw Mickey, and we all jumped a little. It was reassuring, somehow, to know the cops can still be startled.

It was Braynes on the phone. I told him what had happened, and the possible tie-in to Frank Baker's death.

"It's kind of far-out, Randel, but we better treat it like a possible homicide just to be safe. Are there any cops there yet?"

The uniforms had just decided that Mickey was indeed dead.

"Hey, you guys," I said, "Braynes says to treat it like a murder."

They looked at each other and then at me . . . not in a friendly way.

"Marty," I said, into the phone, "you better tell them. They don't believe me."

I handed the phone to the lead cop. She talked with Braynes briefly and then handed the phone back.

I told Braynes I'd be at home if he needed to talk to me, and hung up.

"Call homicide," she said to her partner, "and then call the ME boys."

The other cop reached for my phone. The babe in blue waved him off.

"Use the car radio, Buck. We don't want to run up his phone bill."

We walked back into the living room. I gave her a brief statement, wrote my home phone number on a business card, and started for my car.

"Hey," the neighbor said, "what about the other one?"

"What other one?"

"Him." He pointed to the dog, who seemed undecided about which one of us to follow.

"Better take him home and feed him," I said. "Starving dogs in a neighborhood are hell on property values."

chapter **fourteen**

San Jose's still an early town. Go to bed early, get up early. There wasn't much traffic on the streets. I didn't used to live in an expensive part of town. In fact, when I bought my house, it was in no-man's land, with the great unwashed threatening from all directions. But that was ten years ago, and since then, a lot of the unwashed have cleaned up their acts.

Remember the slogan, Better Flat on Your Ass, Than Middle Class? Life according to the great book of slogans must have gotten boring, because my part of town is starting to look like somebody fed Ozzie and Harriet tapes into a clone machine. The old Victorian houses my generation used to trash up are now getting fixed up and draped out like the Fourth of July. Just when you expect to see a horse and buggy coming down the street, you almost get run over by a herd of jiggling joggers, led by my neighbor from across the street who used to lead demonstrations that burned clothes and books and the occasional police car. I even noticed the outline of a bra strap, one day, under all the spandex. About all that's left of the hippies is their hips, and the joggers, at least, think there's too much of that.

Wasn't it Camus who said that by age forty you could read a man's life on his face? As a general rule, I don't trust a man without gray hair or a woman without wrinkles at the corners of her eyes. The yuppies are trying hard, I'll grant them that, but it's still too easy for most of them. Material success can't buy back the moral authority they threw away. Look around you. Do you like no-fault divorce?

Ask the children of the one-parent families about that. Is sexual freedom your bag? I bet you're pretty lonely these days. Still "doing your own thing?" Did you put that on your résumé?

No, there's still not enough suffering on the faces of too many of the people I see around me. Too many shortcuts have been taken, too much insider trading on the morals market. When I started selling real estate, when nobody would pay me to do anything else, I had a sales teacher who would outline the ten steps to a real estate sale. You have to take all the steps, he said, even if the guy decides to buy the property when you're on the first step, you'll still have to go through the whole process before you finally close the deal.

Life's like that, too. If you want to end up a wise old man of eighty, a guy with enough money but not so much as to corrupt his descendants, a guy with lots of fond memories of wild sins that he repented from, a man with enough wisdom to give sound advice and enough common sense to know when to keep his mouth shut, if you want to end up like that, you have to touch all the bases. There aren't any shortcuts on the way to home plate.

I took some shortcuts once. They got me an ex-wife and two boys I don't see very often, they got me a mountain of debts I just finished paying off last year, and they got me a lifetime membership in a club called Alcoholics Anonymous. I could go on about the true nature of shortcuts, but you get the idea. I was lucky. I got a second chance at the ten steps of life. Mickey Peachton won't get that chance. But then he didn't just skip a few steps, he took a flying leap off the third-floor balcony. Sweet landings, Mickey. I hope the going up was worth the coming down.

I like to wake up at six, but I don't like to talk before nine. Yesterday Frank Baker caught me by surprise. Today it was the telephone at eight. I let it ring through to the answering machine, but when I heard Hilda's voice, I picked it up right away.

"How did you get this number, Hilda?" I'm real friendly first thing in the morning.

"Billy Blake gave it to me. Chase, it's awful. The police picked him up."

"The police picked up Billy Blake?"

"Not Billy, they picked up Tom."

"When?"

"About a half hour ago. They came right to the office and took him to the police station."

"What for?"

"Something about questioning him about Frank Baker's death. They wouldn't say what."

"Hilda . . . how did you find out about it so soon?"

"I was there. We, uh, I worked late on the files, and I fell asleep there."

"Tom slept there, too?"

"Yes, I mean, I guess so. Chase, it was all so sudden."

"You didn't go with him to the police station as his lawyer?"

"He didn't want me to. Besides, I'm Frank Baker's attorney, how could I?"

"I was beginning to wonder if that had slipped your mind."

"What the hell is that supposed to mean?"

"You two looked pretty cozy last night."

"You looked pretty comfortable yourself with Elaine. What time did you get home?"

"I didn't look at the clock, but it was either too early or too late. Look, you know more about conflict of interest than me. I do know you can't sue a man in the morning and sleep with him at night. And you better not look like you're doing it, either, even when you aren't."

Actually, I heard the phone click about halfway into the last sentence. I kept talking because I was curious to see what I was going to say. I guess I should have said the last sentence first. All I know is, it's harder to prove you kept your pants on than it is for someone else to accuse you of taking them off. And why wasn't Billy Blake telling this to Hilda instead of me?

I started on a second pot of coffee to chase down the grapefruit and whole wheat toast, while I chased the crumbs with a paper napkin. This business with Hilda was a bother. I needed some information and I wanted Hilda to get it for me, but it sounds like she's a compromised asset, as they say in the spy books. Well, there is one other interested party who's pretty well connected. I dialed the number while I made up an excuse for the early Saturday phone call I was making, and maybe for the ones I hadn't made, back when it mattered.

"*Eastside Advocate.*" A cheerful male voice answered, just what I feared most.

"Molly Gish, please."

"Who may I say is calling?"

"The Associated Press."

After I started calling again, she stopped coming to the phone.

"Molly Gish." Damn, she sounds happy. Oh well, here goes nothing. The napkin was stretched across the receiver. I wonder if that really does disguise your voice.

"I've got an inside line on the Silicon Investment Group scandal," I said.

"Who is this?" There was more than a question in her tone of voice.

"There's been another death."

"When?" Her instincts as a reporter won out over her nasty suspicious female nature.

"Last night. That's all I'm going to say. If you want to know more, meet me in the bar at the Thunderbird at eleven. I'll recognize you. And come alone."

"Is this—" I ended the call before she could say it. She can think what she wants. She'll be there. There's nothing like a secret to get a woman's attention. Maybe that was my problem with Molly. I was too open, and shared too much of myself. Somehow I don't think that was it. I bet she'll try to explain it to me, no doubt in some detail. I don't think that secret is one she wants to keep, at least not from me.

All that speculation was lots of fun, but it was keeping me from my real work. Yesterday Frank Baker asked me to help him protect some real estate from foreclosure. I agreed to help because he promised to let me handle the sale of a couple of million dollars worth of property. That sale would bring me from sixty to one hundred and twenty thousand dollars in commissions. That income would keep me going for several months at the somewhat slower pace of life I'm coming to enjoy. Frank Baker may be dead, but that hasn't changed

72

the situation much. It just means his widow has to try to clean up the mess Frank left behind. Maybe it'll be easier without Frank—for me, at least.

Frank Baker's phone number and address were unlisted, but I found him with about five minutes of browsing in the real estate microfilm records at my office. There were thirteen Frank Bakers listed as owning property in Santa Clara county, and even three Frank and Betty Bakers, but there was only one Frank Baker who owned thirty-six condos on Fair Valley Place. His listed mailing address (the place they send his property tax bill), was care of Silicon Investment Group. California has a nice little tax break, though, called the Homeowner's Property Tax Exemption; so I just looked on through the records for the property this Frank and Betty Baker owned that had a Homeowner's Exemption, and bingo, I had Frank Baker's home address. I know, I could have telephoned someone and asked for his address, but I'm the kind of guy who hates to stop and ask directions. It's like a defeat, if you have to stop and ask, like you're not in tune with the psychic forces of the universe. Besides, who knows what interesting properties you might see as a result of getting lost.

Usually, too, I make appointments, but Mrs. Baker's probably already had five real estate brokers calling to see if any property is for sale. Some lawyers chase ambulances, some brokers live on probate sales. To those guys, one man's pain is another man's profit. In the animal kingdom, we talk about the scavengers and the end of the food chain. In human society, we talk about "necessary evils" when we're being nice, and mutter "cannibals" when we're not.

Back home we called them buzzards, and I can still remember my dad seeing a dozen or so of them circling in the sky over the pasture down by the creek. He jerked the .22 rifle down off the wall and fired half a box of shells wildly into the sky in their general direction, cursing with a kind of manic energy I had never seen before. I guess he was mad because he knew some animal of ours was dead down there, and he was trying to kill the bearers of bad news. I know two things for certain. When he finished shooting, he had a real weary look on his face, something close to defeat, and it took him a few days to shake that mood off. The other thing certain was those buzzards never even swerved while he was shooting. They just kept up that slow circling until one by one they started dropping down out of the sky on big outstretched wings to land awkwardly, somewhere out of sight.

The Bakers lived on the south side of the city, on a five-acre parcel just below a little hilltop. When they bought it, the property would have been called a "ranchette," in the boondocks. Now you'd say they have a "great big place" down in the Evergreen section. That's a little valley that's almost hidden from the rest of the city by a range of hills that circle it. When you'top the low ridge you used to see a few farmhouses and ranches scattered among the plum orchards that dotted the brown slopes. Now you mostly see red tile roofs on big subdivision homes. Only a few ranchettes have survived the attack of the cul-de-sacs, sitting on the outskirts of the hungry streets.

The Bakers' place was one of the survivors. A winding drive between two rows of Monterey pines led over a saddle of land that hid all but the front of their house from the valley below. I parked on a pine needle–covered pad beside the garage. An old pickup was just nosing out from behind it. There was a slightly sour smell mixed in with the pine scent, and I guessed the pile of debris I saw beyond the truck was a compost heap, because stretching down from the garage and around behind the house was an astonishing array of orchards and gardens and lawns that made the house look like an oasis out of the Arabian Nights.

Around the front of the house there were several carelessly parked autos. A somber black American town car was parked just by the front door, and three casually dressed younger people and an older woman seemed to be concluding a visit from an older man, dressed in a dark gray suit. I waited until they finished. When the older man moved to his car, one of the younger men walked over to me.

"Yes?" he said. He didn't offer to shake hands.

"I need to talk to Mrs. Frank Baker," I said.

"What about?" The kid was broad and muscular, with just a little sag in his face. The kind of kid who was a wrestler in high school, and probably still lifts weights but doesn't watch his calories the way he used to when he had to make the weight limit. He shifted his body across the walk so that he firmly blocked the way to the front door and his mother.

"I spent most of yesterday morning talking to Mr. Baker about his real estate. There are a couple of pretty urgent matters that I need to discuss briefly with her."

"You a real estate man?"

"Yes I am." I handed him my card. "Chase Randel's my name." I held out my hand for a shake. The kid looked at my card, looked at my hand, and then turned his head and spit beside the walk into the big rambling rose bush that climbed up a trellis to the roof.

"If I see one more of you vultures, I'm going to throw up." He looked disgusted. "In fact," he said, "it may not take one more. You may be it."

"Why don't you show her the card first. I think she'll want to see me."

"If she wants to talk to you, she'll call you." He gave me his best tough guy smile. "I wouldn't wait by the phone, though."

chapter **fifteen**

I shifted up onto the balls of my feet. The kid looked nervous. I didn't want trouble, but I didn't want to get sucker punched, either. I looked around at the house, and used the movement to edge just out of his range.

"They made this place really nice."

"I think it's time for you to leave," he said.

"If you want Mrs. Baker to be able to stay here, I would suggest that you let me talk to her—now."

He faked a look over his shoulder and then let fly. I was already rocking back away from him, and the punch missed by at least six inches. After it passed, I slipped behind him, planted a hand in the small of his back, and shoved him into the roses. I kept my hand there and held him up against the bush, where the thorns caught his sleeves and kept his thrashing arms from getting free. The plant was an early bloomer. Petals from the open roses drifted down over us until he stopped struggling.

The other two young males had come running back out of the house and over to us, followed by a broad, balding man in his mid-forties. I saw the older woman stepping out just as I gave my young friend a final push into the bush and stepped away with my hands up, palms out.

"I didn't ask for trouble," I said. "He took a wild swing at me and got himself tangled up. I just asked to talk to Mrs. Baker."

The two boys, in their late teens, waited for the man to speak.

"What's going on, Frankie?" he said, as my attacker pulled himself out of the thorns. His face was scratched and bleeding, and his shirt sleeves were torn and splotched with red.

"He's another goddamn real estate broker," Frankie said, as he finally freed himself.

"It's not a crime, son." The man looked toward me. "I'm afraid we may owe you an apology. We're all obviously very upset. They all loved their granddad a great deal—maybe Frankie, most of all."

"I know it's a hard time for you," I said, "but it's very important that I talk to you and Mrs. Baker this morning. Mr. Baker approached me yesterday and asked me to help him save his properties. I think we should talk about where we stand on this."

Mrs. Baker reached our group then. I don't know what I had expected, but I wasn't ready for the quiet matriarchal dignity that she carried. She was a smaller woman, about seventy, rounded and gray. She walked straight and proud, and carried a figure that suggested her widow status would only last as long as she chose.

"Are you all right, Frankie?" she said. Grandma had her priorities straight. She reached out to him and examined his scratches. She brushed rose petals off his shoulder and out of his hair.

"Thank you for being concerned about my well-being," she said. "Your granddad would be proud of your intentions. With all of you around me now, I don't feel too threatened by this man. He certainly doesn't look dangerous."

Mrs. Baker smiled a smile that would have made the Virgin Mary happy. I've seen that kind of smile before. It only comes from someone who had encountered a great loss and met it with even greater surrender and acceptance. The men all unconsciously rearranged themselves around her. It was obvious who was in charge here.

"I'm Betty Baker," she said, holding out her hand.

"Chase Randel." Her hand was calloused, and her grip was firm. My thumb noticed the bumpiness of her knuckles, so I didn't squeeze back. Arthritis can make the hand very sensitive to pressure.

"I hoped it was you. Frank mentioned you yesterday. You come highly recommended."

"May I come in and review the situation with you briefly?"

"Please do," she said. "You look like you're much more fun than funeral directors and policemen." Her lips held the smile, but her eyes had to blink away some tears. I smiled back and moved slowly over beside her and we started toward the door. The others fell into line behind us.

"You must be quite a gardener," I said. "Your grounds are magnificent. Most of all, I like the strong rose bushes."

"You should be grateful," she said. "Frankie was quite an athlete in high school. But really, my husband was the gardener. I just dig the holes and shovel the manure."

It was ten A.M. on a Saturday morning after a night when I doubted if anyone had slept very much. The house still looked as neat as if the housekeeper had just left. Mrs. Baker led me to a sunny glassed-in breakfast nook just off the kitchen. We sat in cushioned white wicker chairs around a glass-topped table, and she brought out coffee before she let any talking take place.

"It's been a busy day already," she said, as she sat down. "The police were here again at eight o'clock this morning." She paused until she and I had fixed our coffee. Her son was hovering in the corner behind his mother. She sat stirring her cup thoughtfully before she continued, watching me out of the corner of her eye.

"Mr. Randel, my husband told me to trust you." She took a deep breath before she continued. "I think you should know that his death was probably not an accident."

I should have been shocked, but I wasn't. Frank Baker came into my office looking like a doomed man, and nothing has happened since to make me change my mind.

"What happened?" I said.

"The police say fatal levels of cyanide were found in his body. If he hadn't died from the fall he would have died from cyanide poisoning."

"Who told you this?"

"Lieutenant Braynes came out this morning himself to tell me."

"What else did they say about it?"

"Just that they found traces of the poison on the glass he was drinking from before he died." Her voice started to break a little. "Tom Endman gave him a drink and he went out on the eighth floor patio. He . . . he apparently started to drink his drink, had a seizure when the cyanide hit his system, and fell over the railing."

She looked away from me, out through the plate glass doors that opened onto the veranda. There were lemon trees in close to the house. Other fruit trees, probably plums and cherries, were scattered across the back yard, all the way over to some rows of grapevines terraced up the hillside. Mounds of dirt between the trees were covered with vegetables and flowers.

She looked back at me finally, and smiled.

"That's what he loved," she said. "I wish he had stuck to his garden. We didn't need a million dollars. We needed him."

"Why would someone want to kill your husband?" I said.

"Maybe it wasn't meant for him. Honestly, everybody liked Frank. There were only two things in the world he hated."

I kept quiet, encouraging her with a look.

"One was, he hated liars," Mrs. Baker said.

"Did he think Tom Endman lied to him?"

"Possibly. But regardless of whether he lied or not, Tom Endman got Frank in one hell of a mess." She noticed my surprise at her language. "Don't worry," she said, "I'm not as sweet as I look. Now, you wanted to talk some business."

I took a moment to drink the coffee and to fish out a pen and my notebook.

"First, let me tell you that I got a lawyer to stop the foreclosure sale yesterday. With your permission, I'll have the attorney in court first thing Monday morning to get some kind of injunction blocking any further sales. I think we can get thirty days, at least."

"I would appreciate it if you could handle that. Let Frank junior here know how that works out."

She wasn't taking notes, but she didn't look like she was going to forget anything. Frank junior nodded and resumed his stance in the corner after he gave me his phone numbers.

"Now," I said, "it looks like your husband borrowed enough on the duplexes to put them into negative cash flow." Mrs. Baker tilted her head, a classic gesture of uncertainty. "Negative cash flow," I said, "means you're paying out more in mortgage payments, taxes, and repairs than you are taking in from rents."

"Thank you," she said.

"I want to make up an analysis on those properties. My first opinion is that you may want to sell one or two duplexes to pay down the debt on the others to make your cash flow positive again on the remaining units."

"What about the condos?" Frank junior said. "Can we get anything back out of those?"

I turned it over in my head to see if there was any way to soften the news. There wasn't.

"There's only one way you'll get anything back out of those," I said, "and that's to prove fraud and sue someone—and collect if you win."

"What happened?"

"Your dad paid too much. The appraised price he relied on was about twenty-five thousand dollars too high."

"Well can't we sue the appraiser?"

"Not anymore," I said, "he died last night. Maybe of a drug overdose."

"Holy shit," Frank junior said. "He worked all his life to save up something, and just when he needs to start drawing something back out, someone steals it from him. It's just not right."

"No one made him buy the property, Frank junior. Your dad always did what he wanted to do." Mrs. Baker smiled her sad smile again.

"Did he have life insurance?"

"Some. Enough to take care of me."

She didn't look satisfied.

"I don't want to intrude," I said, "but I sense there's something you're not telling me."

"It's Julia, my sister," Frank junior said. "She's the mother of the two younger boys you saw outside. She was in an accident last year. She's in a coma. We don't know if she'll ever get better." He looked away and didn't continue. Mrs. Baker picked up the ball.

"One reason Frank did all this was to create a trust fund for Julia with the profits. Her care is costing us about ten thousand dollars a month." She got up stiffly from her chair. "More coffee?" she said.

"No," I said, getting up, too. "With your permission, I'd like to come back this afternoon or tomorrow and go through all Mr. Baker's real estate files."

"I think that would be a better time," she said. She looked tired, suddenly. I started for the sliding glass door opening onto the patio.

"Can I go out this way?"

chapter sixteen

....

O f course," she said, "I'll walk you to your car." She stopped several times on the way to pick dead leaves off plants.

"Mrs. Baker," I said, during one stop. "You said Julia was one of the reasons your husband bought the condos. What were the other reasons?"

She hesitated, pressed her lips, and blinked her eyes. She took a deep breath before continuing.

"It was his ego," she said. "My husband had a huge ego. I mean no disrespect by saying this. Nothing made Frank more angry than that old saying, If You Can't Do, Teach. He was a teacher all his life, and he wanted to prove he could do something else successfully. He wanted to be a big-shot investor. He wanted to hang around with the celebrities that Tom Endman brought into the Silicon Investment Group."

She stooped and picked a zucchini from a raised mound of dirt inside a redwood box, and handed it to me. It was about twelve inches long, and must have weighed. a pound. It was prickly. I had forgotten vegetables don't grow with wax on them.

"Tell your wife to fry that in butter and garlic," she said, "just like the Italians do."

"If I give this to my wife," I said, "she'll just hit me with it."

"Cook it yourself, then," she said. "It'll make you appreciate her more." She picked two more and kept them, and then looked me in the eye.

"It wasn't that I couldn't understand how Frank felt," she said, "I just wish that what we had could have been enough for him. He wanted me to idolize him. I just wanted to love him. I know Julia's care costs a lot of money. But we would have made it somehow. We needed to all pull together. We didn't need him to be a hero."

I liked Mrs. Baker a lot, but I thought if I saw that rueful smile once more I might say something rude. She wasn't perfect after all. We exchanged phone numbers, too, and then I got in the car.

"Oh," I said, "one last thing. You said Frank only hated two things in the world, and that one of them was liars. What was the other one?"

"You don't forget a thing, do you?" she said. This time the smile was warm and genuine. She leaned over to my window and whispered confidentially.

"It was gophers," she said. "Frank hated gophers even more than he hated liars."

"Gophers," I said, "he hated gophers."

"Oh God, yes," she said. "He trapped them, he made up his own bait. He got up at dawn to shoot them with his twenty-two rifle. He even rigged up a little windmill that made bells ring to scare them."

"Do the bells work?"

"In the daytime, when the wind blows. Gophers, of course, are mostly active at night, after the wind dies down."

This time we both smiled rueful smiles.

"If I see a gopher on the driveway," I said, "I'll run over it. For Frank."

"Thank you," she said. "Do it for both of us."

About halfway down the drive I spotted a little shed I didn't see on the way in. Young Frankie, the grandson, was working there, and I impulsively stopped the car and walked over. There were bins of sawdust, grass cuttings, and other organic materials piled against the outside. Inside, were bags of fertilizers and seeds, and jars and cans of various chemicals and pesticides. He was scooping out handfuls of bonemeal and mixing it in a bucket with peat moss and mulch. He looked up and he didn't smile.

"I just wanted to say I was sorry for what happened up there," I said. "I should have handled it differently."

Frankie stared at me, and then nodded.

"Me, too," he said, finally. "I went off half-cocked."

"Your granddad took his gardening seriously," I said, after a pause.

"I've been helping him since I was big enough to walk," he said. "We were going to mulch the berries today. He'd be disappointed if I didn't get it done."

"What is all this stuff?"

"Granddad figured he could grow plants in solid rock if he had the right stuff to work with. We used to spend half our time mixing up new formulas. He called it brew. We'd brew up good potions to make the plants grow, and evil potions to keep down the pests."

"Like gophers?"

"Especially gophers. Grandma must have told you. Gophers were

Baker enemy number one. He even made me take chemistry in high school, so we could make better brew."

"I don't like gophers, either," I said. "Good luck. No hard feelings, huh?"

"Sure," he said, and stuck out his hand. "Have a good day."

The eternal puzzle, I thought, as I drove off. A good man, loved by a big family, a teacher of children, a man who tends plants, enriches the soil, and guards the earth from gophers, and still he's not satisfied. He still wants the brass ring. American, through and through. No American may rest until he's learned firsthand that material success does not bring happiness. Until then, you're just faking it.

I drove off to confront one of the recent failures of my life. Molly Gish owns a neighborhood newspaper, and, for a time, she occupied a large part of my life. We met when another client of mine died under suspicious circumstances. Molly helped me figure out what was going on. When a fireman pulled me off the burning roof of a five-story building, she took care of me until my burned hands healed enough so I could feed and clothe myself. She got to me the second night when I was still too bandaged to defend myself, and we started a torrid affair that lasted six months. We broke up over the usual silly stuff. It was either over marriage or dirty socks, I'm not quite sure anymore, but it was one of those important issues. Anyway, by the time I realized it was dumb not to want to get married, she couldn't imagine why she ever wanted to, and things just cascaded downhill from there. Now she's got a new fellow, and we haven't spoken for a while, but we're about to. I hope I live to tell you how it went.

I kept telling myself, as I drove to the Thunderbird, that her curiosity was stronger than her desire for revenge. There's nothing she likes better than a good puzzle, I said, and nothing I like better than a good source of information. That's the basis of a solid relationship. Dull, maybe, but solid.

I got there first, just like I planned, and took a seat just around the end corner of the bar, where I could see Molly enter without her seeing me first. Marty brought me a Virgin Mary before I could ask. The bar doesn't make much money on nonalcoholic drinkers like myself, but they say they prefer me the way I am now to the way I was before. I had

this habit of blacking out before I passed out, so I never could understand why people were so disgusted with me the next day. All I could
say was, "I wouldn't do a thing like that, would I?"

I saw Molly park across the street and get out of her little two-seat
Japanese something-or-other. I haven't forgotten her long, slender
legs, but it was a shock seeing them again as she got out of the car.
Molly liked short, tight skirts and blouses without too many buttons.
Today, the skirt was black, covered with flowers in primary colors. A
tight blue-and-green sash reminded me again of her skinny waist, and
her bright red blouse was a button seller's disaster.

She walked straight across the empty room and sat at the bar, and
just as I ducked behind the cash register, I could see from the way
her shoulders moved that she was crossing her legs the way she always
did when she sat at a bar stool.

By the time I took a deep breath and stood up, she was looking
away from me, signaling Marty with a hand in the air. I almost reached
her side before she turned back and saw me.

"Oh, shit," she said, "I was afraid it was going to be you."

I didn't mess around with apologies.

"I need help," I said, "and I know some things you don't."

"You need more help than I can give you, Randel," she said. "But
OK, it's business. I got something you need. You think you know
something I want to know. That's fair. But let's make it fast."

I tried hard to keep it business, but as I pulled my stool over, my
hand unintentionally brushed across her thigh and sent a jolt up my
arm and into the back of my brain.

"Randel, for God's sake."

"I'm tired of playing hard to get," I said.

"Eat your heart out, you jerk. It was yours for the taking, remember,
but it wasn't enough, was it? You wanted to keep your options open,
didn't you? Well, tough shit. This option's closed, to you anyway."

I had thought about giving her the zucchini, but I was glad now
I left it in the car.

"You've still got the prettiest options in town," I said.

Marty brought Molly's drink.

"Thanks Marty," she said. "I thought you had a better class of
drunks in here these days."

"Don't let the clothes fool you," Marty said. "He's not as good as he looks."

"He can pay, then," Molly said, turning back to me. "Now what's this all about?"

I sipped my tomato juice and scanned her body with my eyes, the way I imagined Bogart doing, before I answered. You may be sharing a blanket with some yuppie asshole, I thought, but I remember a part of you that I don't think he'll ever see. I think she knew what I was thinking, too, because beneath that tough-girl veneer, I could see the faintest trace of a blush.

"Here's the scoop," I said, finally. "Silicon Investment Group thinks somebody pawned some doctored appraisals off on them. The same guy who appraised Baker's condos at three-quarters of a million over their real value. His name's Mickey Peachton. Maybe you've heard of him."

"No bells go off," Molly said. "What's Peachton say?"

"Peachton ain't saying nothing, ever again. I found him last night a couple of hours after he died. Maybe an overdose . . . maybe something else."

"All right, I can ask around about him."

"There's more. The cops picked up Tom Endman this morning for questioning. Frank Baker's death wasn't an accident. He drank a cyanide toddy just before he died."

"Where are you getting all this, Randel?"

"Any good broker has his sources."

"So what do you want me to do?"

"I'm coming to that. Notice, by the way, that I gave you my information first, before I asked for a favor."

"God, Randel, you've really changed. Can I still be your mistress?"

"Eat your heart out." I handed her the registration and insurance card from Peachton's car. "I know you've got a source at the Highway Patrol, haven't you?"

"It's my ex-husband, you asshole."

"That's the guy. Anyway, see if he can get us the history on this car. I want to know who owned it before Peachton, and what price he bought it for. Have him check the sales tax data."

"Why?"

"A friend told me Mickey started getting real trendy about the start of last summer, just when he got this BMW. Just about the time Frank Baker bought the condos with the inflated appraisals. Let's see if we can find out where the car came from."

"All right. It'll cost me. I'll have to be nice to the creep. For a half hour at least."

"You can do it. Also, find out for me what the Willow Fund II is. Mickey made a big payment to it every month. I'll try to find out what he paid for his house, and who he got it from. The neighbor said he got it last year, too."

"What's in this for you Randel? Dead men make no deals."

"I'm going to handle some real estate for Baker's estate, and try to find someone for them to sue over that condo deal Baker got screwed on. Also, the people at SIG asked me to try to find out if they had other rotten appraisals floating around."

"Who at SIG asked you to do this?"

Shit. Women. They always know.

"Tom Endman's daughter," I said. "She's real worried about her dad."

"And I was almost worried about you, Randel. I saw her last night. Shapely little thing. Just your type." Molly downed her drink and started getting up to leave.

This time I grabbed her thigh and held it, and it wasn't an accident.

"You're my type, Molly," I said. "I made a big mistake. I'd like to make a big apology . . . and I know you remember just how big an apology I can make."

I thought she was going to hit me, and I tensed up so I could take it, because Molly can hit like a middleweight. Instead, the fury passed, and she sighed and slumped a little.

"That's the trouble, Randel, I do remember." She paused and looked me over the way I scanned her earlier. "You don't make it easy for a girl, do you?"

"I told you the first time I met you, I'm an easy-does-it kind of guy."

She shook her head and stood up.

"You're also a liar and a coward . . . What am I going to do with you?"

86

"Let's be friends," I said. "We can always be lovers again."

"Friends," she said, holding out her hand. "That's it. Nothing more. I'll give it a try. Just this once."

"You won't be sorry," I said, holding her hand until she absolutely had to take it back. "Call me this afternoon with what you find out."

"You want this stuff today?"

"Molly," I said, "what's happened to your sense of urgency? Of course we need it today."

"I just remembered what I like about you, Randel," she said, over her shoulder. "Just about nothing."

I watched her backside sway to the door, and gave her a whistle just as she went out. I may be a chauvinist, but I'm not a pig. Am I?

chapter **seventeen**

I sucked the tomato juice off my melted ice and tried to sort out my next move. My objective was to come up with a strategy that would protect Mrs. Baker's property and also make me some money. The law says I have a fiduciary responsibility to my clients, which is a fancy way of saying I can't recommend things that are good for me but bad for them. New age morality would say that I have to devise a "win-win" strategy. That way you can pretend honesty is a choice, and not an obligation. Too bad social criticism won't pay my bills.

I was sure of one thing, though. The worst thing Mrs. Baker could do would be to put any more money into the condos. No matter what she did, she was still going to owe the lender more than the places were worth. The only way she was going to get any money out of those condos was to sue someone. Maybe she could sue Peachton's estate. That's probably going to be like looking for diamonds in a glass factory. Maybe she could sue the lender. Maybe she could sue the builder, if he's got anything.

Figuring out who to sue is a legalman's job, or legalperson, I should say, but Mrs. Baker's legalperson is entirely too cozy with Tom Endman, the logical person to sue.

Maybe all of them are tied in together, and Mrs. Baker can get a fraud judgment that will set aside the sale and the trust deed notes against the property.

Lawsuits, unfortunately, generate legal fees and not commissions. Still, I'll be better off recommending that she not sell her duplexes in order to save the condos. Then if she does decide to sell them and the condos still go bust, she can't blame it on me. Maybe I'll advise that she sell just one duplex to ease her cash flow problems. That's what I'll do, a little negative sell. I don't think it can go wrong for her, and it's definitely safest for me . . . might even make me some money.

So what do I do now? Molly's tracing Mickey Peachton. I don't trust Hilda Straton any more, I can't help thinking Tom Endman's gotten his busy hands into her pretty young pants. It's too soon to go back to Mrs. Baker's to dig through the files. I guess that just leaves Elaine Endman. Molly's right, of course, not to trust me, but she knows how I am about damsels in distress.

"Thank God you called," Elaine said. "Tom's up at the office in an absolute rage, and he's got that lawyer woman up there with him."

I pressed the phone against my ear so she wouldn't be heard at the bar. The Thunderbird was starting to fill up with the Saturday afternoon crowd of lonely men watching baseball games while they nursed a few too many beers.

"How long did they question him?"

"He said they kept him almost two hours."

"Why so long?"

"All the police told him was that Frank Baker drank cynanide before he died. They were acting like Tom poured it for him, he said."

"Why's he so angry? You do have to admit he is the logical place to start looking."

"Tom would never do a thing like that," Elaine said. She was sputtering a little. Anger is contagious. "Plus which, they got a search warrant for his office and conference room."

"Pretty straightforward approach," I said,

"What do they think he did, poison the man and leave the cynanide laying around the office?" She was shouting now. It seemed safest to change the subject a little.

"Look, I've got some other news. We should talk. How about right now?"

"You'll have to come to the house. I picked Tom up from the police and took him to the office, and that woman was there. I just left him the car and took a taxi home."

"No problem," I said. "I'll be there in thirty minutes."

The Endman property looked even more imposing in the daylight. The house was a large, two-story structure built in an architectural style you might call Mainline Philadelphia, 1927. I saw the style copied many times during a boyhood where you got to occasionally drive through the country club section on a Sunday afternoon, but you didn't get to stop.

As I parked the Merc and ambled up the brick sidewalk to the front door, a loose newspaper page on the walk stirred in the breeze that often comes up in the early afternoon. The warm inland valleys were sucking the moist air off the ocean, and some of it was tumbling down this side of the coastal mountain range. The smog would be gone by Monday morning.

I looked up again at the house before I rang the bell, probably subconsciously looking for the delivery entrance. It gave me a funny feeling. It probably looks great on the inside, I thought, but on the outside, it just looks empty.

It took three rings to bring Elaine to the door. She was talking on a portable phone, and just waved me in with a hand gesture. I closed the door as she walked away, and followed her into a big living room off the entry hall while she listened with the receiver pressed tightly to her head.

"I have absolutely no comment on that now," she said, finally. "We're cooperating with the police investigation in every way we can."

She held the receiver away from her ear, and shot me an angry, exasperated look. I could just hear the voice on the phone, talking in that are-you-still-neglecting-your-mother? tone of voice that reporters work so hard to perfect. Elaine didn't wait for it to stop.

"I've given you my answer, Ms. Gish," Elaine said, almost shouting. "No comment. If you want any further information, you'll have to read it in the *Mercury*, because you sure as hell won't get it from me."

Elaine wanted to slam the receiver down, but you can't do that with a portable phone. She savagely punched the disconnect button instead, and started swearing again.

"You hate reporters that much?"

"That bitch. She made me break a fingernail."

Elaine popped the finger in her mouth. I decided this wasn't a good time to share with her that Molly Gish was helping me look into Mickey Peachton's appraisals. It was doubtful, too, that the timing of Molly's call to Elaine was accidental. Molly likes to stir every pot she can reach. Looks like she made Elaine's pot boil. I hope my fingers don't get burned.

Elaine started to set the phone down when it started buzzing again. Instantly she threw it across the room onto a sofa. It kept on buzzing.

"Can you get me out of here?" she said. "It's been like this all day. Reporters, investors, the police. All they're doing is whipping up rumors. They'll have us selling babies, before they're finished."

"I'm ready when you are"

"I'm ready right now. I'll just grab a purse and a jacket."

"I'll be in the car," I said, and she went out one door and I slowly went back out the way I came. I glanced across to the dining room, kitchen, and beyond. Elegantly furnished, neat as a pin. No evidence of known life forms could be observed. I shook my head and wandered out to the car. I'm glad Jack Kerouac isn't with me. Places like the Endman's give clean living a bad name. We don't know yet, of course, if clean living is a dominant trait of the Endmans.

As I leaned against the car and watched Elaine emerge from the sanitized air of the house into the breezes of a summer afternoon, I felt Jack's spirit beside me, sitting on the trunk of the car with the heels of his shoes up on the bumper. Elaine was wearing black trousers with a shiny green blouse and a matching black jacket slung over one shoulder. Her hair was a lighter shade of dark red when you saw it in the sunlight, and there were some highlights in it that I guessed were natural. There was a single gold chain that hung down between her breasts, weighted by a futuristic airplane-shaped bangle. The airplane was flying just below the blouse's top button, and I noticed a few freckles on the creamy white skin that curved away under the green silk.

"Like my airplane?" Elaine said.

I looked up at her in surprise. I guess I was staring again.

"Actually, I was admiring the landing field," I said. "And envying the pilot."

She raised an eyebrow.

"Watch for crosswinds," she said. "Takeoffs are easy. It's the landings that kill you."

Elaine walked around me and got in the car. I waited for Jack to whisper a witty comeback in my ear, but he just sat there and watched her, same as me. I'm really flying blind with this one, I thought as I got in the car. But at least I'm off the ground.

"How about some lunch?" I said, as we headed down into Los Gatos.

"I'm not hungry," she said, "but I could use a drink."

"Would a Saturday afternoon glass of wine on a sunny veranda do the trick?"

She turned toward me suddenly and actually smiled.

"Yes," she said, "but I get to choose the place. Get on the highway and head for Santa Cruz."

"I hope you're not taking me to the Foghorn," I said.

"It's my secret and it's my treat," she said, brightly. "You just turn when I tell you to. You don't have to make any decisions."

As we got on the highway and climbed up toward the Summit, her mood seemed to lighten. We didn't talk. I opened the sunroof on the Merc, and slipped some Mozart on the CD player. I played the track toward the end of *The Magic Flute*, where they're clucking like chickens, before I started it over at the beginning. It's one of those contagious pieces of music where you don't have to understand anything to pick up the mood. As we got near the top of the mountain, she pulled out a cigarette and lighted it.

"You don't mind?" she asked.

I shook my head.

"Not today."

"I like a cigarette once in a while. It makes me feel adventurous, you know, reckless and off on a journey, not caring so much where the trip ends up as long as it lasts a while."

She blew out smoke, and looked out the window.

"This is just what I needed," she said. "This was a great idea, Chase. Sometimes I think there's more to you than meets the eye."

A withering sarcastic reply was on my lips when an older red Chevy sedan suddenly took all my attention. It had been trying to pass me on the winding mountain upgrade for about a mile. The Merc was doing about sixty-five up the hill, and I didn't think the Chevy had the guts to get around us, but he stayed on my bumper, and I could see the driver and passenger waving and gesturing in my rearview mirror. I eased into the slow lane to let them pass, just as the highway started to level off before the Summit Road bridge.

They shot past us until their rear bumper was opposite my shoulder, and then started to drift into our lane. I hit the horn, but the red sedan kept moving across the front of the Merc, forcing us onto the shoulder of the highway and then onto the broken pavement beside it.

The rest happened in a flash, but I can remember it today like each instant is pasted in a photograph album.

Elaine screamed, and I saw the support for the overhead bridge rushing at us on her side. I guess my teenage training took over then, because my body started doing things my mind had long ago forgotten.

I swung the wheel first toward the bridge and then hit the brakes and swung it back toward the Chevy and floored the gas. The back wheels broke traction when the brakes grabbed, and caught again when I floored the accelerator. The effect was to drop us just behind the sedan, and to point my front end away from the bridge and straight at the Chevy's rear bumper.

My bumper hit theirs a heartbeat later. The driver must have panicked and stepped on his gas, because when I backed off, he was pointed across the road at a forty-five degree angle. His rear wheels caught again and the car seemed to explode away from us, straight toward the bridge tower.

An instant later it hit the concrete and exploded for real.

We were past it by then. Elaine turned and gasped at the fireball, and swung back to grip my right arm frantically.

"Don't stop," she said. "For God's sake, get out of here."

The teenager in me was still in control. I kept the gunsight on the hood pointed straight ahead until the wreck was out of sight.

"They tried to kill us," Elaine said, still clutching my arm like it was a roller coaster safety bar.

There was a half-mile straightaway as the highway crossed the ridge. A pair of restaurants sit on the Santa Cruz side and look out to the ocean ten miles away. I gradually slowed, eased into a left-turn lane, and made a U-turn by the restaurants so that we were going back the way we had come, on the other side of the divided highway. In my mirror I saw a highway patrol car pulling out of the restaurant with his lights flashing.

"Leaving the scene of the accident is a crime," I said, as the patrol car sped past us.

Elaine said nothing as we approached the scene, but sat rigid and tight-lipped, still hanging onto my arm. I forced my arms and fingers to stay relaxed, even though my asshole was puckered clear up to my navel.

"Take the exit," she said, at the last moment.

We veered onto the side road that led up to the bridge over the accident. Below, the patrolman was standing twenty feet away from the smashed Chevy holding a fire extinguisher uselessly in his hand. He couldn't get close enough to use it.

"Go right here," Elaine said. I looked at her briefly and turned south on Summit Road, and headed away from the crash.

"I know you don't need the publicity," I said, "but I'll have to call Braynes and tell him what happened. He'll decide whether to release it to the press."

"Do it later," Elaine said. She breathed some deep breaths, and gradually settled back in her seat. She laced her fingers together and held them between her thighs to keep them from shaking.

"God, do I need to pee," she said, with an ironic smile.

She had me turn off Summit Road and go down a gravel side road that curved back and forth through a field of California oaks and yellowing wild grasses. When the open field changed into bramble and second-growth scrub timber, we turned again up a narrow lane that finally opened into a clearing. We drove up behind a redwood-sided house with steep pitched roofs and a big deck that led off around to the front of the house. I parked and looked over at Elaine.

"What's this?" I said.

"This is the vineyard. Almost no one knows where it is. Tom talks about it, but he practically never brings anyone here. Only a few very special friends."

"What about you? Do you bring special friends here too?"

"You're the first . . . I hope you're special. I hope you're really my friend."

"Let's start finding out," I said, opening my door. "I don't want to be a target for reckless drivers unless I'm doing it for a really good cause."

Elaine led me onto the deck and around to the front door. As we rounded the corner of the house, a gently rolling hillside stretched out below us to the south, dotted with neatly staked grapevines that must have covered eight or ten acres. The vines got smaller as they went down the hill. They had obviously been planted over several years. A row of sheds and outbuildings stretched off to our right, and I suspected some of them opened into cellars cut back into the hillside.

94

I stopped, and looked out over the idyllic scene. Elaine turned and came back to me. She was shivering in the afternoon sun, and I put my arm around her shoulders.

"This is where we really live," she said, "all the rest is just for show. Last year was the first year for our vintage. This year's going to be great."

She looked at me and shivered.

"Come on in," she said. "I've got to have that glass of wine. I've even got some nonalcoholic grape juice for you—organic and home-made. There's a sheltered deck off the kitchen. We'll take our glasses out there. Let's try to figure out what the hell is going on."

I eyeballed the house while Elaine went to pee. It was pretty much what I expected from the outside. We used to call it "redwood chic," which meant vaulted open-beam wood ceilings, white plaster walls, and not too much furniture. It often seemed important, too, that the furniture not be too comfortable.

You were supposed to sit around the fireplace on handwoven rugs from Peru or some-damn-where, lean back against the coffee table, and sip wine. Later, you snorted white lines off the table. I won't talk about what you did on the rug. The important decision was usually whether the hot tub was before or after. I always liked after, myself. Before, and I needed a shower to get going again. The showers were fun, too, of course, so I really couldn't complain.

What happened to those days, the days of wine and blow? What's wrong with the younger generation? They don't seem to be throwing their lives away on much of anything. They've got short hair. They work. They're getting married younger. They're serious about things. Not like us.

I've told you pretty much what happened to me. Unlike our late appraiser, Mickey Peachton, I woke up one day when I was all the way down, and realized I hadn't been going up for a long, long time. I'd just been climbing real hard to keep my head above the surface of the grave.

But what about the bozos we left charbroiled down on the highway? They were just riding the same roller coaster when they got caught, in flagrante delicto. And what about Frank Baker, the guy who died and got me into all this? He was on his own kind of roller coaster when his ticket got punched.

Maybe there will be that great redemption roundup in the sky, and maybe we will all be forgiven. I don't rule it out. I'm just not going to count on it. For me, forgiveness is a second chance. That's why I get up every day and look at that unopened bottle of Jack Daniels up high on my shelf by the cornflakes. Every new day is another second chance.

Elaine came back and I followed her into the kitchen, where she poured me some grape juice and herself some wine from an unlabeled bottle out of a tall white refrigerator that had nothing but liquid in it. She handed over the bottle for me to inspect, while she slipped on her jacket.

"This is our first wine," she said. "It's a white Pinot noir."

As far as I could tell, the bottle was just a green wine bottle, like any one of the hundreds I have broken in my life, but I managed to look impressed before I handed it back to her. She threw some ice cubes in a fancy plastic bucket, ran some water in it, and set the wine and grape juice bottles in it and handed it to me.

"Let's go out there," she said, and stepped through the sliding glass door onto a little redwood deck nestled between two wings of the house. It faced out to the grapevines, so that it got the warmth from the south, but didn't get the west wind that tended to be chilly on this side of the coastal range. There were two wicker chairs and a loveseat, all with deep cushions, clustered around a low table.

"Put the bucket there," Elaine said, pointing to the table, and walked on over to the rail. I put the bucket down and followed her. We both stood with our elbows on the railing, and looked out across the fields, and didn't say anything for a few moments.

"I think you better tell me what's really going on," I said, finally.

chapter **eighteen**

· ·

Elaine stared out across the vineyard and didn't say anything. It was hazy over Santa Cruz, but you could see around the corner of the fog down to Monterey. The way it was rolling in, I guessed we would lose the sun in about a half an hour.

"Did you hear what I said?"

"I heard you."

"Well?"

"I don't know."

"What don't you know?"

"I don't know if I can tell you because I don't know if I know what's really going on."

"Bullshit. You know a lot more than you've told me so far."

"I don't know for sure."

I finished the grape juice and set the glass down on the table. I put my hands on her shoulders and turned her to face me.

"Tell me what you think," I said.

Now it was her turn to empty her glass. She brushed my hands away, went to the bucket and poured herself a refill. She didn't come back to the rail, but started pacing back and forth on the little deck. I leaned back and waited, letting her choose her own pace for telling me the story. She stopped pacing several times and looked at me without speaking. Finally she started talking.

"What I think," she said, "is that you're right. Somebody is trying to make a move on the company, create a panic atmosphere and then buy up our stock on the cheap."

"We got four people dead so far," I said. "This is not your everyday takeover."

"I know." She stopped again and looked at me. Her eyes focused more sharply, and I guessed I had just passed some kind of weird female test.

"This is the part I don't know about," she said, "but I think there's dirty money involved."

"Dirty money?"

"Like in drug money. Like we've been used as a laundromat, and now the owners are coming to clean out the coin boxes."

"What makes you think that?"

"We have some special accounts we use for operating capital. I don't know who they belong to. They just have code names. If we need to fund a loan quick, Tom can draw money out as he needs it. When the loan pays off, the money goes right back in."

"Somebody has to sign the checks. Nobody is going to give you unrestricted use of their money."

She stopped pacing and sent me a sad smile.

"That's where you're wrong, Chase. One day Tom got a checkbook in the mail. The account had a hundred thousand dollars in it. There was a typewritten note, giving a post office box address in Los Angeles. Tom could write a check any time he wanted to. All we did was send the monthly records to the post office box, and put the loan payoffs and profits back into the account."

"When did it start?"

"About five years ago. When interest rates were sky high and nobody had any money to lend. It happened at a real important time for us.

"After we turned the money over a couple of times, other checkbooks arrived. They're still coming. We got the last one about two months ago."

"How much money is involved?"

"We're up to almost four million dollars."

I let out a long, low whistle.

"Why don't you take the money and run?" I said.

"Would you? We think anyone who will give four million dollars to strangers to invest for them will probably be able to find us if we take off. We don't think being found by these people would be a pleasant experience."

"Can't you just give the money back?"

Elaine came back to the railing, and looked out across the vineyard. Her glass was empty again.

"We're not just a real estate company," she said. "We sell all kinds of investments. Tom sold some oil and gas partnerships when we first got here from Texas. Prices went down, the driller went broke, the bank sold the equipment before it went under, the government finally seized the leases when it took over the bank.

"Our investors cried fraud. Tom took back their partnership shares and gave them a piece of a Houston apartment complex we syndicated."

She looked at me and shrugged.

"We all know what happened to Houston real estate," she said. I waited for the kicker.

"You have to understand," she said. "Tom gets physically ill when he thinks about any of our clients losing one cent on any investment we've set up. That's one reason he's been so successful. He genuinely cares about the people we do business with. That's why he's so upset about Frank Baker's death."

Elaine's speech suggested a lot more questions than it answered.

"What's this have to do with giving back the mystery money?" I asked.

"We can't," she said. "We've borrowed it to cover the losses. It's secured by notes against the operating capital of the company."

"Which means if SIG is losing money, that four million dollars is secured by nothing."

"That's one way of looking at it," she said.

Now it was my turn to fill the glasses again and look off across the fields. The fog had just reached us, and it was starting to turn chilly.

"This scandal won't help your cash flow," I said.

"New investment was already slowing down. It'll die now."

"And without new money . . ."

"We're bankrupt," she said.

"Surely the real estate is worth something."

"It is. But I don't think our mystery friends are going to be happy getting back fifty cents on the dollar."

"Maybe the police can help. Isn't there any name on the accounts?" Elaine shook her head.

"They use the names of trees," she said. "There's the Redwood Fund, the Live Oak Fund, the Willow Fund . . ."

"Did you say Willow Fund?"

"Yes. Why?"

"No reason. It just rang a bell, that's all." I thought about the setup. It just didn't make sense.

"Somebody had to set this scheme up," I said. "The bank accounts didn't just fall from the sky."

She nodded.

"Somebody did. Somebody talked to Dad and made a verbal arrangement."

"Well, who was it?"

She just shook her head slowly.

"He won't tell me," she said.

"The person he's protecting may be a killer. If he is, that barbecue back there on the highway won't be the end of it."

She stood at the railing, gripping it with her hands and shaking her head.

"He's in danger, too," she said. I looked at her quizically.

"Tom," she said. "They'll want him, too."

"You can take that bet to the bank," I said.

"Oh, my God. How did it come to this?"

I waited, but she just stared out across the fields. The sun was completely gone, and I was ready for a jacket.

"I'm going to call Braynes," I said. "I'll just tell him about the accident, but you should be thinking about telling him a whole lot more than that."

She didn't answer or look at me, so after a minute I went into the kitchen and found the phone. The dispatcher found him at home. At first he wasn't happy about being found, and then he was unhappy I hadn't found him sooner. It's hard to make cops happy. He wanted us to come in right away, but I told him Elaine was starting to tell me things, and it would be better to wait. Braynes gave me an extensive explanation of the differences between the jobs of cops and real estate brokers, and was starting to become insistent, when I found the right words to slow him down.

"Look," I said, "if you want to spend the rest of your Saturday tracking us down in the Santa Cruz mountains after dark, that's your privilege. Otherwise, you're going to have to wait until we're ready to come back to town."

There was a lot of spewing and sputtering on the other end of the phone line, but I knew he had the message. If there's anything cops hate worse than overtime, it's overtime that might not be reimbursed. Braynes said to call him when we were back. I said OK.

I spotted a lightweight parka on the corner clothes pole. It was too big for me, but so are a lot of things in this life. I put it on anyway. I wanted to tell Elaine about Braynes, but when I stepped back out onto the deck, she was gone.

First I was irritated, and then the worry hit. A quick look around the deck showed me both the wine bottle and her glass were gone, and I relaxed a little. Not many victims carry a crystal wineglass with them to their execution, much less a bottle for refill.

I looked down off the deck toward the vineyard. The air smelled damp and foggy and silty all at the same time. It was a quiet summer Saturday afternoon in the mountains. Not even the birds were singing. The squirrels are still in their nests, the owls are just waking up, and I'm all alone up here, I thought. Nothing else was moving, and that's probably why I finally saw her, just the top of her head, really, moving across one of the terraces toward the bottom of the field.

It looked like she was heading for the group of sheds over by the trees on the north. Not wanting to be at a disadvantage, I filled my glass with grape juice and then set off after her. I left the bottle.

I took a circle route around the top of the field that led me to the sheds from their uphill side. I didn't think she could see me coming, not that I was trying to sneak up on her, but surprises do add spice to life. I walked quietly as I approached the long wooden structures, and finally eased around the corner.

I don't know what I expected, but certainly not what I found. Against the front of the shed stood a four-foot stepladder, and Elaine was sitting on top of it, not ten feet away from me, looking out across the grapevines, holding the glass in one hand and the bottle in the other. She was swaying a little, and singing to herself. It sounded like "Eleanor Rigby." A smell of wine surrounded the shed, making it either a drunkard's vision of heaven or an alcoholic's version of hell. I waited, but nothing else happened, so I stepped out of hiding and cleared my throat to announce myself.

"Like what you see?" I said.

She turned and looked at me carefully.

"Yes," she said.

"Not me, you drunken cow, do you like the vineyard?"

"Are you British?" she said.

"My first ex-wife was."

"No one's called me a cow for years. I kind of like it."

"I called Braynes. Then I couldn't find you. Finally I spotted a bobbing head down among the vines."

"I wanted to take a last look. It's my favorite place in the whole world. I might not ever get to see it again. I . . . I'm glad you found me."

I moved over beside the ladder and tipped the bottle in her hand. It was empty, and so was her glass.

"Do you want some?" she said. "There's more in the shed."

I shook my head.

"I won't tell," she said, smiling.

"I can't fool myself."

She dropped the bottle then, and shifted around on the ladder to face me more directly.

"You're very strong, aren't you?" Her pale gray eyes inspected me from head to foot without embarrassment. "I keep trying to push your buttons, and you don't react."

"Hold this," I said, and handed her my glass to hold in her empty hand. She looked down and took it automatically.

I laced my fingers in her hair then and kissed her. She acted surprised, and tried to pull away. I felt the wineglasses pushing against my chest briefly, and then they slid around my sides and rested against my back. I broke the kiss and stepped back a little to look at her eyes.

"You do react, don't—" she was starting to say as I kissed her again.

This time I ran my lips down her neck to the cleft of her breasts before I broke the kiss and looked at her again.

"Chase . . ." she said. Our eyes locked, and for the first time I could see below their calm gray surface to the restless energy inside her. She moved her arms up until they rested on my shoulders, my neck between her wrists. As I took her lips again, she tightened her arms behind me and held me.

The kiss lasted a long time. My hands touched her face before they slid down over her breasts and body. When my fingers finally pushed between her legs, she pulled my lips down hard on hers, kissed me wildly for a moment and then pushed me away with a violent shudder.

"Chase, we can't," she said. "What if Tom comes here?"

My hand was stroking her face now. Her eyes looked wild. She kept looking over her shoulder toward the house.

"What if he does?" I said. "You're not a teenager anymore."

"But what if he sees us? He won't understand."

"Then let's don't let him see us," I said. I picked her up off the ladder with an arm under her knees and another under her arms, and carried her into the nearest shed.

I frankly didn't understand her concern about Tom Endman, but I didn't stop to think about it either. If it hadn't been that objection, I assumed, it would have been another. Seduction is a lot like selling. The client either stops saying no, or they get up and leave.

The shed was filled with wooden boxes and bales of straw. I set Elaine down on her feet, took off my parka and spread it on the straw. She watched me, motionless. I took the wineglasses out of her hands and set them down.

"If you run, I won't chase you," I said, cupping her face in my hands. She was looking at the ground and didn't raise her eyes. I slid my hands into her jacket, slipped it off her shoulders and down her arms, and then spread the jacket beside my parka on the straw.

I was going to kiss her again, but she was biting her lower lip, so I scooped her up instead and laid her on the rough bed I had just made for us.

Mostly, she just lay there quietly while my lips and fingers explored her body. Only her breathing changed, getting deeper, sometimes gasping a little. Her eyes stayed closed until I opened her blouse and bra and circled her nipples with my tongue. I felt her head pull up to watch me for a moment before she lay back again, breathing long slow breaths under my lips.

She didn't move again until my fingers loosened the waist of her pants, when she raised her hips slightly so that I could slide them down over her legs. Her eyes stayed closed while I stood and slipped out of my own clothes. It was probably getting cooler but I didn't notice. I covered her body with my own, then, and lay with my weight fully on her, and kissed her again. I held her hands and arms flat against the straw above her head. She didn't struggle, but when I eased off her she followed me, answering each of my movements now with her own, exploring me as I had learned her.

When I finally rolled over on her again, she rose to meet me with a passion that surprised me.

chapter **nineteen**

· ·

We lay still and tangled, even after the damp evening air started making goose bumps on my back. Even then, I might not have moved, since it was my bare ass that was exposed and not Elaine's, if I hadn't seen the headlights flash against the treetops down at the end of the lane beyond the house. They passed out of the frame of the shed's window. I slid off Elaine and moved to the door and looked up past the house. The car lights were gone, and I would have ignored it if there hadn't been just the faintest squeal of a car's brakes—the kind of sound you hear when the disk brakes aren't adjusted just right on an older Japanese car. I frowned, puzzled, and then moved quickly back to Elaine.

She was sprawled across our rough straw bed, naked and beautiful. I saw her eyes follow me in the dim twilight, and I fought an overwhelming urge to lay down again with her. Only fear, the strongest passion of all, kept us apart.

"Get dressed," I said, "I think we have company."

"Is it Tom?" she said with a gasp.

"I don't think so, not unless he likes to park halfway down the lane."

She sat up, holding her jacket up over her breasts for warmth.

"It could be somebody looking for a lover's lane," she said.

I took her by the shoulders and kissed her.

"Maybe," I said, "but let's expect the worst while we hope for the best. They could also be friends of the guys in the red Chevy firecracker."

She kept asking questions, but she dressed while she talked. So did I.

"How would they find us up here?" she said.

"The same way they found us this afternoon. Maybe someone knows you better than you think they do."

The parka was dark blue. I slipped it on and went back to the doorway while Elaine finished dressing and got her shoes on. I looked into the blackness of the trees behind us before searching the slope up to the house, to maximize my night vision. Elaine came to the door, and we watched together.

There was nothing for about five minutes. Then I saw a faint light, like from a pencil beam flash, at the glass door of the kitchen that opened onto the deck where we had talked. The light was inside the house and moving out. It was shut off quickly, but I saw a second figure slip up onto the deck from the yard.

I pushed Elaine back around the shed corner.

"I don't like this," I said, in a faint whisper. "What happens if we go down the hill past the end of the grapevines?"

"There's an old barn down there, and a fire road that leads back up to the driveway."

"What's in the barn?"

"Just some tools and an old pickup truck."

"Does it run?"

"It used to."

"Will the keys be in it?"

"I don't know."

"Can you find the way down there in the dark?"

"I think so. It's not far."

I peeked around the corner again. The two figures were not on the deck any longer, and I got a chill up the back of my neck.

"Let's go," I whispered, ducking back and taking her hand. "You lead. Don't make a sound."

It wasn't quite night, and we both had dark clothes. There was a good chance we could make it down past the vines to the barn without being seen. From there we could take the truck, or go on down into the woods beyond and avoid danger, if danger there really was.

It was a good plan, and Elaine did her part with a quickness and grace that impressed me. We ducked down along the edge of the woods until the grapevines were between us and the shed where we shared a bed of straw only minutes earlier. We didn't stop until we eased up beside the blackness of the old barn at the foot of the field. I stopped her then and turned to scan the hillside behind us. I gasped out loud when I saw them, and thought for moment they might have heard me.

The faint little light was inside the shed we had just left, and I could hear voices, though not the words being said. I paused only a few heartbeats and then turned to Elaine to push her on. She probably saw them just as I turned and she froze for an instant, long enough for me to bump into her and push her back against the barn with a thump. I looked back for the light and it was gone. Suddenly we heard running feet.

"The truck," I said, "Where's the truck?"

She didn't answer, but pulled me after her around the corner of the barn. Splinters of wood flew past me as I scrambled, and it took me a second to connect the event with the noise from up the hill. A gun was being fired at us, and not too far away.

The truck was a massive old Dodge one ton. I used to drive one like it on the farm in the midfifties. I pulled down the door handle, hopped from the running board to the driver's seat, and felt for the key. It was there.

"Get in," I hissed at Elaine, and turned the key.

Nothing happened. I hit it again. And again. Elaine was on the seat beside me now, hands at her mouth.

Something's wrong, I thought, frantically, something's wrong.

"Why won't the starter work?" she said, almost crying in her fear.

"The starter," I said. Down on the left, beside the light switch, was the separate starter button that old trucks had. I pushed it, and the engine turned over slowly.

"Where's the choke?" I said, "Where's the bloody choke?"

I found it up above the key, and pulled it out, richening the fuel mixture in the carburetor. The engine coughed, sputtered, and then roared to life in front of us.

"Hang on," I said, then pulled the long stick shift into first gear and eased out the clutch.

The old behemoth lurched forward at first and then surged out of the barn onto the faint track of the fire road. I saw a vague shape moving in the corner of my eye as we cleared the barn and swung the truck toward it and pulled the headlight switch. A man with a gun in his hand was trying desperately to stop his forward motion and pull back away from the oncoming fender. His hand had flown up instinctively to shield his eyes from the headlights; I think that cost him his balance, as I saw his foot slip as the truck rolled past him, and there seemed to be a bump and a scream. I was gunning the engine now, and reaching for second gear, confident of our escape.

Suddenly, we were covered with flying glass from the rear window of the truck's cab.

"Get down on the seat," I shouted at Elaine, ducking my own head and pulling at her arm. There was a second metallic zing as we roared up the rough trail, and then the old Dodge workhorse carried us up into the shelter of the trees. I still squinted through the spokes of the steering wheel at the road, keeping my head as low as I could, but when I shifted up the third gear, I straightened up and shook the pieces of glass off my arms.

"Are you all right?" I said, shouting over the roar of the old engine. I felt for Elaine with my free hand. She straightened up slowly.

"Are you all right?" I said again.

"Sort of," she said.

107

"What do you mean, sort of?" I said, glancing at her as I steered around the curves winding through the trees.

"I'd rather not tell you," she said. "I'm all right."

The trail opened out onto the driveway. I thought about swinging up and trying to get the Mercedes, but only for about half a second. I floored the gas as the road got better and headed out to Summit Road and civilization. Suddenly I eased off the gas.

"Either tell me what's wrong, or I'll stop the truck and look for myself."

"It's all right," she said, "it's just that I think I wet my pants."

I guess it was the tension finding it's way to the surface, but we both laughed uproariously at that well after we turned onto Summit Road and headed for the San Jose highway.

I wasn't in Vietnam, or any other war, but I know there are only two kinds of people in a battle—the winners, and all the others. People define winning in a lot of different ways. Staying alive is what it means to me. Maybe to fight another day. Maybe to be the ultimate victor along with whatever that means. Right now I'll be satisfied just to find out what the hell is going on. And I wouldn't mind some replays of our love scene in the wine shed, although I can do without the action-packed ending.

Elaine looks strangely at peace as I swing the old truck onto the highway toward the restaurant and a telephone. There's straw in her hair, dirt on her jacket, and she's sitting on a seat that's soaked with her own urine. She's rolled the window down and stuck her face out, so that her hair is blowing in the breeze of the highway. Just like a dog I had once . . . but I better not tell that story. You'll think my mind's polluted with revisionist sexist thinking, when all I really care about are good women, good food, and good dogs.

But really, Elaine has a look about her that I haven't seen before. She's right here in the present, right here in the moment, with me. Not in the past, not in the future, not sort of here but really thinking about somewhere else. Like I just grabbed a rebound, fed her a long pass and she hit a tie-breaking jump shot just before the buzzer. I don't know if we're going to any tournaments, I don't know if we have a shot at the championship, but here at this hour, sitting in this old truck, there's no question but that today we're winners.

I called Braynes again from the restaurant pay phone. This time it took a while to speak to him. His wife said he was reading to the kids. I think he was taking a nap. I was into my second set of quarters by the time he got to the phone.

"Somebody wants that little lady dead," Braynes said after I ran down the story for him. He had hung up and called the Santa Cruz sheriff for me, and then called me back. The deputies were going to meet us at the restaurant and accompany us back to the vineyard.

"What about me?" I said. "How do you know I'm not the target?"

"You don't make enough money for anybody to kill you," Braynes said. "You're too busy trying to be a cop. Hell, I may not be the best cop in the world, but at least I get paid for doing it."

Elaine was sitting in the coffee shop. She could see me talking, but she couldn't hear what I said. She had been to the lady's room, brushed her hair with something, and taken the jacket off and tied it around her waist like a schoolboy's sweater. There was no outward sign that she had been horribly frightened a half hour before, or gloriously screwed a half hour before that. Women. How do they do it?

"I've got some ideas about what's going on," I said.

"Nothing like a bullet to shake loose a few secrets." Braynes has a wonderful sense of irony.

"I'll try to get Elaine to tell you herself," I said, "but if she won't, I'll fill you in on what she's told me so far."

The sheriff's car pulled up outside. I arranged to call Braynes later, and took Elaine out to the white-and-green-striped patrol car. There was a sturdy middle-sized balding guy driving, and a sturdy lady sheriff riding shotgun. They followed us back to the farm. Elaine sat quietly on the drive back, and mostly looked out the window, which was rolled up now. It was hard to talk anyway, with the roar of the wind coming in the shattered back window.

When we got to the house, Elaine jumped out and ran back to the sheriff's car. When I got there, the deputies were leaning against the car hood with their arms folded, talking to Elaine.

"It's not up to me what gets in the paper and what doesn't, lady." The male deputy looked irritated. His partner was walking over to the pickup. The patrol car lights were glaring on the old Dodge. The deputy used her flashlight anyway.

"Look, we could have been mistaken," Elaine said, "couldn't we, Chase? Maybe it was just some kids who got us scared, and threw rocks at the truck as it drove away."

She smiled in that self-deprecating way some smart females have of trying to camouflage their real intentions by putting on a bimbo mask. I could feel her fear and her panic reaching out to me, pleading. Her hands dropped to her side, and she looked at me, open, defenseless, promising . . . and somehow, the top button of her blouse had come undone in the truck.

"Let's see what we find," I said to the deputy. "Maybe she's right." God, I hate myself sometimes.

"What I've found is a bullet," said the deputy who was examining the truck. "It went through the tailgate, put a dent in the cab just behind the driver, and bounced down into the bed of the pickup."

She held up a contorted little lump of metal that she had decided used to be a bullet. The deputy walked over and looked me in the eye.

"Good thing for you it was an old American-made truck," she said. "They don't put that kind of steel in imported trucks."

She looked at Elaine.

"Still think it was a kid with a slingshot?" she said.

Elaine shrugged.

"They looked like kids to us," she said, looking at me.

We all walked together to the house. Elaine took my arm and pulled it in tight against her breast. The deputies checked the exterior with flashlights before we went in.

"Was the front door unlocked?"

We nodded.

"Don't touch anything," the man said. "We may want to check for prints."

110

We turned on every light in the house. It looked empty and un-touched. The glass door to the deck was half open. My grape juice bottle was still on the table outside. Just on a hunch I knelt down, slid my little finger in the bottle's mouth, and tipped it. It was empty, and I hadn't left it that way. I shoved a larger finger into the bottle until it was stuck and carried it into the house that way. Elaine was in the kitchen with the officers.

"I need a bottle like this," I said to Elaine. "Mind if I take it home?"

She nodded yes.

"Chase," she said, "they're almost finished here. Can you take them down to the barn when you come back from the car?" She flashed a knowing smile. "I've got to change out of these clothes."

"I'll be right back," I said, to the deputies. Even a scheming female deserves a pair of dry pants.

While I walked with the deputies to the barn, I decided to play it down the middle. I told them that Elaine and I were talking in the shed when we thought we heard burglars in the house, and saw a flashlight. We snuck down to the barn, I said, hoping to drive the truck out and call the police.

"I saw somebody as I drove out," I said, "and then the back window broke. I didn't slow down to ask questions, but got the hell out of there and called Braynes."

We joked about the old truck and how sturdy it was, until we got near the barn. Ms. Sheriff examined the old wood structure as we walked beside it, and her flashlight stopped at a jagged hole in the weathered siding where long splinters had exploded outward from an angling bullet.

"Those kids had some high-powered slingshots, Mr. Randel," the balding deputy said. You could even catch a whiff of pine pitch from where the bullet had ploughed into the siding.

His sidekick walked up the fire road with her flashlight. Some high, dead grass beside the road had been knocked flat. She bent over and felt the ground, and then came back to us.

"There's some blood on the grass up there," she said. "I wonder if it matches the blood on the fender of your truck?"

"There's blood on the truck?" I said.

She looked at me in the light of the flash, which was aimed just at my belt buckle. I had to look away to avoid being blinded.

"Hit and run is just as much a crime as burglary, Mr. Randel."

"Not when you're being shot . . ." I said. I tried to pull the words back into my mouth, but it was too late.

"In other words, you knew it wasn't just kids with slingshots."

chapter **twenty**

I don't know anything," I said. "I hope you find the guy who left his blood up there on the grass. If you prove they were shooting at us, I know you'll put them away. And if they weren't shooting at us, that'll just back up what we thought happened."

I looked at her partner and shook my head.

"I don't get chased by strangers every day," I said. "I'm sorry if I don't have total recall of the incident. But Ms. Endman and I are the victims here, not the other way round."

The deputies turned their backs and talked privately for a few minutes.

"Let's go back to the house, Mr. Randel. We're going to call a tech team out here. We'll let them give us the story if you don't want to."

They started walking without waiting for an answer. I followed them, stumbling just behind the flashlight's golden glaring oval, which ruined my night vision without creating enough light to show the way.

The policemen I have known are open-minded, interesting

creatures—until they sniff out a "significant" fact. Then they revert to a tunnel-vision mentality that doesn't admit the existence of ambiguity. They're like heat-seeking missiles. They do good work when the sky's filled with enemy planes, but they're not worth a damn when the good guys are mixed in with the boogies. You think the police have problems. What about me? I don't know if I'm a target, or if I just keep bad company. I think I'll maintain as much altitude as I can, just in case. As the last few hours have shown, you never know when someone might be trying to shoot a Stinger up your rear end.

Elaine employed the special magic of women while we were at the barn. When we got back to the house, she looked clean and fresh, with her makeup all in place like a coat of Amazonian armor. She'd put on a paisley print shirt and a pair of faded jeans—designer of course—and she smelled just like she did the first time I caught a whiff of her in the SIG building elevator.

She wasn't happy at the expanded investigation, but she didn't show her irritation to the cops.

"Can you lock the house up when you finish?" she said to the deputies.

"You can lock it now, Ms. Endman. We're going to be working outside. Unless there's something stolen in the house, there's no case here if you left the door unlocked. The intruders could simply claim they went in looking for you on some kind of legitimate business."

"I wouldn't think of leaving you up here without a place to make coffee, or a bathroom to use." Elaine looked genuinely concerned. I was proud of her.

"I hope you'll understand my wanting to go back down to Los Gatos," Elaine said. "I think the shock of it all is starting to hit me. Please, call me anytime—tonight, tomorrow, whenever, if you want to ask for any more information."

She smiled at them, and then at me.

"Can we go now, Chase? I'm beat."

We were starting for the door, when the deputy with plenty of hair stopped me.

"There's one more thing," she said. She took me aside, so the others couldn't hear, and lowered her voice. "What do you think interest rates are going to do?"

"You buying a home?"

"We got a home. We're buying a duplex in Rio Del Mar, and they want us to get an adjustable rate mortgage. What do you think of those loans?"

"Don't worry about it," I said. "The only reason rates go up is to stop inflation. If there's inflation, that means rents are increasing. So you'll get more rent to make the bigger mortgage payment with. Meanwhile, inflation is also driving up the value of the property, but the mortgage is getting smaller, plus you're paying it off with inflated dollars. You can't lose."

"I didn't understand all that," she said.

"Just buy the place. Don't worry about it. You're doing the right thing."

I gave her one of my cards.

"Don't put this card in the case file," I said. "Keep it in your Rolodex. If you ever need any advice about real estate, I'm your man. It's on the house."

Cops. They always want just a little freebie. An apple off the fruit stand. A cup of coffee on the house. A bit of free advice. The thing for us is that we often think it's buying us something. The problem for them is drawing the line. But then that's a problem we all share.

I waved at them and joined Elaine outside. I put my arm around her as we walked to the car, but she didn't snug up to me this time. She was distant, as though our earlier closeness was now an inconvenience. We got in the car and started back to San Jose. I made sure all my rearview mirrors were adjusted just right, and I spent a lot of time checking them as we drove. We slowed as we turned onto Highway 17. The crash site on the other side of the highway was almost cleaned up. In the darkness, I could only see some broken glass, and a great black smudge on the bridge support tower the car had burned against.

"The garbage men cleaned it up real quick," I said, glancing at her out of the side of my eye. She was huddled against the door, looking the other way, and didn't reply. I thought about what could

114

be bothering her, and took a shot as we started down the winding highway.

"What did Tom say?"

"What did Tom say when?"

"When you called him from the vineyard."

"What do you know about who I called and who I didn't?" She sat up straight, threw me a dirty look, and stared out the window again. "Just take me home."

"What did he say?"

"Are you hard of hearing? I told you, who I talked to is none of your business."

I drove on through Big Moody curve (an aptly named stretch of road, if tonight is any indication), and didn't say anything until we reached the fire station pull-off just above the reservoir. I slowed and pulled to a stop in front of the pay phone there. I sat back with folded arms and watched her.

"I'm waiting," I said, finally.

"Oh, for God's sake, this is ridiculous. You got what you wanted tonight, but getting into my pants doesn't give you a ticket to the rest of my life."

I was across the seat before I could stop myself. I grabbed her blouse with one hand and her face with the other, pulling her around to face me.

"I don't care about the rest of your life, but I do care about the parts of it that might get me killed . . . and you, too, for that matter."

I don't know what I expected, but what happened certainly wasn't it.

Elaine's expression suddenly collapsed in fear. Her eyes moved erratically from side to side, avoiding mine. Her hands and arms covered her breasts protectively, and her whole bodily presence seemed to diminish.

I loosened my grip a little and watched. Her knees were drawn up toward her belly, and she was starting to shake. There was just the hint of saliva seeping out of the corner of her mouth. The yellow tint of the streetlight outside the car glared off her face. Images of the heroine of *Queen of the Zombies*, starting her nightly ascent from the coffin in the cellar.

"I'm not going to hit you," I said, letting go of her blouse and stroking her cheek lightly as I moved my hand. "I'm trying to keep us from getting hurt."

She slid away from me to the corner of the seat, her arms and legs still drawn up protectively, looking like she wanted a teddy bear to hug more than anything else in the world. Which makes me into the bully down the street who's just been caught by the parish priest.

"I'm sorry I scared you," I said. The traffic outside was mostly heading the opposite direction, toward a Santa Cruz Saturday night. Their headlights kept bouncing shadows inside the Merc like a Java puppet show. Each time they bounced off Elaine, she seemed to change. The obvious pain she felt right now was giving the lie to the power I knew she carried in her person, and lying under both I remembered the passion of earlier tonight.

I could have played father confessor right then. She may have even been grooming me for the role. But this bird is too old for her. I've seen too many facades come and go. Elaine is one of those women with a secret, and she survives by holding it close and tight inside her, safe from the light of day. No matter how many skins you peel off the onion, no matter how many times she pulls out a new secret and waves it at you like a bullfighter and says, "Here it is, here's the awful truth, now do you understand?" you can bet the real "awful truth" is still tucked away in there somewhere.

If I had a few more lifetimes in the bank, I would be tempted to take the bait. If she gets me in the wine shed again at sunset, I'll be more than tempted. But that's the secret with women like Elaine, you pick the fruit you can reach. Even then, you better look for wormholes before you take a bite. Earlier tonight, I bit at the apple without looking, and the worms almost got us both. Now, I'm looking, and I'm not reassured by what I see.

"Look, let's forget about what happened between us tonight," I said. "You're a beautiful woman, but that won't do you or me any good if we don't stay alive to enjoy it. I just want to know who knew we were up at the vineyard, and who knows where we're going right now. Just so I can keep you safe. And me."

"Just take me home, please," she said. "Tom will know what to do."

116

"Is Tom at your house now?" I watched her face as I started the engine again. "Or is he still with Hilda down at the office?"

Her eyes blazed for an instant, and then she looked away.

"You bastard," she said, to get even. "Just take me home."

Those were the last words she uttered. I pulled back on the highway and made it down the hill in record time, driving to the tunes from a Kate Wolf CD where her beautiful earlier classics were almost ruined by the new-age country feminist nonsense of her later songs. It reminded me of my relationship with Elaine. The beginning was a lot more fun than the end.

I got off at the second Los Gatos exit and took a roundabout route to Elaine's house in Monte Verde, just on the faint chance someone was watching for my car to approach her house. I came back down from the north, switched the headlights on bright, and scanned all the parked cars for the last block or so before the Endmans' driveway. I didn't see any suspicious heads sitting in the parked cars, but there was one thing unusual. A white Rolls-Royce was parked just around the corner on a little side street. When's the last time you saw a Rolls parked on the street? This is a better neighborhood than I realized.

Elaine had it back together by the time I stopped at the front door. She turned toward me and leaned over and touched my arm, as I shifted the Merc into park.

"Forgive me," she said. She made her eyes get big and soft, and she left her hand lying lightly on my arm. I could just sense the perfume again. The porch light came on then, and bathed her face in a soft white light.

"I do care about you, and the last thing in the world I want is for you to get hurt. I feel better now that I'm home."

I looked at her quietly, and then opened my door.

"I'll walk you up," I said.

She smiled as she got out of the car, and took my arm and held it snugly against her again. She stopped and stood close to me at the door.

"Call me tomorrow," she said, and smiled again and touched my cheek just as the door opened behind her.

"Daddy," she said, as he stepped out and pulled her to him in a tight hug.

"Thank God you're home," he said. He stroked her hair with his eyes closed. After a moment, he pushed her in the door, and turned to me. His smile was wide and his eyes were narrow.

"Let's talk tomorrow about what happened," he said, patting me on the shoulder like a paperboy who's just been paid. He took Elaine into the house, then, and shut the door firmly.

If I were a poet, I could probably make "Let's talk tomorrow" rhyme with "Let's have lunch." I'm not a poet, but I'm not stupid, either.

I turned north again as I pulled out of the drive, just on the faint chance someone was watching for my car to go down through Los Gatos. I was starting to run a hundred questions through my mind when I turned up the side street on a whim and took a closer look at the white Rolls-Royce. I sat across from the front bumper and studied the car with a frown before I drove on toward home. It was a long time since lunch, and a grumbling stomach is a terrible companion for a troubled mind.

Why, I wondered, as I drove along, has Frank Baker's death stirred up such a commotion?

Where did the cyanide come from?

What happened to Mickey Peachton? Appraising real estate used to be a pretty low-risk business.

But then, so did selling real estate, and I've given death the finger twice today, and maybe yesterday as well, if you count the fight at Frank Baker's condos.

Why does someone want Elaine Endman dead? She may be a woman with a lot of different talents—some of which I like very much—but I hardly think she's the brains behind anything.

And Tom Endman. What's his racket? The real racket, I mean. Or is he just a man of too many talents, some of them tainted?

And how did the bad guys know where to find us today? I better have my car checked for bugs tomorrow. Maybe there's a homing device stuck under a fender, and I'm the carrier pigeon in someone's homicidal scheme.

It's the newest question that keeps popping up in my mind though, as I roll the Merc down the freeway again. Is there any connection between all of the above, and the fact that the white Rolls parked around the corner from Endman's house carries a personalized license plate that reads "WMBLAKE"?

chapter **twenty-one**

I don't lock my car doors anymore as I drive into my neighborhood. That's how much San Jose has changed in recent years. My house on Eighteenth Street used to be right on the border with encroaching slums on the north, east, and south sides. Now the frontier's moved at least six blocks east to Twenty-fourth Street, and fingers of pacification are jutting even farther east. I know, gentrification is a bad word in a lot of places, politically incorrect and all that, but you should have been here before the gentry came back. But you weren't here, of course, you were too scared to be here. You were probably tuned in to listener-supported FM stations, playing songs about the romance of the slums. It's a love story best appreciated from a distance of three or more miles, and at least two generations.

Now I expect everything in my neighborhood to be normal. Exceedingly, boringly normal. No junk cars on the streets. No hookers on the corner. No postteenagers hanging out. No armed robberies in progress. Stifling, bourgeois boredom. That's what I expect now.

What I don't expect, seeing as I live alone, is to drive up and find the lights of my house on, looking friendly and lived in.

Now what? I was thinking as I rolled into the driveway, when I saw the little Japanese two-seat whatever parked across the street. That's one of the things I like about Molly, she makes herself right at home. Women. There's always one lurking about somewhere, eager to please and hard to appease. Were we just talking about boredom? I should be so lucky.

Molly barely looked up when I looked.

"Where have you been?" she said. She looked at my face and frowned. "You know I still have a key, don't you?"

"I do now."

She was staring at my computer screen, and hitting the buttons like she knew what she was doing. The printer suddenly started rattling away. There was a long string of printed pages on the floor behind it already. Molly watched it run for a minute, and then got up with a satisfied look on her face. She gave me a kiss on the cheek and headed for the kitchen.

"I'll put the kettle on," she said.

I followed her into the kitchen, opened the fridge, and took out some ham and cheese, a carton of milk, a loaf of French bread, and a hard-boiled egg.

"I see your diet hasn't improved."

"My cholesterol is one hundred and thirty-one. I can eat what I damn please."

"Your waistline must love that philosophy."

I gave her a dirty look, and put extra slices of ham and cheese on the sandwich.

"My, you are hungry," she said, pouring the hot water through the coffee filter. "No supper?"

I shook my head in midbite.

"Well, then, just where have you been?" she said, stepping back a little. There was an ominous shift in the timbre of her voice, and a certain careful coolness in her eye that I seemed to associate with past memories of big trouble.

I walked to the round oak table in the nook by the window and sat down before I answered. I matched her suspicious gaze with a steely look of my own before I answered.

"I almost went to the morgue," I said, finally. "Twice."

Molly didn't look impressed.

"Who did you go with?"

"Almost went."

120

"Who did you almost go with, sweetie? Twice."

There was no way around it.

"Elaine Endman."

"That must have been nice for you. Twice. I mean, two is company, isn't it?"

"I'm touched by your concern for my well-being." I waved the sandwich at her. "Shouldn't we have a feast to celebrate my safe return?"

Molly threw down a dish towel in disgust and started for the door.

"I'm just going to kill the fatted rat," she said. "I'll be right back."

I caught her arm as she passed. I hung on and slowed her by the computer and finally stopped her by the door.

"You shit," she said, "just when I was starting to like you again."

"Will you come listen to me?" I said.

"Send me a confession on my fax machine."

I held on, though, and she didn't try for the door.

"Come back and have a cup of coffee, and let me tell you about it. Stop being so neurotic, and so suspicious . . . stop acting so much like a woman, and let's talk this thing through, man to man."

"If you weren't acting like a man, we wouldn't have to talk anything through."

"That would be incredibly boring, and you know it." I led her back to the kitchen.

Molly's still a sucker for a story. First I gave her a quick version, summarizing my day in about two minutes. Then we went through a more detailed account. Finally, she made me tell it all again, in great detail, while she made notes. As she started writing, her anger dissipated. All the versions I gave her were rather heavily edited when we got to the part about Elaine and me and the wine shed.

Women. How can a woman be jealous about a man she kicked out of her life months ago? Easy.

At the end of the story, she sat nodding her head and tapping the table with her pen.

"Very interesting," she said, over and over, mostly to herself.

"You can tell me," I said, finally. "Remember me?"

She looked up at me with surprise on her face, as though she had forgotten I was there.

121

"Chase," she said, smiling brightly, "I'm sorry, I was just putting some things together in my head."

"I don't want to intrude," I said, "but maybe you could tell me what you're doing in my house, typing on my computer, and printing on my printer."

She looked at me and then looked at her watch with a start.

"Oh, Lord, look at the time. Ron will be wondering where I am."

"Molly, for God's sake . . ."

"No, you're right, I've imposed on you enough, and unlike some people we know, I do have someone waiting for me."

"Molly . . ." She is a beautiful woman. Maybe not according to *Vogue*. Maybe that's why I'm not a subscriber. But the magic's still there, and it pulls at me like a magnet. I'm trying to be cool, but . . .

"Molly . . ."

"It's OK if I stay?"

"Of course you can stay. . . ."

"I might hold you to that."

I looked at her then, across the table, her eyes full of mischief. Really, it's just a front; underneath it all she's a shy little girl . . . in some ways, at least.

"Let's save the talk for later, then," I said, staring at her. I leaned forward across the table, as if to get up. Her smile suddenly got cautious, but she didn't look away.

"You mean it, don't you?"

I just nodded, slowly. She leaned back in her chair, folding her arms and studying me. I silently cursed myself for not putting some music on and getting a glass of wine in her hands, earlier.

"We better talk now," she said, finally, "but I appreciate the thought. Let's keep an open mind, shall we?"

She thumbed back through the steno pad she was writing on, to some earlier notes, and got right down to business.

"Mickey Peachton's BMW was previously owned by one J. Paddington Moss. On the side of his truck, it says Jay Moss, Builder. He built the condos at Fair Valley Place.

"Bingo," I said. "We've got a connection between the bogus appraisals on the property Frank Baker bought, and someone who stood to profit from the inflated sale prices."

122

"Here's a picture of his truck," she said. "I took it this afternoon."

The photo was of one of those monster pickups with the dual back wheels. You usually see them hooked up to horse trailers where the animal flesh they're hauling can be worth more than the truck, trailer, and driver put together.

"Where did you take this?"

"It was parked in front of his new house on Dry Creek Road."

I whistled. Dry Creek Road is a span of a couple of hundred of the most expensive houses in San Jose.

"So," she said, "I did a little poking around. That's what I was doing on your computer." She smiled at me.

"Why didn't you use your own computer?"

"It was too hard getting any work done at my house. You know how men are on a Saturday night."

I looked around at my kitchen and the living room beyond.

"I've just about forgotten," I said.

"Anyway, I didn't have the entry codes to your real estate data base, so I came over here."

"And dug through my desk until you found my codes."

"You have a file on your disk called Codes. It wasn't too hard."

"OK, Molly, what else?"

"I developed a very interesting calendar. Listen to this. In June and July of 1988, Frank Baker bought thirty-six condominiums at Fair Valley Place. In August of 1988, new homes were purchased by Mickey Peachton in Willow Glen, and by Jay Moss, Builder, on Dry Creek Road. Also, a 1986 BMW was transferred from Jay Moss to the ownership of Mickey Peachton."

"Molly, you're wonderful. I'd forgotten just how good a reporter you are."

"I'm not just a reporter, Chase. Don't you remember what you told me the first time we met?"

"I know, you're not just a reporter, you're a woman reporter."

"And don't you forget it."

"There's a problem, though. This information just confirms what we suspected anyway. It doesn't give us anything new to suspect."

Molly turned to a new page on the steno pad.

"There's more?"

She nodded. She looked quite pleased with herself.

"Let's see," I said, and got up and moved my chair around beside hers. In my eagerness to see her notes, my elbow brushed her arm, and my knee ended up against her thigh. Molly has the greatest arms, lightly tanned, with taut muscles and lots of little blonde hairs.

"That's terrific," I said, studying the pad.

"You always said you couldn't read my writing."

"I've gotten new contacts."

"Does it help when you look in the mirror?"

She twisted on her chair, and crossed her legs, moving away from the pressure of my knee. She did not, however, move her arm or her chair. Two out of three, not bad for a first attempt. Even Casanova said it was a numbers game.

"I could only find two possible connections to follow," Molly said. "The data base shows the former owners of the properties they bought and the lenders who financed the trust deeds on the properties."

"Any luck?"

She shook her head.

"Neither of the sellers rang a bell. The lenders might be related. They both have tree names. Willow Fund and Live Oak Loans."

Bingo again. I didn't tell Molly what Elaine had told me about the mystery accounts. At the time, it didn't seem that she needed to know it.

"I couldn't follow those trails any further today. Maybe on Monday, or maybe the cops can."

"That's wonderful work. I couldn't have done that well myself."

I was just easing over closer to her, when she stopped me with a withering look.

"Particularly since you weren't here."

She flipped another page. I tried to read it.

"There is more," she said.

"I took a step back and looked at the records on Baker's condos. The lender on those was Shorham Commercial Savings. We knew that already. Some address in Pasadena. Dead end, except . . . I looked them up in the phone book here. Just a phone number and a post office box, usually that means they have a relationship with a mortgage broker."

She stopped talking and studied her notes. I cleared my throat. Then I tried drumming my fingers on the table.

"So what?" I said, finally.

"Chase, do you have that big book where they show the phone number and then list the address where the phone is located?"

"My reverse directory?"

She nodded.

"You want to look up the Shorham Commercial number?"

"Good idea," she said.

I got the directory. I pay almost two hundred dollars a year to rent it, and it's never made me a dime yet. Today it either saved my life or almost caused me to lose it. If you figure out which, I'd like to know. It's almost time to renew the subscription.

We opened it on the kitchen table. It's about the size of those photo books they use to hold down flying coffee tables. We found the number. Shorham Commercial, Suite 417, 1609 the Alameda.

"Is that in the SIG building?" I said.

"I think it's down the street."

We went to the front of the directory, where they list addresses first, and then show the phone numbers at that address. There were numbers for three businesses at that address: Shorham Commercial Savings, Doubletree Insurance Brokers, and Arbor Financial. Molly and I looked at each other. I even forgot to accidentally brush against whatever parts of her were close to me.

"What does the word 'Arbor' mean?" I said.

"Two things. It means trees, and it means you're thinking the same thing I'm thinking."

Our eyes stayed locked.

"I hope we're thinking the same thing," I said, and reached out and took her hand.

chapter **twenty-two**

···

Chase . . ."
"I swore I would never miss anyone again the way I've missed you."

"Chase . . ."

"When I saw you last night at the seminar, I felt like I did the first time we ever met. Now I can't imagine why I ever left you."

"Chase . . . I kicked you out. Remember?"

"Molly, what happened would never have happened again."

"What about today?"

"What *about* today?

"You. Screwing that Endman woman."

"Molly . . ."

"Isn't that what really happened? It's all right, Chase, you can tell me the truth. It's not like you were cheating on me."

All my best instincts told me to lie, but the words just wouldn't come out. All I've ever wanted was to be loved for what I am, appreciated when deserved, forgiven when necessary. I sat there looking back at her, silently hoping that this might finally be the time. Molly's eyes finally looked away.

"Shit," she said, "I thought maybe you had changed. But you'll never change. Look at you."

I didn't look.

"I bet you haven't even washed her smell off you yet."

Not my fault.

"Why on earth I ever let my feelings get tangled up with you is something I'll never understand. What a waste."

She got up. Her face looked stricken. I felt guilty—for a minute, then I jumped back into the character she knows and loves. Four guilty feelings and a quarter will still buy you a local phone call, but not much else.

I got up, too, and moved to stand in the doorway that led to her escape route.

"Don't come on like the vestal virgin," I said. "You moved that creep into your house before the sheets were cool on my side of the bed."

"He's still there, too. And he's waiting for me right this minute. And that's where I'm going. So move."

"I'll move in a minute. But just for your information, I didn't go looking for what happened today. She practically dragged me up there with her."

"And I suppose she tied you up and raped you, too. You make me sick. Get out of the way."

I put my hands on her shoulders.

"Just a couple more things, then I'll move."

I took my hands away deliberately, and held her with my eyes.

"I almost got killed this afternoon. I saw the two men who tried it go up in smoke. Later, she was drinking, and I was, well, I guess I was thinking about my own mortality."

Molly's eyes never left mine.

"If I had you to come home to, I never would have been with her in the first place."

Her gaze drifted across my face and then down my body before she looked at my eyes again.

"That's a nice thing to say, Chase. But you don't have anyone to come home to . . . and I do. And that's where I should be going. Right now."

Neither of us moved for a moment. Then I stepped up and kissed her. She didn't kiss me back, but she didn't not kiss me back either. I held her against me then for a long time before I kissed her again. When I stepped back, her eyes were still closed.

"I have to go," she said.

I nodded.

"Don't forget what we said earlier."

127

She raised an eyebrow.

"Let's be friends. We're working together on this thing. Let's just keep going and see what happens."

She smiled thinly, stuffed her steno pad in her purse, and nodded at me as she went to the front door.

"I'll call you tomorrow," she said.

I didn't say anything until she was half out the door.

"Molly."

She turned and waited, as I walked over to her.

"Does Ronnie really sleep on my side of the bed?"

She grinned mischievously and shook her head.

"I changed sides," she said, and walked out toward her car. Once again I watched her sway away, going home to Ron von Yuppie. This time, though, I had to smile. If he thinks he's going to get a good night's sleep there tonight, he's dreaming.

It's been a hell of a day. When my feelings are stirred up the way they are now, it's vital to remind myself of where I've come from. It helps to put away the worries about the future. Up in the cupboard, the unopened bottle of Jack Daniels is still looking down at me, like a sentinel. I may not know where it's all going, but I do know where I am. That's something I haven't always been able to say.

It's been a quiet life, these last few months. After Molly and I split up, I carried on for a while like it didn't matter. Then I realized just how empty the house was when I got home each night. It wasn't always empty; I do still get around a little, although there's not too much demand for a graying, dry alcoholic with big support payments. There's not much patience in me, either, for the boy-girl games associated with adolescence and the dating racket.

Apparently, Tom Endman could give me lessons. First I meet a pretty lady lawyer who has real possibilities, once you get past her weak stomach, which really isn't a problem since who wants a woman hardened to the ugliness of life. So I meet a pretty lady lawyer, she meets Tom Endman, and suddenly, he's the cat who's getting milk poured in his saucer, and my legal eagle's perched on his fist like a tame falcon. I mean, I knew beforehand that cats feed on birds, but

128

I thought Hilda was big enough to protect herself. She looks all grown up to me. Apparently I was wrong. Instead of a sharp-clawed eagle, she turned out to be just another chick who got pushed out of the nest too soon on unproven wings, desperately needing a safe place for a crash landing.

What I know is that she landed at Tom Endman's side. What I don't know is how safe a landing it was. I hope I'm wrong, but I'm afraid Hilda is going to leave some tail feathers sticking in Tom's nest.

It's her business, of course. I just thought of it because I was comparing my own attractiveness to Tom Endman's. Elaine turned out the same way. We seemed to get real close this afternoon. Brushes with death will do that to you. Then as we started cutting through the bullshit to get to the place where a man and woman can start making some connections that might last a while, it was, "Take me home to Tom, he'll know what to do." Why do I feel like Butch Cassidy, looking back over his shoulder. Who is this Tom Endman guy? He's pretty good.

Right in the middle of all these worries about virility, another *ity* word pops in my mind. Mortality. All guesses so far indicate that Elaine Endman was the target of the attacks that happened today, but the mathematics give these guesses only a fifty-fifty probability. It's equally likely, mathematically speaking, that I was the target.

There's nothing like sudden, growing, naked fear to spoil a good night's sleep.

I slipped quickly from room to room, putting out the lights, and checking the window locks. The doors are all solid wood, with "case hardened, one-inch dead bolts." I called the phone company number to check the time, just to make sure the phone was working. I would have put the dog outside, but he died last year of old age. He had lost the skill of barking in the last few years anyway. Use it or lose it. Fido lost it.

When the security precautions were finished, I stood in the kitchen doorway and looked around at the rest of the house, imagining the possibilities.

If someone came through a window, you might allow five seconds to break the glass, five seconds to reach in and unlatch the lock, five seconds to raise the sash, five seconds to climb in, and maybe ten

129

seconds to find me in the bedroom. If I allow ten seconds for waking up when I hear the glass break, and ten seconds to realize what's happening, that leaves about enough time for half the Lord's Prayer before the intruder blasts me away.

If, on the other hand, my assassin is a big guy, and not too subtle, he could kick in a front-door panel and get to my bedroom in about twenty-three seconds, which leaves me just time for "Our father, who art . . ."

There's a little light in the room from the street lamps outside. On the kitchen wall is a framed needlepoint sampler from my great grand-mother. It says There's No Place Like Home. I'm sure you're right, Grandma, and when my time comes, I want to die at home in your bed, the one in my room, just like you did. But tonight doesn't feel like the right time to die, and the more I look around, this doesn't feel like a safe place to be.

I moved fast, once my mind was made up. I keep a little bag packed with all the essentials. Actually, I haven't touched it in years, but it's still there in the closet. I grabbed it, made sure I had my wallet and credit cards, put on a dark windbreaker, and slipped into the garage. I could take the Merc, but I'm not James Bond. The only tail I can spot is the kind that walked out my front door a little while ago. So I left the car parked out front, and strapped my gym bag on the back of my fifteen-year-old's eighteen-speed mountain bike. He left it here the last time he came for the weekend, whenever the hell that was.

A back door from the garage opens onto an alley behind my house. It's an old-fashioned neighborhood. I eased the door open, and stepped out into the darkness. Nothing moved, and after my eyes were ad-justed, I lifted the bike out into the alley, shut the garage door, and peddled off into the night.

The air was cool, and a little damp. There'll be fog by morning —the moist ocean air's getting sucked all the way in over Silicon Valley. It used to make the plum orchards blossom and the cherry trees bear fruit. Now it makes an inversion layer to hold in the smog, and a moist blanket to water the garlic fields twenty miles to the south. Sometimes the smells of the auto exhaust and the garlic harvest get mixed. I tried calling it glog, but the name never caught on.

130

Tonight, though, it just smells fresh, as I headed uptown on quiet rubber wheels.

I called Braynes early on the portaphone and left a message, then ordered a room service breakfast. Grapefruit and a bowl of cornflakes are the usual breakfast items, but today was Sunday, and I was holed up in the downtown Fairmont, so it's bacon and eggs and hash browns and toast and Danish. It was gray outside in the early fog, but it will burn off by ten. If you're wondering why I don't go for a walk by the downtown shops and have coffee and a croissant at a sidewalk cafe, it's because you haven't seen downtown San Jose. We've come a long way in five years, but not that far. Or maybe I should find a room in a bed-and-breakfast joint in one of the quaint Victorians with antique furniture and pretty curtains? You think about it while I sit propped up in bed on four pillows with a room service breakfast on one side and the Sunday *New York Times* on the other, flicking through the television channels with the remote, looking for a basketball game.

There's not much that surprises a night clerk at a downtown hotel, but a middle-aged guest arriving at midnight on a mountain bike did raise an eyebrow. They were nice, though. Took my American Express card with only three other pieces of photo identification, and the bellman carried my bike up to the room for only a five dollar tip. I'm glad they left the light on for me.

It was a pretty quiet night. They were wrapping up a Mexican wedding reception downstairs when I arrived. The music was mostly salsa, but there were a few sweet trumpet fanfares toward the end that helped me get to sleep. Memories of Rosarita Beach. It's not San Blas, but it's not bad, either. A little later the guest next door had a falling out with his hooker, er, girlfriend (I forgot, they don't have hookers at the Fairmont), but it wasn't too loud, and things settled down toward dawn.

Braynes called me back toward the end of my second cup of coffee. I had hoped he would wait, but the ball game wouldn't start for another hour, and I'd spilled milk on the op-ed page, so boredom wasn't far off.

"Where the hell are you?" As usual, Braynes got right down to business.

"I decided I needed a change from the routine."

"I checked your house earlier when I got the news."

"What news?"

"About your friends who crashed on the highway. They weren't American citizens, but a certain government agency was familiar with their fingerprints. A federal agency."

There was a pause while I finished a bite of toast. This was one coincidence too many.

"Sounds like it's time we had a chat," I said.

"That's what we're doing."

"I mean in person."

"I would, if I knew where you are. You're not holed up with that Endman broad, are you?"

Braynes loves to talk like he thinks a cop should talk. All he needs is a cigar and a hole in his pants.

"I'm holed up in a downtown flophouse. Come on by."

There was a sigh of disgust at his end of the line.

"Where are you?" he said.

"Room 402 at the Fairmont."

"You're shitting me."

"Be polite at the desk, won't you. If they won't let you come up to my room, have them call me."

"I think I can handle it, Randel."

"No gun waving, now, there's a good fellow."

Braynes was there in thirty minutes. I was out of the shower and ordering a second pot of coffee when he arrived. The quick getaway bag had everything from shampoo to shaving gear. It also had a reminder of the past. A little square-sided pint of Jack Daniels. What would you pack if you were leaving in thirty minutes, maybe never to return? For me it used to be ninety proof mouthwash. I think I'll leave it as a tip for the maid.

"What the hell are you doing up here?" he said.

"I got nervous."

"You should be. You left some top talent roasting up there on the mountain."

"Who were they?'

"South American. DEA says they're known around Long Beach and San Pedro. *Pistoleros*, but good ones."

"Why are they after Elaine Endman?"

"That's what I want you to tell me. And if they're after Elaine Endman, why are you up here at a hundred and fifty dollars a night?"

The bellman brought the coffee, and left with a nice tip, even though it seems less and less likely that I'll make any money out of this deal. Right now I'll settle for living to deal another day.

Braynes and I swapped information. The facts uncovered so far led to a lot of guesses, but there was no solid trail to follow to a predictable end. We thought that camouflaged money had gone into Silicon Investment Group. Some of the dead bodies lying around indicate that drugs are involved. Was it just a simple money laundry scheme where some of the washermen got hung out to dry?

Another angle was the bankrupt S&L, Shorham Commercial Savings. Somebody paid off Mickey Peachton. Who knew what he did? And who paid him to do it? Was the fraud investigation at Shorham tied into the rest of Silicon Investment Group?

"What about Endman?" I said. "Is this just a side show, or is the whole business in trouble?"

"I can't answer that yet," Braynes said, "but my guess is that the more we find out, the worse it's going to smell."

We sat and drank coffee quietly. Braynes helped me finish the toast.

"Marty, I almost forgot," I said. "Frank Baker was my client. Where the hell does he fit into all this?"

"He's the odd man in, so far. If he hadn't died falling off the eighth-floor patio, he would have died from cyanide poisoning. Endman says Baker came in his office threatening him. He was on the telephone. He says he told Baker to pour them both a drink and that they would talk on the patio when he hung up. Baker put a drink on his desk, he says, walked out on the patio and waited. He hung up, took his glass and joined Baker outside."

Braynes paused for a gulp of coffee, and the last bite of whole wheat.

"Endman's story from there is that Baker raised his glass and said,

"Here's to a debt-free world," and knocked back half his drink. End-man was going to join him, when the phone rang. He walked inside, answered it, looked around, and saw Baker staggering across the patio to the railing. He backed into it, toppled over, and he was gone."

chapter **twenty-three**

···

That's a hell of a story."
"He tells it like he believes it."
"Where did the poison come from?"

"There was enough cyanide in that Scotch bottle to kill a polo team. Endman's glass was full of it, too. The fingerprints on the Scotch bottle belonged to Endman and Baker. If he wasn't so smart, it would be pretty incriminating. But I just can't believe he's dumb enough to leave hard evidence lying around like that."

"Baker was getting to be a problem for SIG."

"But what does killing him solve?" Braynes said. "In such a clumsy way? It doesn't make sense to me. We're checking the guy out, but so far, it's too good to be true."

"So you let Endman go."

"We might have kept him longer, but Billy Blake came down and "suggested" we had asked him enough questions without an attorney."

"Is Billy Blake his lawyer?"

"Yeah, I thought you knew that. Has been for years. I wondered about your using that young Straton woman as Baker's real estate lawyer. If there wasn't a conflict of interest on Friday, there sure as hell is today."

"That is strange," I said. "It must have just slipped by. It's new lawyer time on Monday, and hopefully, no harm done. That's not like Billy, though."

"It's not like you, either." Braynes looked at me carefully, and then at the luxury hotel room we were in. "You've been living alone too long. It's a shame to waste all this on a guy like you."

"Believe me, Marty," I said, as I walked him to the door, "it's not my idea."

The mountain bike made it to the elevator without the bellman's help, although there were a few strange looks in the lobby as I rolled it across the marble floor to leave my keys at the desk. I waved at the doorman and the parking valet, and pushed off in a whisper of rushing air. My first night at the Fairmont. If the hotel has its way, it'll probably be my last.

The street around my house was clear of watchers, so I swung up the alley, put the bike in the garage, changed clothes, and backed the Merc out for a Sunday spin.

Getting a rental car might have been smarter, if I was being watched, but if something is going to happen, I like for it to happen in the daylight. Hiding would just prolong the agony. Besides, the old Mercedes is almost like driving an armored car. That's what I like about the Germans. They may not know much about style, but they make a damn good steel.

I rang Baker's widow on the portaphone and got her to agree to let me go through her husband's real estate files right away. I thought I knew how they worked the scam on him, but I wanted to be sure I wasn't overlooking any of the players. As yesterday showed, carelessness could be a fatal mistake in this deal.

Mrs. Baker left for church before I arrived, but the grandson I'd scuffled with on Saturday let me in and showed me a dining room table piled with manila file folders. He was friendly today, and after offering me some coffee, he left me alone with the files while he resumed his gopher work outside.

Paper. They've been calling it obsolete for twenty years, but don't you believe it. The creation of paper was the seminal event of modern trade. With it, you could easily carry the records of transactions from one place to another, and the written signature transferred authority from both place to place and person to person. It still does. You can take all your electronic signals and beam them out into space; when you want to do business, it's the pen and paper that gets the job done.

And when you're down on the street, all the plastic cards and wire transfers don't mean diddley. If you want action, it's the twenty-dollar bills that command attention.

That's why all data banks and all the hard disk memory in the world couldn't have done for me what thirty minutes with Frank Baker's plain paper files did. Because when they record the real estate records on microfiche and in electronic memory, there is only so much space for each type of information. For instance, the owner record on Baker's condos would say, "Baker, Frank Edward and Betty Ann, as joint tenants in . . . ," and you're out of spaces on that line. The hard paper deed, however, didn't stop there. It said, "Frank Edward Baker and Betty Ann Baker, as joint tenants in an undivided 99% interest, and Thomas Houston Endman, as joint tenant in an undivided 1% interest . . ."

Every condo deed was like that, all thirty-six of them. So were the deeds of trusts that secured the Shorham Commercial Savings loans against each property. Each file also had a copy of the escrow papers for each transaction, where all the expenses of the purchases and loans were listed. The papers were standard, except for the Tom Endman entry at the top, and they confirmed what I suspected.

Mickey Peachton got paid two hundred dollars for an appraisal on each property. Arbor Financial got paid twenty-four hundred dollars (two points) for arranging the loan on each property, and about four hundred dollars in additional processing fees. That's more than a hundred thousand dollars in loan fees. Shorham Commercial Savings made the loans at a twelve percent fixed interest rate. That would have been about one percentage point over the going rate in the summer of 1988. They did OK. And finally, Doubletree Insurance got paid four hundred and eighty dollars for each fire insurance policy, and a hundred and eighty dollars for some additional item called "Lloyds." That should mean insurance, also, but I couldn't imagine what it would mean on a real estate deal. Just another rip-off, as far as I could see.

Bad news is very tiring. After thirty minutes of reviewing the theft that took Frank Baker's retirement security, and eventually his life, I was ready for a break. Young Frankie was energetically digging into the hillside above the house. Every so often, he would stoop, take something out of a tray, stick it in the ground, and pat some dirt on top of it. There may be more fun things to do on a Sunday than poking around in the dirt, but after what I had just read, the dirt outside seemed a lot cleaner than what was packed in those manila files.

He looked up and smiled as I approached.

"Find what you wanted?" he said. He had that distracted look that people sometimes get when they haven't quite realized the finality of the death of a loved one. Frankie was gardening just like he expected his granddad to pop out of the house and help him any second.

"I found pretty much what I expected," I said. "What are you doing?"

"Granddad thought he had discovered a final solution to the gopher wars. He cut up old mushrooms, soaked them in his special goop, and then put them at the mouth of their tunnels and covered the hole with a little dirt."

"What's the goop?"

"His secret recipe. It's the one thing he wouldn't share. He made it up out of some pesticides and some other stuff."

"Where did he learn to do that?"

"I guess he started out as a chemistry teacher."

"Does it work?"

"Granddad said he never again saw fresh dirt at a tunnel he baited with goop."

"I hope he wrote down the recipe."

Frankie smiled sadly, and shook his head.

"This is the last of it," he said. He looked self-conscious. "It's just a silly ritual," he said, "I guess it's my way of saying good-bye. "

I put an arm across his shoulder for a moment.

"It's important to say good-bye," I said. I stepped back and watched him work for moment until I saw Mrs. Baker driving up the lane.

"I'll see you at the funeral," I said. He looked up sharply at me, and then back to the ground.

"Thanks," he said, finally. "I wasn't going to go. I made up some good reasons, but the real one was I didn't want to say good-bye. But . . . I think you may be right . . . see you there."

I met Mrs. Baker at the door, and walked in with her.

"Why is Tom Endman on title on your condos?" I asked her, after she joined me at the files on the table.

"I wondered if you would find that unusual. Frank was afraid of the deal. And rightly so, as we now know. Every time he told Tom about his concerns, Tom talked about how much money Frank was going to make, and gave us another bottle of wine. Frank was usually a bit tipsy after a meeting with Tom Endman."

She talked in little bursts, and seemed glad to have someone to share her memories with.

"Finally, Frank wasn't going to do it, and Tom said he would buy it with Frank, so they'd both be responsible."

"One percent wasn't a whole lot of responsibility for Endman."

"What he said was that one percent of his reputation was worth as much to him as our money was to us. He said with his name on the deed, there was no way he could afford to let the deal go bad."

"What did you think of that?"

"It sounded good to Frank."

"But what did you think?"

"I thought it was worth about as much as Endman was paying for it."

"Why did you go along, then?"

"Frank wanted it so bad. He wanted to provide for Julia, and he didn't want us to have to scrimp in our old age. As I told you yesterday, he wanted to prove he was master of whatever situation life dealt him. So, I went along, hoping for the best, trying not to think about the worst." She sat back in the tall dining room chair, and paused.

"But never in my fears, did I imagine anything like this."

"No," I said, "I'm sure you didn't."

138

The discipline of a thousand deals let me accomplish then that hardest of all tasks—keeping my mouth shut. Mrs. Baker sat and reflected, keeping company with her memories. When someone dies, their image persists. We imagine talking to it, like a holograph, like a friend who's just gone to the store to get some ice cream and is going to be back any minute. Old conversations are remembered, are reconversed with different beginnings and different ends. If it had taken place in the garden instead of the kitchen, if only I'd waited until after dinner, thank God we got it straightened out then and didn't wait, the last words I said to him were "I love you. . . ." Memory. That's what's left. Over time it fades, gets stuck on the top shelf, far from eye level, gets packed away in crates for the children to go through when they settle things up, gets sold finally at auction, or given away to the secondhand man, that nice man who isn't going to charge anything for hauling all this junk away.

Memories that fade and recede across the mind's horizon, that's all that's left. Memories and tombstones, that settle and tilt, while the carved names erode in the sun and the weather. Finally, no visitors come any longer. Just other people's children, who run fascinated from grave to grave, reading the names and marveling that anyone walked the earth so long ago, shaking their heads at the folly that brought the deceased to this end. How careless of them, the children think, to lose their lives. We won't make that mistake, and picking up a stray clod of earth, they throw it at the robins sitting naturally atop the carved granite blocks, waiting for the bugs to come back when the children leave.

"I'm trying not to hate him," Mrs. Baker said, finally.

"Tom Endman?"

She looked at me impatiently.

"Frank," she said. "I don't care a pig's winkle about Endman. But Frank . . . I lived with him for forty-five years, and now he's left me all alone with a big house, a daughter in a coma, hocked up to my eyeballs, and a bunch of dear sweet grandchildren who can't do anything but hunt gophers."

She looked at me appraisingly.

"And now you're telling me that the lawyer you got for us is not good, and that there's probably nothing you can do anyway. . . .

You've been very kind, and I do trust you, but really, what good have you done?"

I was going to make some brilliant excuse for things turning out the way they had so far, but she stopped me with an upraised hand.

"It's all right," she said, "I'm just tired. Frank and I always took a nap after church, and I think that's what I should do right now."

She smiled evenly at me.

"Do you ever work with that big real estate company?" she said. "The one that has all the little offices everywhere."

"Century 21?"

"That's the one. Could you call them about the condos for me? Maybe they could do something. They probably do a lot more of that sort of work than you do, being so big and all."

We got up from the table. My smile was even, too. Even thinner than hers. Be kind to widows and orphans, my mother taught me, and I didn't disobey her now, even though I did think briefly that the world would be better off with one less widow and a few more orphans.

Mrs. Baker had that faraway look again.

"I wonder if they know about duplexes, too," she was saying, as we got to the door.

"They know a lot about advertising," I said, with a straight face. "They always have big yellow page ads. Look in there and you'll find their number real easy."

"I still want you to work on this," she said. "I just need to have a second opinion. I learned that much from Frank, anyway, always get a second opinion."

Mrs. Baker eased me on out and shut the door. The sun was bright now, and getting warmer. There were a few white fluffies overhead, but mostly it was another perfect day in the land of silicon. The walk out to my car seemed a lot longer than it had going in. I sat behind the wheel and stared back at the Baker's house before I started the engine.

For what it's worth, Frank Baker is a little easier to understand now. It wasn't the world around him that he was trying to prove something to, was it? He must have gone quietly and desperately crazy trying to be the successful man of the world his wife expected, while providing and protecting the affluent life-style she demanded. Try being a security conscious risk-taker sometime. It'll drive you round the bend . . . or over the edge, as it did in Frank Baker's case.

So where does that leave me? Forty-eight hours ago I was aiming for a hundred thousand dollars in commissions from selling Frank Baker's duplexes, and maybe a lot more than that if the condos were salvageable. Now I know I can kiss the condos good-bye for a couple of lifetimes, or at least a couple of lawsuits, and Mrs. Baker wants to talk to Century 21 about the duplexes.

Some people see their past flash through their mind when they get in a tough spot. When I get in a jam, like losing a deal, I see the future, and it's never pretty. No Mercedes. No beach house. No athletic club. No hiding out at the Fairmont. No portable phone. Working for a living. . . .

Just then the portaphone rang, and interrupted the orgy of imagined doom. The voice on the phone made the imagined fears seem comforting, compared with the real thing.

"Where the hell have you been?" Molly sounded pissed.

"What gives you the right to ask that question?"

"I'll ask what I damn please . . . unless you'd rather I hung up . . . forever."

"I'm about to leave Frank Baker's place."

"I don't care about now. Where were you last night?"

"I was with Elizabeth Taylor at the Fairmont."

There was a pause at her end, and for a moment I thought I lost her. Then I heard a breath.

"Last chance, Randel."

I had eased the Merc in gear, and it was rolling down the drive. I waved at young Frankie. There was something I needed to ask him, but the left side of my brain was scrambling too fast to cover the right side's ass.

"Molly, I got scared. I rode Eddie's bike downtown and stayed at a hotel. *Raintree County* was on the late show. Channel Three. I fell asleep just where Liz and Montgomery Clift are down by the river."

"What else, Randel?"

"Nothing else. Ask Braynes. He saw me there this morning. I was alone with the *New York Times*."

"I will ask him, Randel. And I'll ask the desk clerk if you were alone. And I'll ask the maid if there were pecker tracks on the sheets. If I find out you're lying, Randel, you're dead meat."

"Ask anything you want, but tell me this. How do you know I wasn't home last night?"

"Because I came back, you dumb shit. I came back to finish seducing you, and you weren't there. I walked out on the yuppie, and then I had to go back home again. God, was he snotty about it, too."

"Where are you now?"

"I'm at your house. I decided to give you another chance."

"I'm on my way. Make yourself useful, in the meantime. Look up who owns the building where Shorham Commercial Savings and Arbor Financial are located. I'll be there in fifteen minutes."

Unfortunately, they had Highway 101 torn up again. Traffic backs up even on Sunday, when they have it cut down to two lanes. It was closer to an hour before I could fight my way back downtown. I tried calling, but I only got my machine. When I got home, Molly was gone. There was a note.

"Chase," it said, "I decided not to wait. I'm checking something out. Have a wonderful life. Molly."

It was a mysterious and disappointing turn to the day. Instead of a friendly Sunday afternoon with an old friend who I suspected was going to make me feel a lot younger, it was cops and robbers again. She left the microfiche reader turned on, so I checked the building's ownership myself. I was not reassured. The bad smell was coming from an unexpected direction, like finding out that your fiancée farts in her sleep just after you sign the prenuptial agreements.

The little flashing light on the answering machine was working full-time. I usually don't listen to messages on Sunday. A man needs a day of rest. Unlike Jagger, I don't always get what I need.

"Chase," Elaine's voice said, "I just wanted to apologize for last night. There was simply too much going on. I hope you'll give us another chance." There was a pause. "Yesterday was really wonderful." Another pause. "Please call me when you hear this . . ."

142

She might have gone on talking. The machine has a thirty-second cutoff. She was right, though. Yesterday was special. More than just a roll in the hay. The memory was rolling through my mind like fluffy white clouds across a blue Seattle sky, when a thunderhead boiled up over the horizon.

Would Molly have listened to my messages? Can a fly stay away from a garbage can? Holy shit. Women. One is crazy jealous, and the other may just be crazy. Suddenly the lawyer woman was looking better and better to the memory's eye. Was that just two day ago that I met honey-tongued Hilda? Time was racing by.

While time is racing, I suppose Molly is running. Away from me and lovey-dove messages on the answering machine. Not much point in waiting around. Molly might be gone for days. Or forever. One thing's certain. She'll stay on the story, even if she does decide the script no longer needs a leading man.

I shook my head, pondered fate for a few seconds—which is about all the time fate-pondering deserves, looked up some addresses, and headed out. I may be a designated victim, but old mother fate better be able to hit a moving target.

chapter **twenty-four**

....

There were several possibilities for the next move. I decided to use sequence, the old step-by-step approach. It's not an easy decision. Should I check out each link in this imaginary chain of criminal actions, or should I jump to the possible end and tie up the loose ends later?

The classic quandary. Lots of wars have been fought over sequence and order. Do you ask the priest, who asks the bishop, who asks the pope, who asks God? Or do you go directly to the source? The problem with answer two is, who do you blame if you get it wrong?

J. Paddington Moss, Builder, was the next step on the path of logic. Somebody paid Mickey to phony up his condo appraisals, and Jay Moss, Builder, is the most obvious beneficiary of the fiddle.

Dry Creek Road isn't Beverly Hills posh. It attracts people who have worked hard for a living and have been damn successful at it. Pickup trucks are not unusual on Dry Creek Road, but even the gardeners drive four-by-fours with custom cabs and top-of-the-line sound systems. A real "dirty clothes, clean hands" neighborhood. I don't think many lawyers live here. I know for damn sure there aren't many real estate brokers.

Jay's truck wasn't in sight. It was hot, even for June, and the sweat beaded on my forehead and dripped off as I waited for someone to answer the doorbell. It was a long wait. Finally, there was a voice from the gate in the redwood board fence at the side of the house.

"Who is it?" she asked.

I didn't answer until I walked to the gate. I knew she heard my shoes hitting the brick walk.

"I'm looking for Jay," I said. "I'm a real estate broker."

When you tell them that, they either open the door or check the lock. She opened the gate.

"You don't sound too dangerous," she said.

"Do I look dangerous?"

"Looks can be deceiving."

She'd obviously walked up from the pool, and her looks were not deceiving. She was not tall, although her straight brown hair created a vertical impression. You could tell from her tan that she spent a lot of time in the sun. The absence of strap marks and the even skin color on her breasts all the way to the bikini fabric made me suspect she liked to take off the top half of her bathing suit. Her figure made this an interesting subject to speculate about. I couldn't tell about the bottom half, but speculation isn't limited by facts.

"You look hot," she said. She got that right.

"I really do need to find Jay," I said.

"Well you sure as hell won't find him here," she said. "And just between you and me, looking for Jay Moss is a dumb way to spend a Sunday."

She looked at me impatiently. A little hiccup snuck out past the hand covering her mouth. "Jay's at the project," she said.

"Where's the project?"

"All the way down Meridian, right on Rebel Way, at the end on the left. Jay will be the one with the blueprints stuck up his nose."

I took one last look, just to tide me over.

"I wish I could swim," I said.

"I wish you could lie."

"I know how you feel," I said, heading for the car. I did, too, know how she felt. But this wasn't the time for empathy.

The project turned out to be an acre full of condos, pretty much like Frank Baker's condos, except in a better part of town. The neighborhood looked half deserted. Everyone's gone to Santa Cruz for the day, probably. They're either sitting in traffic trying to get there, waiting in a line at the parking lot entrance, or carefully stepping over body parts and blankets to get to the water. Today it's their problem.

Sometimes I think if I see another condo I'm going to throw up. There was a time, for about eight or nine years, say 1955 to 1963, when there seemed to be enough of everything in America. Then our perceptions changed, people started reading the world news, the Club of Rome invented the population bomb, and some guy in Los Angeles invented the condominium. We've been imitating sardines ever since.

The planners love condominiums. I finally figured out that condos max out the number of building permit dollars that can be squeezed out of an acre. Those fees of course go directly to pay the salaries of planners. It's a variety of intellectual mercantilism that Adam Smith would be proud of. But what the hell, condos max out the amount of real estate commission dollars per acre, too. It's just that the planners claim it's all for the common good. Which is probably why so many real estate people act so common—they know it's for their own good.

I didn't drive into the project but parked down the street and ducked in through a hole in the chain-link contractor's fence surrounding the construction. The builders sometimes put holes in the fences so the neighborhood kids won't get hurt climbing over. I walked through some unfinished back patios to the end of one set of units. Jay Moss's big pickup that I had seen in Molly's Polaroid photo was parked in front of the next building. The units looked ninety-five percent finished, although the grounds were still cluttered and the landscaping wasn't done. There were muffled voices coming from inside. A look in a window showed nothing but an empty room. Jay was probably upstairs. I went on around the corner and tried the door of the unit his pickup was parked in front of. It was locked, so I knocked and waited.

All at once it got very quiet. Even the traffic out on the street seemed to have vanished. I looked around, waiting, but nothing happened until I stepped back and looked up at the second-story window. I saw the face watching me before it ducked away. After a moment, the window slid open, and a head stuck out.

"What do you want?"

"I'm looking for Jay Moss."

"And who are you?"

"I'm Chase Randel. I'm a real estate broker. Are you Jay?"

"What if I am?"

"What if I want to buy a bunch of condos?"

"They're not finished yet."

"Not these. I want to buy Fair Valley Place. Can I ask you a few questions about it?"

The face ducked back inside without answering. I waited. Finally, he said, "Stay there. I'll be right down."

Jay Moss didn't rush right down to see me. He must be having a conference with his confidant upstairs. There was a blue Chevy sedan parked in front of Moss's truck. I walked over and was glancing inside when I noticed someone glancing back. His face was Hispanic and looked familiar. A pair of crutches in the backseat jogged my memory back to the confrontation at Baker's condos on Friday. I turned quickly and walked back to the front door, took out a business card, and wrote a phone number for "Lt. Marty Braynes, SJPD," on the back.

Moss opened the door about halfway and didn't invite me in. He appeared to be a big man with a beer drinker's paunch and broad shoulders that were starting to roll forward from lack of use. His eyes looked cloudy and he blinked a lot.

"What can I do for you?" he said.

"I've been asked to take over Fair Valley Place," I said, "and I heard you built those units. Is there anything special I should watch out for?"

"It's not a very good neighborhood," he said. "I'd stay out of there if I was you."

"I heard you did all right in there."

"Not really. I just finished them up for some people. They handled all the money stuff. I guess they did all right, though."

"Who could tell me more about those places?"

"I don't know. I guess you might try the mortgage broker. He put the whole thing together."

"Who's that?"

"Morris Payne. He's got an outfit called Arbor Financial, over on the Alameda. Try him."

I looked around the project.

"This is about the same design as Fair Valley Place, isn't it? What do you think these will appraise for?"

The question and the change of pace seemed to lull his alertness.

"The appraisal depends on who does it," he said with a laugh. "You're a broker. You ought to know that much at least."

"I know," I said, "but who are you going to use now that Mickey's dead?"

"What?" he said. He looked confused. Fast changes of mental direction were not his forte.

I pretended not to notice.

"Why don't they give you an office, too," I said, "over on the Alameda along with everyone else?" Jay's eyes were narrowing now. I still don't think he understood completely what I was saying, but he sensed that he shouldn't like it.

"Arbor Financial's there, Doubletree Insurance, Shorham Savings, Silicon Investment Group . . . hell, even Billy Blake's just down the street if you get legal problems."

Moss started coming out the door, but he looked undecided about what to do. He looked nervously over his shoulder and up the stairs. I was starting to share a little of his apprehension, but I wanted to give the knife a final turn.

"You'd like it over there," I said. "Mickey sure would have liked it."

"Get out of here," Moss said. "Get out of here right now or we'll both be sorry."

I held up my open hands to placate him—and to slow him if he made a sudden charge at me. I backed off and pulled the card out of my pocket.

"Here's my number," I said. "Or you can call my associate on the back, if you remember anything you think you should tell somebody."

I gave him the card, waved, and moved quickly around the corner. When I got past the window, I darted behind the adjacent building and sprinted for the hole in the fence. I didn't expect gunfire to follow me, but Jay Moss and his friends weren't going to get any better shot at me than mother fate was.

If I were a detective I would have figured out a fancy next move, instead of just following along after whatever came up. I was pulling away in the Merc with no clear direction. I knew more than I did when I woke up in the morning, but the reasons for Frank Baker's death were no more clear, and the probability of my earning some commissions out of all this seemed to be slipping ever further away. Going home and taking a nap was getting strong consideration when the portaphone rang. It was Elaine Endman, and what she told me got the Merc pointed north in a hurry.

A group of investors, she said, had forced Endman to meet them at the SIG, and had demanded repayment of all their investments within twenty-four hours. When Endman refused, she said, there had been an ugly scene with shoving and a few ineffectual punches being thrown. Finally, Endman had to slip out a back door to evade the crowd, which had grown to two dozen or more by the time the meeting broke up.

I was only about ten minutes from Los Gatos, and I could smell the fear in her voice, reaching out to me like a radio beacon. I kept her talking so I could follow the beam on in.

"Who kicked up the fuss?" I said.

"Maxie Turbot."

"That'll look good in the papers. I can read it now. Ex-linebacker puts big hit on financier. Don't you have any low-profile investors?"

"Chase, how fast can you get here? Tom's locked himself in the library." Her voice was starting to break now. "I'm afraid he might try something foolish."

"I've been heading your way ever since the phone rang."

I heard the little gasp in her voice.

"Oh my God," she whispered. "They're here."

"Ten minutes, sweetheart, I'm on my way."

chapter **twenty-five**

I parked on the street and walked up the curving drive to meet Elaine. There was a black Cadillac limo pulled up in front of the house. A driver was sitting behind the wheel smoking, with his arm out the window draped over the mirror. I eased off the drive and slipped up the edge of the property to the side of the house. The driver didn't see me.

The gate in the adobe wall that surrounded the veranda was open. I walked quietly on up the path and around the house until I found the back door. The pool looked inviting. It also looked unused. No wet towels, no inflatable rafts, no rolling wet bars and no soft music from south of Panama. I thought of Mrs. Jay Moss. She was probably still working on her suntan. It might have been fun to spend a day with her by the pool—until Jay came home, at least.

The back door was unlocked, so I let myself in. I vaguely remembered the layout of the house from my brief visit the day before. The back door opened onto a porch and storage room, which then led to the kitchen. From there you could see through to the dining room. Elaine was sitting at the end of the table with her head in her hands. Angry voices could be heard farther in, too muffled to be understood. Elaine saw my movement in the corner of her eye, then turned with a start until she recognized me. I waved for her to come out to the kitchen. She looked away toward the library, then got up quietly and walked toward the kitchen, glancing over her shoulder as she came.

She was shaking and tense, sucking her lips in to suppress a twitching cheek muscle. I held out my arms without speaking and pulled her close to me. After a moment, she moved back.

"What's going on?" I said.

"I'm not sure, but I think they want the money."

"So does everybody else. Which ones are these?"

She looked at me sharply.

"They want the special money."

It was a moment before I guessed what she was talking about.

"The money that came in the mail?"

Elaine nodded. I frowned.

"Holy shit," I said. "Have you been missing payments?"

"Never."

I walked over to the arched doorway between the kitchen and dining room. The rooms were painted in whites that had tints of pink mixed in. The color was almost subliminal, but the walls seemed to radiate energy. It was one of those houses where there is more life in the walls than there is between them.

The double doors to the library were still closed. The voices stopped and the doors opened. Two short, slender men in tailored dark suits walked out with Tom Endman between them. The two men looked vaguely Hispanic, and very sure of themselves. Endman looked accommodating. They walked on out the front door toward the waiting limousine.

I turned back to Elaine. She looked rigid with fear.

"Relax," I said. "Tom didn't look worried. Why not let him handle it."

She came over to me and I held her again.

"How deeply are you tied into all this?" I said, when we eased apart.

"Something's wrong with the money," she said.

"That's pretty obvious. It's hard to get anybody to send you clean money in the mail with no strings attached."

I asked her again.

"How much do you know about it?"

"Just what I told you."

I held her at arm's length and studied her face. I guessed she was telling at least some of the truth. Say, seven-to-three odds on the lady. I've bucked worse odds on females. If I was right, the reward side of the equation looked unbeatable. It was the risk factor I was unsure of. I gave the dice a roll.

"Let me get you out of here," I said. "My place in Santa Cruz should be safe for tonight. We'll figure something out from there."

"You hardly know me."

"According to the Bible, I do."

Her eyes softened, and there was almost a smile.

"You always make me laugh, don't you?"

It was a wild idea, wild and romantic. To take each other's hands and run down through the trees to the car, and escape to the ocean hideout. Tomorrow we'd drive down the Big Sur coast, lunch at Nepente, hole up again that night at the little inn at Whaler's Cove, make love to the sound of the breaking surf, and . . .

"Do you think it would work?" she said. She looked younger, not innocent, more like a perennial flower putting out new shoots for springtime.

"Just give me five . . ."

Her eyes darted away, toward the front door. Endman opened it and then turned back to talk to his visitors. Elaine frowned as she stared at him. She let go of my hands unconsciously, and clenched her fists together just under her chin. After a moment, she looked back at me and forced a smile.

"I'll just see what Tom's going to do," she said, and started walking slowly toward him. He finished talking and shut the door when she was about five feet away. He turned to look for her, not seeing me at first. He forced a smile, too, but not before I saw the panic and fear wash across his face. Elaine wrapped her arms around him and buried her face in his chest, holding back her sobs.

"Tom, Tom," she said, "what are they going to do?"

He stroked her hair with his eyes closed.

"Shhh," he said. "It's going to be all right."

Suddenly she looked up at him, digging her fingers into his shoulders.

"What's going to become of us?" she said. "You're all I have."

Endman looked up and saw me. A look of shock, and then fear crossed his face. He stepped away from Elaine, and pointed at me.

"How long's he been here?" Endman said.

"Only a few minutes," she said. "Don't worry, he just wants to help. Don't you, Chase?"

She stood beside Endman, with one arm still around him. Back in the dusty closets of my mind, a small, dim light bulb clicked on. I wasn't exactly sure what was going on, but I did guess that I wouldn't need to go home and pack my travel bag. Still, a theory's just a theory until you test it.

"I was just suggesting to Elaine that she take a little vacation . . . step out of the line of fire, as it were."

There was sudden shock on Elaine's face.

"I can't do that, Chase. I can't leave when Tom needs me the most." She looked up at him. "You do need me here, don't you, Tom?"

I still can't describe the look on Tom Endman's face, like a vampire, perhaps, racing to close the blinds at dawn, and every time a beam of sunlight hits, a little more of the mask falls away. Guilty, sad, defensive, belligerent, scared, grateful, they also flashed across the screen. Finally, he looked down at her.

"I think you better stay," he said.

Elaine tucked herself tightly under his arm and looked at me.

"Thank you for offering, Chase. You're very sweet. We still need help, don't we, Tom?"

It's a strange world. I don't pretend to understand it. You let a mouse out of a trap and it goes back for the cheese. We're all addicted to something, I guess, and we cling to the pain we know rather than risk an unfamiliar world that may contain . . . who knows what?

I need some help, too, I thought. I need evidence of fraud for Frank Baker's widow to use in a lawsuit, and there's no better place to get that than looking over Tom and Elaine Endman's shoulders.

I held out my hands, palms up, and smiled.

"I'll be happy to do whatever I can," I said.

"Thank you," Tom's voice said. His eyes said something different.

"I don't know your business," I said, "but I know how to think. Why don't I ask you some dumb questions. Sometimes we overlook the most obvious conclusions because they're too simple." Salesmen love mental gadgets. Tom shrugged his agreement. He couldn't seem to think of a graceful way to get rid of me.

"I have a meeting at the SIG building in an hour," he said, "but we can talk for a few minutes."

I walked to the dining room table, sat down, and looked up at them expectantly. They slowly came over and sat down opposite me. When you're selling, you want the opponents, uh, customers, to sit beside each other where you can see them both. Otherwise, they'll be shooting each other significant looks and signals when you're not looking. They might even imagine they're in control of the situation. God forbid.

"Let me take a couple of wild guesses," I said. "You stop me if I'm wrong.

"Those guys want their money." I paused and looked at them both before I went on.

"You don't want to give it to them." There was an awkward shift in the feelings.

"Scratch that. You don't have it to give to them." Nobody stopped me. Tom and Elaine sat wrapped in a space warp. They were listening, but they didn't seem to be fully part of this reality.

"They want their money. Maxie Turbot wants his money. But you've invested it in the company and you can't pay it back right now." It felt funny again. I looked at them carefully.

"Your company has been growing, hasn't it?"

Tom nodded.

"We've shown twenty percent growth for four years running."

"You pay the highest rates in town, and nobody's ever lost a dime until Frank Baker's deal."

I literally scratched my head.

"I don't understand it," I said. "It sounds too good to be true."

Tom suddenly looked like he was going to be sick. I suddenly thought I knew why. I sat back and stared at him and didn't say anything. He waited, fidgeted, looked at Elaine and back at me. He gradually regained his composure.

"If that's it, Chase," he said, with a rueful smile, "thanks for trying, but I don't really think we're accomplishing much here."

"That's it, isn't it?" I said. "It is too good to be true. It's a what's-his-name, isn't it? What's-his-name, Tom, you know what I mean."

Tom was getting up, and pulling Elaine up with him.

"I've really had about enough of this," he said. He wasn't smiling now.

I snapped my fingers at him.

"That's it," I said, "it's a Ponzi, isn't it? You pay off the old investors by getting new money from new investors. You had to grow, didn't you? And when you didn't, you used the funny money to keep things going. And now the funny-money men aren't laughing."

"That's a damn lie, Randel," Endman said. "And if I hear you repeat it in public, I'll have you up on slander charges." Endman pulled away from Elaine and stormed from the room.

"Chase, you can't believe that," Elaine said. I stood up as she came around the table and took my hands.

"No matter what you believe," she said, "if you repeat that in public, a lot of people are going to get hurt in the panic. Innocent people."

"Give it up, Elaine," I said. "You can still get out of this alive."

"I can't leave him now," she said. "You can see how much he needs me. How could you possibly suggest such a thing?"

"Just run-of-the-mill stupidity," I said. "Don't worry about me. Go take care of Tom. Give him what he deserves."

"I'm sorry, Chase," she said, "there are just a few things you don't understand." She turned and walked into the library after Tom and closed the double doors.

I stood and looked at the doors for a moment, but they didn't swing back open. I took that as my cue to leave. I had part of what I needed. I knew what was wrong at Silicon Investment Group. I knew at least one party that Frank Baker's widow should sue. What I didn't have was proof, and I sensed that the longer I took finding the proof, the more elusive it was going to become. I sat in the Merc thinking, then picked up the portaphone and called my answering machine. Maybe it knew something I didn't.

It did.

"Chase," Molly was saying, not thirty minutes earlier, "you should get your faithless ass over to Arbor Financial as fast as you can. They're loading up a rental truck with cardboard boxes. I suspect our paper trail is about to turn into spaghetti."

Suddenly I was smiling again. Molly Gish. Who else could make jealousy seem like a healthy, wholesome emotional experience? I put the Merc in drive and rolled through the rich Sunday streets of Los Gatos. I didn't look back at the Endmans' house. Home is where the heart is, and right now I was happy to be putting up a vacancy sign.

chapter **twenty-six**

Braynes wasn't happy again about being called at home on a weekend. You could smell the smoke from the barbecue over the phone.

"The hell with it, Randel," he said, when he finally answered the phone. I could hear kids screaming in the background. "We can play cops and robbers again tomorrow. Frieda says bring your girlfriend, whichever one of them it is, on over and we'll have some steaks and a beer."

The traffic was getting heavy again on I-880, as the beach goers started to return from Santa Cruz. The reception on the cellular wasn't very good, the afternoon smog was starting to build, and I'd already had about one too many confrontations for a Sunday. Steaks with Marty and Frieda Braynes sounded awful good. But . . . Molly was probably waiting and watching, and she was right. The evidence might be rolling off into the sunset if we didn't act fast.

I told Marty what was happening. He swore a few times and didn't promise anything.

"Just get a black and white to roll by, Marty. And tell them who the good guys are, in case we need some help."

Braynes hemmed and hawed some more, and finally promised to get something moving just as I took the exit for the Alameda. It was after six o'clock, and the temperature was starting to cool a little, although there was still plenty of sunlight.

Arbor Financial was located in a two-story Spanish-style stucco building that had probably been a residential duplex at one time. There was a dark brown sign with tan lettering on the building's front, set against the off-white walls, that told us this was the home of Arbor Financial and Doubletree Insurance. It sat on the corner of the Alameda and Villa Drive. There was a little parking lot in the back, and I glimpsed a rental van there as I drove by.

A right turn at the next three corners brought me up Villa so I could park on the street a hundred feet behind the building. I pulled in behind a little red two-seat Japanese something-or-other that I knew belonged to Molly Gish.

Molly wasn't in the car, and I didn't see her lurking anywhere nearby. There was activity in the parking lot, however. Two men were loading cardboard boxes in the van while a third was walking back in the rear downstairs door of the building. The van looked pretty low on its wheels, as though it had quite a load of paper in it already, and one of the loaders was reaching to slide shut the side cargo door.

"Hold it," I said, "there's been a change in plans. The boss said to leave everything right where it is until he gets here."

The pair looked at each other and then at me.

The bigger one walked over toward me, while the skinny one

"That's funny," Payne said. "He didn't mention anything about you when he was here ten minutes ago."

"Things change fast."

"They sure do," said leather jacket. His hand had already slid into his jacket and was now on its way out. "I bet one thing that's just changed is your plans. Why don't you get in the van and go along with us. The man himself can tell us if we're making a mistake or not."

Payne nodded at leather man, and he motioned with the pistol he was no longer concealing under his jacket.

"No way," I said. "I wouldn't be caught dead in that van."

"Don't count on it."

Payne put his hand under my arm gently.

"Don't worry," he said. "If anything's crooked here, Mr. B. will straighten it out. In the meantime, do what Lonny tells you. It's safer that way."

With Payne's hand under one arm and Hefty guiding me from the other side, I was eased through the cargo door and onto a pile of boxes. Lonny got in after me, a little smile on his lips, which he kept wetting with his tongue. It smelled dusty in the van, but it didn't completely cover the smell of Lonny's stale sweat. So Mr. B. is going to straighten it all out, is he? It was hard to imagine a healthy outcome from the facts I knew so far, but the sun was still shining outside, and my heart was still beating inside.

Payne's instructions to the driver cut through some of the comforts of philosophy.

"Wait for us at the landfill," he told Hefty, who was driving. "Use the back entrance, like I told you. The gate will be unlocked."

Payne looked back at me.

"You're Randel, aren't you? I was warned you might be poking around."

"Warned by who?" I said.

"Who do you think?"

"What did he tell you to do about it?"

"He said not to let you cause any trouble."

"You're making a mistake, Payne. The cops are on their way here right now."

158

reached for a leather jacket that was hanging over an open front door of the van.

"Who are you?" the larger man said.

"It doesn't matter who I am, it's what you do about it that counts. None of this stuff is to leave here until you get further word."

"Word from who?"

"The boss," I said, with my most menacing gaze.

"Who says we have a boss?"

"If you mess this up, you won't have one. Where's Payne?"

The skinny one had his jacket on now, and walked over to join us. It seemed too hot for leather, and he seemed too skinny to have such big bulges in his jacket.

"You sure you got the right place?" the skinny one said. His hair was an oily blond, and the oil wasn't natural. He ran his fingers through it a few times. He held his other hand lightly inside his jacket, pointed toward the bulge.

"Listen guys, I don't blame you for being suspicious, but I'm telling you what the man said. If you don't like it, take it up with him when he gets here."

"Who is this mysterious man?"

The voice came from behind me, and I confess I jumped a little. I hadn't heard him approach, but I moved around so I could see all three at once. I figured the third man was Morris Payne. He looked like an ad in a Macy's Sunday supplement. He wasn't sweating like the other two were, and I suspected the heaviest thing he had carried was some bad vibes.

"Are you Payne?" I said.

Mr. Suave nodded.

"Then you must know the man doesn't like have his name spoken casually."

"Say it anyway," he said, "we've got short memories."

I moved back a step, and not just for dramatic effect.

"Do what you think best," I said, "but if this van rolls out of here, Mr. B.'s not going to be happy."

"Do you mean Mr. Blake?"

"What do you think?"

"Too bad you're going to miss them. Roll it," he said to the driver, and slammed the door. I must have been trying to get up to have a final word, when Lonny mistook my intentions, and pulled the gun out and laid it lightly across my head above the ear. I stumbled back against the boxes. Lights flashed for an instant, and a pain seared down my temple and neck. As the van started moving, I looked at Lonny in astonishment. He was still half crouched with the pistol ready for another swipe. As we started toward the street, I only vaguely saw the little red something-or-other pull out and head for the front of the van.

"Jesus, you bitch," the driver shouted, as Molly's car headed toward him. He jerked the wheel toward the right and the van swerved and tipped out the driveway entrance, half up on the sidewalk. He missed Molly's car by what must have been inches.

The elm tree, however, was a different story.

I saw it coming and dived to the floor. Lonny must have thought I was going for him, because he was swinging the gun around as we crashed into the tree. Suddenly he was flying over the front seat and into the windshield. The police said later that the impact probably made him pull the trigger. His gun arm by that time was up by the steering column, and the bullet went sideways through Hefty's guts as he hung over the wheel and halfway out the shattered glass in front of him. The cops said his face was so messed up he might not have found life to be much fun anymore, anyway. Still, he probably would have wanted to make that choice for himself. Unfortunately for Hefty, that was an option he didn't get to explore.

The black and white Braynes called made a timely appearance just then. Morris Payne split the scene, but somehow he didn't seem the type to get very far on his own. I was shaken and bruised, but a few minutes earlier these were options I didn't expect to have. Molly made the explanations to the cops, who called Braynes. He said he was on his way. I told the cops to tell him to bring the steaks with him. They didn't get the joke, and he didn't get the message.

"Thanks," I said to Molly, when the cops had finished with us. She looked scared shitless. "Thank God they missed you. I don't see how they did it. You were coming right for us."

She buried her head in my chest and had a good sob. My shirt was hardly dry from Elaine's cry earlier. When Molly looked up, though, she appeared to be guilty about something.

"I couldn't do it, Chase, I'm sorry, I couldn't do it."

"Do what? You did great."

She shook her head and hugged her arms close to her chest.

"I hit the brakes," she said. "I hit the brakes and turned the wheel. I couldn't do it. I was too scared."

I pulled her to me again, and stroked her head.

"You saved my life," I said. "You want to be a hero as well? Give yourself a break. You got the job done. That's all there is to it."

She didn't say anything and gradually calmed down. I had a good shake myself, as the delayed shock surfaced. I think we were going to talk about dinner when I noticed the light on upstairs in the little office building.

"Was that light on earlier?"

Molly looked up and frowned and shook her head.

"Earlier it was broad daylight, and now the sun's going down," she said.

"As long as we're here . . ." I said, and started for the stairs.

The office of Doubletree Insurance was upstairs. The entry door at the foot of the stairs was locked, but I could hear a radio playing softly inside, so we knocked loudly and waited. There was a bell by the door, which we rang also. Finally, there was a voice saying wait a minute. The voice seemed to come from below us, but we waited anyway.

When the door opened, a youngish, brown-haired man stuck his head out.

"You know we're closed," he said, "so I suppose you want something special."

Molly gave him her best hello smile.

"We're sorry to bother you," she said, "but I have a question about my father's insurance coverage."

I looked at her in surprise, and waited my cue.

"I'm Molly Baker," she said, "Frank Baker's daughter, and this is our real estate broker."

"Wallace Blake," he said.

160

I shook his hand and gave him my card.

"You're Billy Blake's nephew, aren't you?" I said. "You must have been engrossed in your work."

"I was down in the vault in the basement," he said. He looked out the door with surprise on his face.

"It's late," he said. "You can't tell if it's night or day down there."

The tow truck was just hooking up to the wrecked van.

"What's that all about?" Blake said.

"Traffic accident," Molly said. I looked in the door and down the stairs.

"You share space down there with the mortgage people?"

"No, just with my uncle. He owns the building. I've just got a little space for my master policy records."

Wallace Blake paused and looked back and forth at us.

"I'm very sorry about your father," he said to Molly. "Was there something you wanted to ask about his policies?"

"Well, yes there was," she said, and turned to me. "Maybe you can phrase it better than I can, Mr. Randel."

"You covered Frank Baker's condos. Did you write the coverage for his other properties?"

"No, just Fair Valley Place."

"Was there anything special about his coverage there?"

"Not that I can remember." Blake shrugged. "I write a lot of policies."

"Any special death benefits riders, or anything like that?"

"No, I'm sorry," Wallace Blake said, looking over to Molly sympathetically. "I'm sure it was just standard fire insurance."

"I saw an insurance billing called 'Lloyds' on the escrow statements. Can you tell me what that was for?"

Wallace Blake laughed then. His face looked young and innocent. He looked concerned about Molly, but he didn't look worried about anything else.

"Oh, that's right, he had the 'double trouble' coverage," he said. "Sometimes they asked for that."

"What's the 'double trouble' coverage?"

"Tom Endman dreamed it up," he said. "Every once in a while he'd have a client who was afraid he was going to die before the investment plan was finished. So we worked up this policy with Lloyds so that if the client and Endman both die within thirty days of each other, the client gets his investment money paid back."

"I don't understand," Molly said. "Why not just get life insurance for them?"

"A lot of these guys . . ." he stopped and hesitated. He was young and exuberant, and he was having trouble being restrained in deference to Molly's loss.

"I'm afraid this was true of your father, as well," he said to her. "A lot of these guys couldn't get insurance if the premium matched the benefits. This was a wonderful gimmick. I used to listen to Tom present it. 'Listen,' he'd say to the clients, 'I'm going to stay on title along with you. Now I know,' Tom'd say, 'if I die that you'll be able to handle this property. And you know that I'll do the same for you if something happens to you.

" 'What we're both worried about,' he'd say, 'is what happens if both of us die and somebody we don't know has to step in. That's what this insurance is for. I already know I can count on you, and you know you can count on me. And if we both are gone, we can count on the insurance to take care of things.' "

Blake stopped and shook his head. Recalling the scene brought a look of admiration to his face.

"It never failed," he said, "It was as sweet a close as I ever saw." His eyes lit up abruptly. "Now I remember," he said, "Tom had me come specially and explain the coverage to Mr. and Mrs. Baker. She wasn't going to sign without it."

"Would the policy actually pay off?" Molly said.

"Good as gold. Of course Endman looks awfully healthy, I'm afraid."

"Today's the last day of the rest of somebody's life," Molly said. "Maybe today's his day."

Blake looked confused.

"SIG's investments were so good, though," he said. "I don't know why the clients were always so worried."

"You'll hear more about that tomorrow," I said. "Thanks for the information."

I tugged gently on Molly's arm and eased her back out the door.

"Here's a sales close I like to use," I said, and as he looked at me quizzically, I shut his door in his face.

We walked over to the sidewalk and around toward Molly's car. One cop was giving orders to the tow truck driver as he got ready to haul away the van. The light was soft and gold, and dying in the west.

"It's the new morality," I said. "Situation ethics, you know, what's yours is mine, and what's mine is mine. He's probably a child of a child of the sixties."

"It's enough to make you believe in birth control," Molly said.

I put an arm around her.

"Let's get a hamburger," I said. "The Cozy Cafe's just up the street, and they have the best burgers in town."

Her red car looked safe in the parking lot, so I walked her to the Merc, and we turned north toward the Cozy. The SIG building was a couple of blocks up on the way, and I slowed to a creep as we approached it. There were a lot of lights on. I stopped by the curb in a no-parking zone. The cars in the parking lot included a white Rolls and a dirty blue Chevy sedan, as well as a black Caddy limo and a red Corvette with the personalized plate that said "ENDMAN."

"They're still at it," I said, and was about to pull away when the door burst open, and a woman came running out.

"It's Elaine," I said, and opened my door and stood up.

"Over here, Elaine," I yelled, and started toward her. She heard me and ran to the car and grabbed me frantically. Her hands were shaking and her eyes were wide and unblinking. She looked disorganized and out of control, and scared of being that way.

"Elaine, Elaine, what's happened?" I said, shaking her.

"They're going to hurt him," she said. "Oh God, don't just stand there, do something. They're going to hurt Tom."

chapter **twenty-seven**

···

I held her back at arm's length. Molly was getting out of the car and walking toward us. It seemed a poor time for comforting embraces.

"Slow down," I said, "and tell us what's happening. Where is Tom and who's going to hurt him?"

Elaine saw Molly. Her body went rigid, and her eyes snapped with anger.

"What's she doing here?" Elaine said. "She's that noisy bitch who caused so much trouble at the seminar Friday night."

"Calm down," I said. "She, wants the same thing we all do, to find out what's going here, and why people are getting killed over real estate deals."

"It's her fault," Elaine said. "If people like her would quit stirring up rumors, all this wouldn't be happening to Tom."

"It's happening to you, too," Molly said.

Elaine almost snarled at Molly.

"You want him, too, don't you? You're like that other one, the little legal lady. Well, you're not going to get him," she said, smiling with a knowing look, and shaking her head. "Neither one of you are going to get him."

I was still holding her shoulders. My hands gave her a little shake to get her attention, and I eased my body between between the two of them to break their eye contact.

"Elaine," I said, "where's Tom?"

"He's with them."

"Where?"

"In the conference room. They're saying awful things to Tom."

"Why did you leave?"

She looked away, a little guiltily.

"I wasn't in there," she said. "I was listening from Tom's office."

"Can we get back in his office?" I said.

Elaine nodded.

"I think so," she said.

"Let's go, and find out what's going on."

"Not her," she said, pointing at Molly.

"She comes along," I said, "in case we need an impartial witness."

I tugged on her shoulder and turned her toward the building before she had a chance to object further. We walked quickly across the lawn to the entrance.

So SIG had the conference room bugged. It sounded like a car dealer's closing room, and I had to suppress a laugh. No matter how high-class the clientele, they were still susceptible to high pressure and low-down dirty deals.

The front door was unlocked and unattended.

"No security today?" I said.

"Someone sent him home for the day," Elaine said.

We got in the elevator and started up.

"Who's with Tom?" I said.

"Those Spanish men are there." Her voice trailed off.

"Who else?"

"The lawyers are there."

"Hilda?"

"Not just her. Billy Blake's there, too."

"Anyone else?"

"There was another Spanish man, but he left. He was different."

The elevator opened, but I didn't move at first.

"How was he different? Was he a thug?"

She nodded.

"Let's be real quiet," I said, "and let's go down to Tom's office and find out what's going on now."

It was an odd time for it, but I think I was more aware of Elaine's physical presence as we walked down the hall than I was at any other time I was with her. There was a mixture of courage and fear in the air that rooted us absolutely in the present instant. My hyperalertness to external threat also made me aware of the way her body moved, the way each breast extended with the swing of her arm, and how her thighs stretched the fabric of her pants as her legs moved. The excitement of the hunt, I suppose, but it would have seemed the most normal thing in the world to have swept her off into a closet for ten minutes, and then to have returned to the venture without missing a beat.

Molly was following a step or two behind us. I looked back at her once, expecting to see her eyes shooting fire, but she was strangely subdued, almost sympathetic. I opened the office door quietly and closed it behind us. Elaine went to a console hidden in a drawer of Tom's desk and turned up the volume. The "conference" sounded like it was coming to a close. There was an Anglo voice doing most of the talking.

"Are we all straight about what's going to happen?" Billy Blake was saying.

There was a murmur of voices too faint to distinguish.

"Tom, you and Hilda and I are going over to my office. You're going to deed over this building, the Los Gatos house, and the vineyard to Arbor Financial. Also the condos that Jay Moss is finishing up. That's step one. Are we all clear on that?"

"That's a good beginning," said a Hispanic voice talking softly. "But it leaves about three million dollars more to go, *sí?*"

"That's correct," Blake said. "It's only a first step.

"Tomorrow, Hilda is moving over here and she's going to handle the mortgage payments coming in." Blake's voice changed, like he was turning away from the bug that was feeding our sound system. I watched Elaine. She was sitting rigid and staring out the window. Molly stood by the door, arms folded, face noncommittal.

"Hilda's going to turn up the heat on everyone that owes SIG money," Blake was saying. "Every penny that comes in goes into the special accounts."

Endman interrupted Blake.

166

"I really don't think that's necessary," he said. "Having Hilda working over here could cause some problems."

"Your daughter's the problem," Blake said. "If she can't handle it, she'll have to take a vacation."

The Hispanic voice said something about deeds.

"Here?" Blake said. There was a mumbled consultation. "OK, sign the deeds now and Hilda can do the notary seals at my office later."

It was quiet again. I guessed they were signing papers. Signatures used to be a noisy business, but the fountain pen was quieter than the quill, and ballpoints make no noise at all.

Molly moved over closer during the silence. When the Hispanic voice spoke again Elaine got up and strode quickly to the back of the office, opened the connecting door to her office, and left. I heard a lock click behind her, but the voice coming through the speakers had asked a fascinating question, and I wanted to hear the answer.

"And you, meester Blake, what are you going to do? I don't theenk the mortgage payments are going to make three million dollars."

"It's the best we can do tonight," Blake said. "As the situation develops, we'll find ways to pull more money back out."

"I hope you're right," the voice said. We head a door open. "Wait five minutes," it said, and then the door closed with a solid thud, and it was quiet next door for a moment. Molly and I exchanged looks, and I held out a hand to her. She looked at me blankly, and then walked over slowly and slid her arm through mine.

"You really know how to pick them, Randel," she said. Maybe if I'd had an hour, I could have come up with a suitable reply. Tom Endman's voice saved me that fruitless search.

"For God's sake, Billy," he said, "what have you gotten me into?"

"You're the one who should be answering that," Blake said. "I helped you out with money when you needed it, and what did you do with it? You've screwed up, my friend."

"I don't think that's fair, Mr. Blake," said a female voice that sounded far away. "Tom didn't know the money was coming from crooks."

"You've done great so far, Hilda," Blake said. "Don't screw up now by trying to understand what's going on. It's not your specialty."

"We will screw up if Tom doesn't sign my notary book for these property deeds."

"Sign it for him."

"You know the law, Mr. Blake. He has to sign it himself. If he doesn't sign, I won't stamp the deeds with my notary seal, and that's all there is to it."

I looked at Molly.

"That's my legal eagle," I said.

"I'll say it again, Randel, you really know how to pick them."

We heard the sound of a door opening. I could picture Billy Blake with his hands raised in capitulation, like the emperor agreeing to follow correct legal procedure in signing the execution warrant of an innocent man.

"All right, Hilda," he was saying, "we'll go do it right now in my office."

Molly squeezed my arm.

"Now what?" she said.

The opening of the door to our hiding place answered that question for us.

"I just need to get my . . ." Tom was saying, when he walked into his office and saw us rabbits with our big little ears.

"I'll be right there," Hilda's voice was saying from the conference room. The sound system was picking her up real good now. Tom looked at us and then at the speakers hung up in the corners near the ceiling for good stereo effect.

"Billy," he said, "I think you better step in here. We seem to have another problem."

chapter **twenty-eight**

··

C hase," Billy said, when he walked in, "what a surprise."

I hadn't seen Billy in the flesh for a few months. I'd only talked to him on the phone. He was different than I remembered. The bald spot was a lot bigger now, and the remaining hair a lot grayer. He seemed to have lost some weight, leaving wrinkles around his eyes now that were deeper and that seemed to cast shadows across his eyes as they flicked back and forth between Molly and me. There was an air of menace about him that I'd never noticed, probably because I'd never before seen a gun in his hand pointed at me.

"You should have stuck to open houses, Chase. I don't think big-time real estate is quite your style."

Hilda walked in with her briefcase, and her eyes got big.

"Chase," she said, "what are you doing here?"

"That's a good question," I said.

Tom Endman decided to provide the answer.

"Stand here and listen, Billy," he said. He left the office and a moment later we heard his voice over the speakers.

"If you can hear this, Billy," Endman said, "you can imagine what Chase heard."

"Yes, I certainly can," Billy said, in a musing voice.

Tom came back into the office. Billy backed away so he and his pistol could see everyone in the room.

"Why was this sound system turned on, Tom? You weren't making a tape or anything, were you?"

Tom looked at us quizzically.

169

"How the hell did you get in here, Randel?"

I almost jumped when I heard Molly's voice beside me.

"I'm not used to being ignored," she said. "I can break into offices as good as he can. As it happens, we came over looking for Tom, found the doors open, no security, and we were coming up to look for someone to tell about it. We just walked in about thirty seconds ago."

"You must be the woman reporter I've heard about," Billy said.

"Good news travels fast."

"I admire your confidence. I've got some interesting people I want you to meet." He was reaching for the phone. "I'm sure you'll find them equally fascinating," he said.

Billy put the receiver to his ear, frowned, reached down and punched the disconnect switch a couple of times, listened some more, and frowned again.

"How do I get an outside line?" he said to Tom.

"You just dial it. Try it again."

"Then there's a problem with your phone," Billy said. He looked momentarily confused. I'd never seen him look that way, except when he was discussing women. Finally he shook his head, stretched his eyes wide open, and looked at all of us.

"Here's what we're going to do," he said. "Hilda, write this number down." He gave her a phone number and she wrote it down.

"Take Tom over to the office and get him to sign the notary book so those deeds are legal. Put them in the safe until morning." Billy glanced at Tom to see how he was taking all this.

"When you get to the office, call that number and tell whoever answers where I am, and that I need some help over here."

Hilda had a blank look on her face.

"What kind of help?" she said.

"Don't worry about it, they'll understand the message."

"But I am worried. Will it be those same men who were here?"

"I'm not paying you to think, Hilda, just get the papers notarized and make the call."

"You don't even know if they heard anything, and besides . . ."

Billy's voice snapped like a whip.

"Hilda!" he said. "Get the fuck over there and make the call."

"Tom and I aren't calling anyone, Mr. Blake." She moved over between Endman and Billy, and took Tom by the arms.

"Let's get out of here," she said. "You don't have to be a part of this."

Tom looked sick.

"It's not that easy," he said, glancing nervously over at Billy Blake.

"But's it's not worth murder," she said. "He's talking about having these people killed."

"Hilda!" Billy's voice snapped again.

"Oh fuck off," Hilda said. "You're not going to shoot us all. Not even a lawyer like you could explain that." She turned her attention back to Tom.

"Don't you see," she said, "I don't care what you've done. I'll help you. I'll defend you. I'll wait for you, if I have to."

She had Tom's full attention now.

"I love you," she said. "I'll stand by you. Leave with me now. Don't you see? I love you."

"How touching."

Elaine's voice sliced into the room ahead of her as she stepped in from the hall. She, too, had a gun. It was pointed at Billy Blake, and even an amateur at reading body language could see that Elaine meant business. Billy, who was a master at body language, and who could see that Elaine would probably shoot him three times before he could get his pistol swung around toward her, set his gun on the desk without even being asked.

"It was you, wasn't it?" she said to Blake. "You sent those goons after us in the car, didn't you? You're the only one who's been to the vineyard. You're the only one who knew where I'd go."

She glanced at the gun on the desk.

"Pick it up again," she said. "I'll give you a fair chance."

Billy smiled weakly and shook his head.

"You're not going to kill us all, either," he said.

"You're damn lucky. I'd shoot you in a second. And her. And her." Elaine's gaze panned the room, stopping briefly at Hilda and Molly, and then moving on. She looked me in the eye and smiled.

"But not him," she said. "Not him."

There were at least four collective sighs of relief breathed in the room. We all saw that Elaine was a walking terrorist bomb. Who could tell when her timer might go off.

Elaine looked at Tom.

"I killed the phones, and I've got the cash from the basement," she said. "We can lock them in here. They might be here all night . . . unless one of them wants to jump off the balcony and go get help."

Hilda pulled at Tom's arms.

"You don't have to listen to her, either," Hilda said. "If you run now, you'll always be running."

"You're a little late, sweetie," Elaine said, not unkindly. "Tom's already been running for a long time. Haven't you, Tom?"

Endman took Hilda's hands off his arms, one at a time. He brushed her cheek with his hand.

"Thanks anyway," he said, "but like I said, it's not that easy."

Tom looked at Elaine.

"I guess it's just you and me again," he said. "My car's in the parking lot. We can take it."

He moved over beside her. The gun never wavered in her hand. She motioned with it at Billy Blake.

"Over there," she said, pointing toward the balcony door. When he moved, she picked up his gun and gave it to Tom. He didn't seem to know what to do with it, and finally stuck it in a jacket pocket.

"They'll find you, you know," Billy said. "And when they do, you won't enjoy it."

"They already know where you are," Tom said. "Be sure and take notes on your legal pad, so you can tell me all about it."

Hilda stood paralyzed, arms crossed over her breasts, a stricken look on her face. Molly seemed to have disappeared into the background. I leaned against Tom's desk, watching the drama unfold, wondering how many innocent trusting sheep were going to take an unexpected financial bath now that Tom Endman was pulling the plug on the SIG money machine.

"Enjoy yourselves," Elaine said, as they backed out the door to the hallway. "There's wine, cheese, whiskey; take whatever you like. There's even grape juice for you, Chase. We'll send you a postcard from . . . somewhere."

The door shut, we heard the key in the lock. Billy Blake moved to the door with unexpected swiftness and shook it fruitlessly. I stayed where I was. I had already seen that the lock was a double-sided dead bolt that needed a key to open it from either side.

Billy grabbed a side chair from beside the desk. He swung it at the door as hard as he could, but the legs broke on impact with the solid mahogany door. Billy dropped the broken chair, holding his stinging hands in pain.

"Help me, Chase," he said. "We've got to get out of here."

"Help you, Billy? I think I'll wait to be rescued. Somehow I feel safer with you up here than I would with you out there."

The balcony door opened behind me. The air changed and smelled cool and damp. Molly was going outside, and I turned and followed her. Hilda came out, too, and after a minute, so did Billy. Nobody said anything. I supposed we would all yell when we saw someone walking below.

I looked down at the sidewalk, and suddenly thought of Frank Baker. He was, after all, the reason I was stuck up here with an ex-girlfriend, a woman-child lawyer, and a shyster who used to be a friend and was now a dope money launderer and probably an accomplice to murder.

Frank Baker had seen this view. In fact, it was the last thing he ever saw, unless his convulsing brain processed the images as he fell a hundred feet to the concrete below. Try though I might, I just couldn't figure out how his death fit into all this, and it was his death that started the whole chain of events two days ago.

It was late twilight now. The mercury vapor lights in the parking lots were coming on. There was movement below and I was about to shout down for help. It was Tom and Elaine, however, walking quickly arm-in-arm to the red Corvette. The Rolls was still there, but the limo and the dirty blue Chevy sedan were gone.

We could just hear them as they got in the car. Tom and Elaine were laughing. He opened the passenger's door for her, and she stuck a large attaché case behind the seat before she got in. Elaine made a great fuss with her handbag on the car's floor. *Probably arranging her gun so it would be close,* I thought. Tom walked briskly around the car looking down at the tires before he got behind the wheel.

They both carefully fastened their seat belts, and Tom was reaching for the ignition, when Elaine caught his arm. She must have sensed us watching from the balcony, because she pointed as she spoke to Tom. Then they both looked up and waved. I was sure they were laughing, even though it was getting dark and they were a hundred feet below.

Just your average upper-middle-class couple going away on a long vacation, I thought. Not a care in the world. I'm sure they were still laughing when the explosion ripped the big muscle convertible apart. I doubt they even felt the fireball that swallowed the car an instant later, and I'm sure they didn't choke on the acrid smoke that followed.

No, Tom and Elaine died laughing, and I suppose from some points of view, it wasn't a bad way to go.

Like Billy Blake's, for instance.

chapter **twenty-nine**

Hilda had run back inside in terror. I didn't see that there was anything for us to be frightened of, but Hilda apparently doesn't need a reason for the things she does.

Molly stood transfixed at the railing, whispering "Oh my God," softly over and over under her breath.

But Billy stood grasping the ornamental iron railing with a gleeful look on his face, saying something like "Burn, you bitch, burn," and apparently not caring who heard it.

I'm normally a tolerant man, but this was going a little too far, even for me.

"Isn't your celebration going to be rather a short one?" I said, in my absolutely most caustic tone. My ex-wife was British, so I have a lot of experience with caustic comments. But like a true lawyer, Billy didn't even notice the insulting tone I used.

Billy held out his arms and beamed at me like nothing had happened.

"They were the only ones who could ruin me, Chase. With them gone, there's no one who can . . ." Billy stopped for a second and looked at me and Molly. "They were the only ones," he said, continuing after a second's deliberation, "who could possibly slander my name in such a way as to damage my standing in the legal community."

"What about your tequila-breath friends? I imagine they'll have a thing or two to say."

"Somehow I don't think the arms of the law will be quite long enough to bring them back from where they're on the way to now."

This was discouraging. If he got any more smug, I might consider throwing him off the balcony myself. Some cars were stopped below, and I heard a siren in the distance . . . again. It was almost time to start shouting for help.

"Morris Payne might not be so far away," Molly said. "The police already have all his records."

Billy was really enjoying himself now.

"One of the keys to a successful law practice like mine," Blake said, "is an excellent memory. I almost never write down anything really important. Nor do I forget things of importance. It's a gift God gave me, I suppose."

He looked thoughtfully at Molly, and then at me.

"Good memories are not for everyone, though. There are some things, my friends, that it would pay you to forget. Then we might all live to enjoy the fruits of our work."

I could hear the fire trucks pulling up below. There was probably a cop car or two, also, but I didn't look. The short balding man on the balcony drew my attention like nothing had since I gave up whiskey.

"You think you're going to get away with it, don't you?" I said.

"If you plan to make accusations," Billy said, "I suggest you have overwhelming evidence on your side. Otherwise, you will be spending all your time and money in court defending yourselves from slander suits.

"Now," he said, "why don't you start yelling to attract some attention up here? I'll go inside and switch the lights on and off, so they'll be able to spot us in the dark."

He turned and walked toward the office without another word. A man at peace with himself. Walking back to his law practice, his golf clubs, his forgiving artist of a wife, his Los Gatos opulence, his white Rolls-Royce, his house on the beach in Santa Cruz, just five doors down from me. I could live with all of it . . . except the vision of him as a neighbor.

"Billy," I said, as he was starting back into the office. He stopped and turned back to me.

"Yes, Chase?" he said, in an almost fatherly tone.

"What about the money?" I said. "What are you going to do about the money?"

"The police will not find one written document to tie me to the money, Chase. I guarantee it."

"I'm not talking about the police. I'm talking about the money. I don't think your friends from the south are going to be too understanding about losing four million dollars . . . dirty or not."

"But I didn't lose it."

"Your friend did. The man you recommended to run the laundromat stole the money. He used it to keep his business growing when he couldn't attract enough regular suckers."

"I did what I could. They chose to blow the guy up instead of working with him to get the money back."

"Maybe some things are more important to them than money."

"What are you trying to say?" Billy said. I had his full attention now. He looked puzzled. A real smart guy who was getting a hint that sometimes being the smartest guy around isn't enough. One of those guys in the Dick Tracy comic strip who looks down and sees round holes of daylight in his body, and realizes suddenly that the holes are connected to Sam Ketchum's smoking gun.

"What I'm saying is that those guys can afford to lose the money. What they can't afford is to lose respect. What they can't afford is stories about some San Jose shyster who steered them into a swindle, and walked away smiling."

Billy wasn't smiling anymore.

"Don't worry about me, Chase."

"I'm not, Billy, I'm worried about pollution. I'm worried about you washing up on our beach some morning, sewed up tight inside a burlap bag."

Finally, finally, Billy Blake had nothing to say.

"Just remember, Billy, each day may be the last day of the rest of your life . . . so keep smiling."

Molly and I started yelling then, to the crowd down below. Billy went on inside, but he didn't flick the lights the way he promised. Some people you just can't count on to do anything they say they're going to.

Eventually a fireman came up, and chopped the door open with his ax. Billy Blake pulled his officer of the court routine, and got himself and Hilda excused to go home for the night and to come back and make statements to the police in the morning.

Lieutenant Braynes arrived on the scene not too long after. Apparently it takes two homicides in one place to get him away from steaks and beer on a Sunday night. He hadn't stirred at the news of the shooting earlier at Arbor Financial. Probably because the dead victim was a hood, and the intended victim was a real estate broker, neither of whom is important enough to spoil a cop's Sunday night at home in the backyard.

Molly and I talked to Braynes at the scene. We told him what we saw happen, and what we thought were the reasons for it. Then we too got to go home with the promise of returning on Monday for full written statements. When we left, Braynes was on his way to talk to an assistant district attorney. Getting search warrants and going after a prominent city attorney was not going to be easy. Billy Blake probably plays golf with half the judges in town. I wished him luck.

It was too bad about Billy Blake. I was going to miss my coffee and apple turnovers at his office, and the occasional stroll by his house on the beach at Santa Cruz. The beach house may not be as much fun for Billy anymore, or his wife. What the hell, she wasn't a very good painter, anyway.

I drove Molly over to pick up her car.

"Follow me home," I said, as we stopped.

"I should go to my house and see what the yuppie is doing. He's probably worried about me."

"It'll do him good to worry. Make him appreciate you more."

"Will it?"

"Follow me home."

"I don't know if that's a good idea, Chase."

"It's not an idea."

"What is it, then?"

"Passion."

"Shit. I was afraid of that."

"Here's an idea," I said, putting the shift in drive again. "I'll bring you back to get your car in the morning."

We didn't talk much on the drive to my house. Hell, it only takes five minutes, and what can you say in five minutes? It was what she didn't say that counted, anyway, and what Molly didn't say was "no."

At first we didn't talk much after we got to my house, either. We held hands walking to the front door. Inside, she sat down at one end of the couch, while I brought us glasses of grape juice. She must have started thinking while I was in the kitchen, because after I saw the way Molly was sitting, I wished that I had some wine for her. Her arms were crossed firmly over her chest, and her legs were crossed away from me. She didn't reach for the grape juice, but only glanced at me and then stared away. she looked angry.

"Making up is harder than breaking up," I said. I'm a master at breaking the ice. The thing about broken ice, though, is that it's still awfully cold.

"Aren't you sorry it's not her?"

"Not her what?"

"Not her. Here. Instead of me."

"Molly, the woman was crazy. She was in love with her stepfather."

"That didn't seem to matter to you before."

"I didn't know before. Besides, if I'd known there was a chance of seeing you again, I never would have looked at Elaine."

"I saw the way she looked at you today."

She looked at me angrily, and reached for her glass and took a sip. She made a gagging sound and I thought she was going to spit the mouthful back into the glass.

"Grape juice," she said, scornfully. "I suppose this came from her, too." She slammed the glass down on the coffee table. The liquid sloshed over the top and ran across the glass top and off onto the carpet. Molly didn't seem to notice.

"Take me back to my car," she said. "This is outrageous. I don't know how I ever let myself get talked into a situation like this with you . . . again."

I was just on the verge of a good rebuttal when she got up, walked out the front door, and slammed it behind her. It must have been something I didn't say, I thought.

While I tossed down the rest of my grape juice, I thought of Elaine, poor screwed-up Elaine, choosing the evil she knew and thought she could control over the uncertainty of a new and unknown future. I said a quick prayer for her. I said one for Tom Endman, too, in one of those little "there but for the grace of God . . . " vignettes that flash across the mind and that we would dismiss as sentimental claptrap if it wasn't for the intensity of the feeling of the moment.

Molly was sitting in my car. I could see her outline in the streetlight's yellow glow. The moisture in the air made everything seem hazy, and bathed the Merc in a sparkling halo. I tried to think of something to say on the way to the car. Somehow I didn't think explaining her unreasonableness to her was going to work, but I was having trouble coming up with anything else.

"Chase," she said, in a tentative voice as I opened the car door.

"Molly," I said, in a tone so conciliatory it almost sounded phony, even to me.

"Chase," said a third voice as I eased into the driver's seat. The third voice didn't sound tentative or conciliatory. It sounded familiar, a bit crazy, and very, very dangerous.

chapter **thirty**

....

That sounds like my old friend Billy Blake," I said. "What brings you out again on a night like this?" I was starting to turn and look at him when I felt a hard object behind my right ear.

"Look straight ahead and keep your hands on the wheel, Chase," he said. "Then start the car, and back out real easy."

I made a familiar, unconscious movement, and felt the gun jab sharply into my skull.

"What are you doing?" Billy said, half shouting.

"I'm putting my seat belt on," I said. "The car won't start unless I do. It's a special option." I felt the gun ease back away from my head.

"Relax, will you, Billy," I said. "You're really getting stressed out." I pointed to Molly after I connected my lap and shoulder harness. "She has to buckle up, too," I said. "Otherwise the car won't start. I got a special insurance rate for having the system installed."

"I never knew you were so concerned about safety," Billy said.

"It's important in my business. You better buckle up, too."

I heard a chuckle. It was more like a snicker, really.

"I'm going to live dangerously tonight," Billy said.

Molly fastened her harness without a word.

"You obviously need a ride, Billy," I said. "Where can I drop you?"

"Let's drive to Santa Cruz," he said. "It looks like a nice night at the beach. Foggy . . . and mysterious. We'll build a fire, and talk about what we're going to do."

"Do about what?" Molly said.

180

"You . . . and him."

I felt the gun barrel jab lightly again.

"Let's go," he said.

I started the car and backed out.

He didn't start talking until I got out on the highway.

"I didn't want things to turn out this way, Chase. You were a good friend to me when I needed one. I thought I could control things through Hilda. I could have, too, if that silly little twit could have kept her pants on."

"Tom could be quite a persuasive fellow," I said.

"He sure fooled the hell out of me. I helped him out with money when he needed it, and all the time he was stealing everyone blind."

So even lawyers get fooled sometimes. An occupational hazard. Lawyers don't ever initiate anything. They react to events. They try to get you out of trouble after you're in it. They try to help you cover up or minimize what you can't hide or walk away from. They hold your hand and stroke it comfortly, especially until you've paid their bill. It's not a very creative profession, really. It's one that looks for opportunities. It doesn't create them. A second-order discipline. Always a step behind, counting on court orders and legal process to slow you down until they catch up. It works fine for the lawyers until they meet someone like Tom Endman, who's not just a step ahead, he's already gone around the track and is pulling out to lap you when you first notice he's in the race.

I thought about Tom . . . and Elaine . . . as we passed the Los Gatos exit.

"How did you get involved with him in the first place?" I asked.

"The most innocent thing in the world. I won a case for some clients, and they asked me if I knew of some investment opportunities. I referred them to Tom Endman."

"Secret investments don't sound innocent, Billy. What did you tell Tom about where the money was coming from?"

He was pretty confident now. His guard was down. He talked like he might be telling the truth. He didn't use the work "alleged" once in our whole conversation. I expected him to be more careful. I'm sure it never occurred to him that I was tape recording our conversation. The recorder's in the trunk. The switch is beside the receptacle for the seat belt buckle. The mike is behind a fake stereo speaker. I got offered a bribe once, to cover up some construction defects in a shopping center. I had a hard time proving I didn't take the money; I've been careful ever since. Braynes knows about the system, too. If Molly and I don't get out of this in one piece, neither will Billy Blake, though right now I don't find that thought very comforting.

"It's not my business where clients get their money," Billy said, after a pause. "The law's real clear about that."

"Tell it to the kids in the crack houses," Molly said.

"Moral dilemmas aren't our problem right now," Billy said. "There's a much more immediate, practical problem that's got me baffled."

"Give it up, Billy, it's your only chance. You know the district attorney. Find a way to make it politically popular for him to go easy on you in return for full cooperation."

We passed the turnoff at the Summit where the first two goons had crashed while trying to run Elaine and I off the road. I saw the restaurant up ahead where I had called the cops from.

"Let's pull in up here, Billy, there's a phone we can use. Braynes will help us set it up."

The gun nudged my head again. It felt big and round and cold.

"I wish it were that simple, Chase. But I'm afraid there are still a few things you don't understand."

Why does everybody keep telling me I don't understand what's going on? Maybe it's because they're right. But like I've said before, understanding is the booby prize. There was something about the gun, though, that was starting to break through to my subconscious.

"Jesus, that feels like a big gun, Billy. What have you got, a silencer on there?"

"That's right. It's the best one made. This thing's as silent as a cobra. And just as deadly."

"Where's a guy like you get a silencer?"

"The same place you would. Order it through your neighborhood gun shop. It's just for sporting purposes, you understand."

We passed the restaurant and started to drop down into the fog. I slowed for the curves and for the cars ahead that kept popping up out of the mist like ghosts.

"It was you, wasn't it, up at the vineyard?" I said. "The first shot. I never heard the gun, just the impact when the bullet hit the barn."

Billy didn't say anything.

"You probably had a key, too, didn't you? Got it from Endman's house, didn't you? That's why the Rolls was parked there. What were you so afraid of? Making trouble for you was the last thing I had on my mind that afternoon."

I felt Molly's sudden glare. I'll have to be more careful, I thought. No sense getting out of one deadly situation to get caught in another.

We were passing the Scotts Valley exit just north of Santa Cruz before Billy answered the question.

"I was afraid of you, Chase, afraid of what that stupid little twit would tell you." The gun tapped me lightly on the side of the head. "You're smarter than you think you are. You could have been a lawyer if you had put your mind to it."

"I thought you were smarter than to get messed up with drug money, Billy."

"It was just business. They paid well, and very promptly, I might add. Everybody was happy until Endman started stealing the money. Then they got very unhappy."

I took the Highway 1 exit south without being told. We were getting close to the beach. I was running out of road, and out of time as well.

"And you tried to take an uninvolved posture, the way American lawyers do, and they didn't buy it. Did they?"

"I'm afraid the legal concepts of the third world lag far behind our own."

"You got them into it, right, and they expected you to get them out of it."

I heard a long sigh behind me.

"They still do, Chase . . . expect me to get them out of it. That's why we're here, I'm afraid."

Suddenly the time seemed very short. I couldn't see the sign for our exit because of the fog, but I knew it couldn't be very far ahead. There was just time for one more question.

"Billy," I said, "why was Frank Baker killed?"

"You got me there, Chase. I was as surprised as you were." I felt him edge up between us, straining to see the exit sign through the fog. "Be careful, now," he said, "our turnoff should be coming up any second now."

The people who planned the freeways had a tremendous sense of order. Straight roads, long sweeping curves, gently arching exits, big clear signs lighted and suspended over the roadway to direct us into the next centuries.

What they didn't plan on was the tremendous disorder of the average driver. The freeway planners put those beautiful legible signs on big round steel posts, and they sunk the steel posts in the vee between the freeway and the exit. It works most of the time. But every so often, say once in every ten thousand cars, a driver would get caught in indecision between going straight and turning off, and the cars would plow right into these poles holding up the signs.

Not to worry. Low tech to the rescue. The planners just stacked these garbage cans full of sand in front of the steel poles. Mr. Indecision hits the sand cushion instead of the steel, and comes to a soft landing.

The system works great, if you're wearing your seat belts. If you're not, the way Billy wasn't, the stop can still be quite sudden.

"There's the turnoff," Billy said, as the arrow for the Forty-First Avenue exit popped up out of the mist.

"Where is it?" I said, pretending to look from side to side.

"There, you idiot, turn there."

I held the car straight until Billy reached up to grab the wheel, and then I turned toward the barrier and floored the gas pedal.

Billy screamed something just before we hit. I couldn't understand what he said, and I didn't get a chance to ask him to repeat it. We were probably only going forty-five when we hit the sand-filled garbage cans. Even so, the impact snapped Molly and I forward into our restraining harnesses so hard that we both had bruise marks across our chests from the straps. The straps did stop us, however, from going through the windshield, and the sand barrels stopped the car from hitting the steel pole.

Neither of these facts proved true for Billy Blake, however. He was just in the act of lunging for the steering wheel when we hit. The impact propelled him through the windshield and on over the hood of the car and into the round smooth steel of the freeway sign pole. The aerodynamics of the thing must have pulled his arms down to his body so he was moving through the air like a swept wing jet fighter. He probably hit the pole headfirst, they told me later, because the top of his skull was compressed down to the level of his eyebrows.

Molly and I were covered with glass, and later, with bruises, but otherwise we were unhurt. My door was jammed, but Molly's still opened, so we got out that way. Billy Blake lay crumpled on top of the scattered sand cans, looking like a sack of broken bones. If he wasn't dead, I knew there was nothing I could do for him. Earlier, at my house, I had locked the portaphone in the trunk. I got it out and called the highway patrol, and then called Braynes. He was pissed. So what else was new?

When I hung up, I absentmindedly handed Molly the phone and walked around the car to see how bad the damage was. The front end was smashed up pretty bad. I guessed that the frame was bent on the driver's side. Inside, there was a big dent in the instrument panel. Probably where a knee hit. Billy's gun was lying on the front seat, looking every bit as deadly as it felt when it was poked in the back of my head.

Molly gave me a funny look as she handed me back the portaphone after my inspection tour.

"You better hang on to this," she said. I stuck the set in my jacket pocket as I went to talk to the highway patrol officer who had just arrived. The phone would come in handy. I would probably need a good word from Braynes to avoid spending most of the night answering questions at the Santa Cruz Sheriff's Office. I was right. It took three calls and about forty-five minutes before I got permission to have the car towed, and to leave the scene myself. I was just calling the tow truck when Molly came up to me again, and tugged on my arm.

"Chase," she said, "I'm leaving now."

"How did you get us a ride?" I said.

"I got me a ride. I called the yuppie to come get me."

I didn't answer, but I guess the expression on my face said everything I would have if I hadn't been so slow on the uptake.

185

"I'm sorry," she said, "but I've had enough for one night. Maybe I'll call you after things calm down." And with a tight little smile, she was gone.

Which left me and the highway patrolman to wait alone in the fog for the Triple-A truck. He borrowed the portaphone to call his wife and explain why he'd be home late off his shift.

"Thanks," he said, "there's nothing like a phone call home at the right time to keep things peaceful."

I thought about calling my office and listening to my message on the answering machine, but decided against it. It's too cheerful a message, I thought. The guy must be a phony. I thought about that one on the seventy-five-dollar taxi ride to San Jose. As we got near my house, I called the message, just to see how it sounded. I wasn't reassured.

chapter **thirty-one**

I spent most of Monday in bed, after meeting Braynes at the police station to make a statement early in the morning. I didn't hear from Molly.

Frank Baker's funeral on Tuesday afternoon was a big event at the Evergreen Valley Community Church. I would have missed it if I could have found a convenient excuse, but I couldn't find one so I didn't miss it.

I got to the church service a little late, and had to stand outside. I guess half the people in the south side of San Jose had someone in their family involved with Frank Baker's school at some point in their life. Apparently they had good memories of Baker, because they sure turned out for the funeral.

Braynes showed up at the church a little after I did. We couldn't hear the service inside, so there wasn't much else to do but talk shop.

"This is the only sad part of this whole situation," Braynes said. "As far as I can tell, most of the people who lost money at the Silicon Investment Group won't miss it too much. And nobody's going to miss the other people who died. So that just leaves Frank Baker. The poor guy didn't know what he was getting mixed up with."

"He really died of cyanide poisoning?" I said.

"He sure would have, if he hadn't fallen off that balcony and hit the cement when he did. I got the written autopsy report this morning. Enough cyanide in his system to kill a you-know-what. Unusual chemical structure, apparently. The coroner sent it on to some chemical lab for more analysis . . . not that it matters much now."

"How do you figure it?" I said.

"My guess is the drug boys sent it up hoping to get Endman and his daughter."

"Stepdaughter," I said.

"Yeah, right. We talked to Endman's ex-wife, you know, down in Texas. She wouldn't say anything about the relationship between her daughter and her ex, but . . ."

"But what?"

"But she didn't want the bodies sent down there, not even her daughter's."

"Maybe she tried to poison them."

"Maybe. The whole thing was strange. Endman always had this one liquor store come in once a month or so and restock the bar up in his office. Apparently he closed a lot of deals over a drink. Anyway, on Thursday morning, this bottle of Scotch got dropped off by a delivery service with a note from the liquor store saying it was left out of their regular order. Endman's secretary just stuck it up on the shelf with the other bottles."

"Did the store send it?"

"Nope. They never heard of it."

"Where did it come from?"

"Delivery service picked it up at the Holiday Motel. A maid found the package in front of a room with a note saying to hold it for pickup, and had an envelope taped to it with money for the delivery service.

Somebody called the service, said they had to catch a plane, and asked that it get picked up at the motel."

"Pretty hard to trace."

"Yeah, it was well thought out. Kind of a scattergun approach, though, if you ask me. Anybody could have drunk that stuff, even the cleaning people."

"Maybe that was Endman's favorite brand of Scotch."

Braynes frowned and looked off into space.

"Endman told me he didn't like to drink, he just did it to make people feel comfortable. What he really liked was that wine he was making up at the vineyard. That's what other people told us, too. They said Endman would always let you order first, and then order what you were having . . . even at parties. He was just like an actor, apparently, always on stage."

"Just like a salesman is more like it," I said.

Just then the church doors opened. Baker's family came out first, his widow flanked by her son and grandsons. Even though the men bent down to her, she seemed to be the central post that was holding up the family structure. She saw me standing with Braynes, smiled, and spoke briefly to young Frankie. He walked over to us quickly.

"Grandma wants to invite you up to the house after we leave the cemetery, to have some food and stuff," the kid said.

"Thanks," I said, shaking his hand. "I'll see you up there."

Braynes waited until the family was getting into the black funeral limousines, and then took my arm.

"Make my apologies for me, will you Chase," he said, "I've just got too damn much to do. Hate to miss it, though. They always poured good Scotch in that house."

"Was that Baker's drink?"

"I never saw him with anything else."

"If you change your mind, I'll see you up there," I said, as he walked away.

I wished that I had something else to do. A big deal to close. A hot date. A day at the beach with my boys. Hell, I'd even take my ex-wife along. Even nice and neat Emma, who could be so naughty, and was, at least once too often.

But instead, I was going to watch them bury a man I hardly knew, and then to drink to his memory, his eternal good health, I suppose, and then I'd turn my rental car back toward town, probably in time to catch the end of rush hour. Even Mrs. Fuentes, the housekeeper, would be gone by the time I got home. The basketball season was over, there were reruns on TV, I haven't seen a video I liked in at least three months. I don't know. Maybe it's time to get a dog again.

There were hundreds of people at the graveside service. The pastor was apparently a friend of Baker's, and he spoke at length about how much he would be missed. The members of the immediate family sat on chairs arranged under a square awning for shade. The rest of us stood in the sun. It was hot enough to make you sweat a little. The son and grandchildren listened intently while the pastor spoke. The widow gazed out at the crowd, turning her head slowly, noting who was there, I supposed. Familiar faces perhaps calling up a memory of the day when Frank and her and he and she did this or that. A fine black lace veil covered her face, so I couldn't see her expression. She held a pale blue handkerchief in one hand, but I didn't see her use it.

When the service finally ended, the family stood as the coffin was lowered into the grave. The grandsons were crying openly now. When the little motor shut off, the funeral home attendants shook the straps loose and backed away. Mrs. Baker stepped to the grave's edge, unpinned the carnation on her lapel, dropped it into the grave, and walked firmly over to the pastor and began speaking to him. The men and boys behind her were doing their part to fill up the grave by throwing in flowers and handfuls of dirt.

More quickly than I expected, Mrs. Baker gestured to the family and started walking slowly through the crowd, touching hands, exchanging little formal hugs, whispering a brief, earnest word. She seemed to be giving comfort, rather than receiving it. The family strung along behind in a ragged line, passing through the valley of comforting handshakes and soft-spoken words until they disappeared into the limos for the ride back home.

The crowd at the Bakers' house looked almost as big as the one at the graveside. I had to park about a half mile down the hill. There were some oleander bushes blooming in among the pine trees that lined the drive. The poppies on the hillsides were just about finished. The grass would be turning brown soon, but for now it was still good pollen weather, with lots of stuff blooming. Everything I ever planted seemed to grow well, but I could never remember the names of the damn things. You'd think they'd wear name tags.

The little gardening shed stood back from the last curve before the driveway shot up the hill to the house. It looked a lot cleaner than it had on Saturday when I stopped to talk to Frankie junior. The shelves were cleaned off, and there were two bulging heavy-duty garden trash bags sitting at the side of the shed. A tag on one said, Hold for Toxic Pickup. A movement past the shed caught my eye. Young Frankie was walking slowly down the hill, stopping at little dried mounds of dirt, occasionally kicking one and making a little cloud of dust.

He smiled when he looked up and saw me.

"How's the gopher war going?" I said.

"It was going great," he said.

"Was?"

"Grandma made me throw away all the goop," he said. "She said she didn't want any more poisons around. I can't blame her, really, after what happened to granddad. But this hill will be covered with tunnels in six months if we don't control them."

"So grandma shut down the goop factory."

"Cleaned it out. Chemicals, beakers, burners, the whole works. She said it made her feel sad when she saw the lab and remembered him. That's how they met, you know, in the chemistry lab at college."

I patted him on the arm.

"I better go up and pay my respects," I said. "Though, really, I'd just as soon stay down here."

Frankie smiled.

"Don't tell anybody where I am," he said.

I left him with his memories of gopher hunts past, and walked slowly up the hill to the house. The five o'clock sun was still bright and warm. It looked like a middle-class crowd. A lot of the men had taken off their jackets and loosened their ties. That's one of the meanings of middle class. You dress up for half the day and then you kick back. Most everybody had a glass in their hand. Alcohol is still the drug of choice for this crowd—which is a pretty smart move, in my opinion, even though I was a drunk. If God had wanted people to use drugs, he would have given us other kinds of tubes and valves. A little faucet on a handy vein, a third lung with special smoke-resistant lining, a nose with a noncorrosive membrane, things like that.

I made my way through the patio crowd, and found a glass of grape juice. Nonalcoholic wine, they call it. A nice looking blonde tried some small talk, mild seductive stuff. We were just getting down to some serious repartee, when a six-year-old girl ran up to tell her about the crimes of an older brother. A husband followed a minute later, and the lady introduced us with a tag line about my being a real estate broker. I slipped away before things got awkward. A few minutes later, I caught her eye across the room and sent her a wink, just to keep her spirits up.

I hadn't had time to tell her that the only blonde I was interested in right now was wasting her time and mine with a trim-bodied, well-heeled, sweater-wearing dumb slob of a yuppie. They're probably in bed right now, trysting between his well-pressed designer sheets. After he hears about me, the despicable son of a bitch will probably forgive her. Some people you just can't offend.

Frank junior found me just before I was about to do something I would have regretted, which was to go talk to the blonde again.

"Mother would like to talk to you for a few minutes, Chase, if you don't mind."

The way he said the word "Mother" made it obvious that the leadership of the family had not passed to the eldest surviving son.

Mrs. Baker was waiting for us in the little library off the living room on the west end of the house. The French doors opening out to the patio were closed. The room was dim, brightened only by some indirect lighting above the bookcases. Mrs. Baker had taken off her veil. She wore enough makeup so as not to appear pale, and there was a suggestion of perfume in the air. She looked good in black, like she had been practicing all her life to play the queen mother role.

She was sitting in one of a pair of leather-covered chairs bunched in the corner around a little antique walnut table. She motioned me over to the empty chair.

"Frankie, be a dear, and make Mr. Randel a drink. And bring me a glass at the same time, would you?"

"Just club soda for me," I said. Mrs. Baker raised an eyebrow. "I'm on a strict diet," I said.

Her son opened some club soda for me, and brought his mother her glass. There was a bottle of Dunroamin on the table beside her. She obviously shared her late husband's taste for single malt whiskey. She didn't invite her son to pull over a chair.

"Thank you, Frank," she said, after a minute. She smiled at him sweetly and didn't say anything else for a minute. When Frank didn't leave, she added, "We'll only be a few minutes." This time he got the message.

When we were alone, she aimed her smile at me.

"It's an ill wind, Chase, that doesn't blow some good somewhere." She saw my little smile, even though it was gone in an instant. "Did I get the quote right?" she said.

"Close enough for a chemistry major," I said.

"The English teachers hated me," she said, "I could remember the ideas, but I never could get the words right."

She sat back smugly for a moment, wrapped in a fifty-year-old memory.

"Anyway," she said, finally, "I got the most marvelous news this morning. The insurance man called me and said that Frank had taken out this unusual policy when he bought the condos, and that it was going to pay me some money."

"What kind of policy?"

"He called it a 'double-trouble' policy."

"That's a funny name," I said, suddenly paying very close attention to every word Betty Baker said.

192

"And how appropriate," she said. "How sadly appropriate." She stared off into space again. I drank some club soda, and my movement broke her lapsed attention.

"You were telling me about the insurance," I said.

"Apparently Frank took out this strange insurance against the possibility that he and Tom Endman would die within thirty days of each other. If that happens, the insurance pays back Frank's investment."

The room was still dim, but her face seemed bathed in a glow of genuine surprise and wonder. There is a God after all, she seemed to say, and he's a just God, taking care of his own in the way she'd always expected.

"Didn't Frank tell you about this insurance?"

"No, the poor, sweet dear. He was afraid I wouldn't be able to cope with things all on my own." There was another significant pause. "He's taking care of me still, just like he always did," she said.

"That was very farsighted of him," I said. She reached over to the table for a leather-covered checkbook before she continued.

"Now, Chase," she said, "I know you've worked hard for us on this condo mess, even if it was only for a couple of days. The insurance money, of course, means that I don't have to sell any property just yet, so I'm afraid we won't be listing any property with you, not at this time anyway."

She gave the benefit of her very best I-know-you-understand smile.

"I want to give you a check anyway, though, just to let you know how much we appreciate your efforts." She tore a check out of the book and handed it to me. Apparently it wasn't an issue we were going to negotiate on. The check was for a thousand dollars. She watched me read the numbers, and then sat back and smiled.

"I know it's not what you hoped to make on the sales, but believe me, we'll keep you in mind if I do decide to sell someday."

I studied the check and then looked over it at Mrs. Baker before I answered her.

"That's quite a story about the insurance money," I said, "and this is quite a check for only a couple of days work.

"Let's see, now, Friday noon, I had a fight with some goons out at your condos. Friday afternoon I got to see the remains of your husband on the sidewalk. Friday night I found the body of a dead

193

appraiser. Saturday morning I had a scuffle with your grandson. Saturday afternoon some out-of-town talent tried to run me off the Summit. Saturday evening Billy Blake and a hit man tried to shoot me up in the Santa Cruz mountains. Saturday night I spent almost this much staying at the Fairmont, because I was afraid to sleep at home." I waved the check at her.

"Not much happened Sunday until a mortgage broker tried to give me a one-way ride to the landfill. Then I watched Tom and Elaine Endman blow themselves up. When I tried to make up with the lady I love, we got kidnapped by a crooked lawyer who ended up spreading his brains on a freeway signpost while my Mercedes turned into an accordion. My girlfriend left me for a schmuck whose biggest virtue is that he has quiet weekends. I spent two days answering police questions and trying to get this old body to recover from the bruises of that auto accident, and now you want to pay me this magnificent sum."

Mrs. Baker was sitting back in her chair in stunned silence. I don't know what reaction she expected, but this obviously wasn't it. She was watching me, though, from somewhere behind those old pale-blue eyes. I felt like the kid on the Nintendo game who makes it through to the third level. Only seven or eight more to go.

I held the check up and examined it.

"I couldn't take this," I said, "even if it had two more zeros on it." I made sure she was looking and then I tore the check in two.

"I was working for your husband, really, and it wouldn't be very loyal of me to take money from his murderer."

Her jaw dropped when I said that, and she lurched forward in her seat. Her eyes didn't change, however. They covered me like a surveillance camera, unblinking, scanning silently from side to side. She still hadn't poured herself a drink.

"The first thing a salesman learns, if he's any good, is to only make his pitch to someone who has something to gain by listening. Everytime I thought about Frank's death, that question kept coming to me. Who had something to gain by his being dead? What if Tom Endman wasn't the target? What if Frank Baker's taking poison wasn't an accident? What if he really was the target all along? There was only one answer. You. The widow. The beneficiary of the insurance policies."

"But I didn't know anything about the insurance."

"That's not what Wallace Blake said."

"Wallace Blake?"

"C'mon, Mrs. Baker, Wallace Blake, the insurance agent. Wallace said Tom Endman told him the only reason you signed the condo papers was because of the 'double trouble' coverage."

She was sitting back in her chair again. She looked a little threatened, but not too worried about it. Yet. She reached over and poured a good-sized belt of whiskey into her glass.

"You sent that bottle of Scotch up there, didn't you? You knew Frank would choose that if it were there, and you knew Tom Endman would drink whatever Frank was drinking. That's what made it so perfect. It wasn't just Frank, or Tom, who was the target. It was both of them. At once."

There was a little smile on her lips now. I was glad I had seen her son open the bottle of club soda. I'd heard the seal break on the twist-off cap. Even so, I kept my eyes on the old lady, just so there wouldn't be any newspaper stories tomorrow about a real estate broker getting killed "while examining an heirloom gun," or something.

"The police would laugh you out of town with that story," she said.

"Not when I tell them you're a chemistry major," I said, "quite capable of extracting exceedingly lethal doses of cyanide from rodent poisons.

"You've got it all," I said, "motive, method, knowledge. I don't think Marty Braynes will find it too hard to believe. Neither will a jury."

Now it was my turn to sit back and see what happened.

"My daughter needs that money," she said. "Would you really tell a string of lies like that, and possibly cheat her out of the care she deserves, just because you didn't make a commission off my poor dead husband?"

She was good. She didn't give up.

"I'm just going to tell the truth as I know it," I said, "I'll let the law decide what's to be done."

When she didn't answer, I got up and backed toward the door. Silly, really, but why take chances? I was reaching for the knob when she said her last words.

"I suppose you think I'm terrible," she said. I didn't answer. "I do, whether you do or not. Even though Frank was throwing away our retirement, our security, everything we ever worked for." She looked up at me, asking for understanding, I suppose.

"I know," she said, "stupidity isn't a capital crime. Maybe if he'd just admitted that he was wrong, that he'd made a mistake. But he was such a pompous son of a bitch."

She shook her head sadly.

"I didn't ever imagine, in my wildest fantasies . . . that I would miss him like I do. The bed is so empty at night."

This part I could understand.

"After fifty years, Mr. Randel, a lonely bed is a terrible thing. Especially when you've enjoyed sharing it as much as I have."

Her eyes were starting to shut down. I guessed she was about to get it off her chest. I wanted to call Braynes, but I was afraid to break the spell of the moment.

"You won't prove it, you know," she said, softly. She was cradling the drink in both hands, holding it just above her lap.

"I'm sure you'll look very hard, but you won't find any traces of cyanide in those bags of trash. And you won't find any connection between me and that bottle of Scotch in Tom Endman's office."

"What about Wallace Blake and the insurance policies?"

"There's a word for that, Chase; you're the word man, you should know it."

I looked at her quizzically.

"Hearsay," she said. "It's not admissible in court. Is it?"

I didn't answer. Her facial expression was changing now. She almost looked like she was crying.

"You do what you think best," she said. "Just tell young Frankie how lonely his grandma was."

Then with another of her famous little smiles, she tossed down the Scotch in about a second and a half.

I couldn't have done anything even if I'd guessed what she was going to do. Which I hadn't, being genetically slow on the uptake as I am.

One thing I could do, however, was not watch. I've seen enough death in the last few days. I suppose she wanted comfort, and understanding in her last minutes, and I was the lucky fellow. She'd played her cards pretty well, right up to the end; but if she wanted me to give her comfort in her dying, she was going to go to her grave with her last wish unfilled.

A silly thought came to mind as I walked out of the room and closed the door behind me. It was from the wedding ceremony: "For richer and for poorer." Mrs. Baker hadn't been able to handle the second part, even after fifty years of the first. Not my problem anymore. Maybe she and Frank will get a second chance to work it out.

What happened next was just what you might expect. I called Braynes, the wake was spoiled, I had some poignant moments with the grandson, I told Braynes what I thought happened and how it would never be proved and how it would be best for everyone if we just kind of dropped the whole thing, and he told me to mind my own business, and then he told me thanks, anyway, for the good advice, and if I ever wanted to grow up and be a cop to go somewhere else.

The good news was that I missed rush hour traffic. There wasn't as much time to think about Betty Baker's words about empty beds. I hadn't gotten to tell her that not only had the whole scene cost me six months worth of commissions and my lovely Merc, which was totaled and which I really couldn't afford to replace, but that the scene had also cost me the woman that I'd been ready to fall in love with again.

You wonder what the point is, sometimes. You work your ass off for a client, you get half killed, you end up with less than you started with, and you find out that the client assumed that would happen all along, and furthermore, didn't particularly care.

And what's the point of all these modern relationships, anyway? You find a woman who's really everything you ever wanted—maybe a little skinny on top, but other than that, you know what I mean. Pretty, witty, sexy, independent, cuddly, smart, somewhat broadminded, but not too much so. The list could go on and on.

You find a woman like that, and she leaves you for some guy you could pick off the shelves in the generic foods section in some upscale market.

So, yeah, to some degree, I know how Betty Baker felt. Alone. Cold bed at night. No one to understand the old jokes you repeat. No one to tell you to go on a diet. No one to say, "Oh what the hell," when you go off it.

The late evening joggers were out in force as I turned down Nineteenth Street toward home. They still jiggled in all the right places, but I didn't feel superior anymore. The only time I would run that hard would be if someone were chasing me. Right now that didn't seem like such a bad idea. At least I'd have some company. At least I wouldn't be driving up to a cold, dark . . . shit . . . who parked that car in my driveway? What's a little pissant two-seater Japanese something-or-other doing parked in my drive at this time of night? And what's that light doing on? Jesus. The next thing you know I'll be smelling dinner on the stove.

Women. Who can understand them? But like I said before, understanding's the booby prize.